Temptation Has Green Eyes

Emperors of London Series

Lynne Connolly

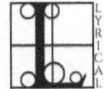

LYRICAL PRESS
Kensington Publishing Corp.
www.kensingtonbooks.com

First Electronic Edition: February 2015
eISBN-13: 978-1-61650-570-7
eISBN-10: 1-61650-570-2

First Print Edition: February 2015
ISBN-13: 978-1-61650-594-3
ISBN-10: 1-61650-594-X

Printed in the United States of America

There's more to love than meets the eye…

The daughter of a wealthy merchant, Sophia Russell has no interest in marriage, especially after a recent humiliation—and especially not to Maximilian, Marquess of Devereaux. But it's the only way to save herself from fortune hunters—and those who wish to seize a powerful connection she prefers to keep secret—even from her future husband…

Marrying Sophia is the only way Max can regain the wealth his father squandered on an extravagant country palace. And while Max and his bride are civil, theirs is clearly a marriage of convenience—until a family enemy takes a questionable interest in Sophia—one that may lead all the way to the throne. Forced to become allies in a battle they hadn't foreseen, the newlyweds soon grow closer—and discover a love, and a passion, they never expected…

"Lynne Connolly writes Georgian romances with a deft touch. Her characters amuse, entertain and reach into your heart. This book is a Must Read."
--Desiree Holt

Books by Lynne Connolly

Emperors of London Series
Rogue In Red Velvet, Book One

Published by Kensington Publishing Corporation

Author's Foreword

In 1745, Charles James Stuart, aka Bonnie Prince Charlie, fled the country. Legend says he never returned. But he did.

Chapter 1

Maximilian Wallace, Marquess of Devereaux, strode through London's crowded streets, feeling completely at home. With the dexterity of a seasoned Londoner, Max dodged past an urchin who appeared determined to collide with him—and probably relieve him of his purse at the same time. That boy's Wednesday haul would be absent one fine linen kerchief and a purse heavy with guineas.

Max reached his destination and flattened his palm over the weathered paint of the door to Lloyd's coffee house. As he shoved it open, he breathed in the intoxicating fragrance of coffee and tobacco.

A group of men sat in the worn leather-upholstered chairs by the fire, puffing on long-stemmed churchwarden pipes. More sat at the long, plain tables, making deals that would cause even a duke to gulp. Max had made many in his time.

This place had been part of Max's life since he'd attained the age of sixteen and discovered the state of the family's finances.

Spotting the man he'd come to meet, Max made his way past the tables and cubicles to the one Thomas Russell occupied, in the corner, where they wouldn't be overheard. Men nodded to him and he returned the acknowledgement. He was well known here, despite his title, not because of it. Men of the City had little time for aristocrats. He liked the busy hum of people doing business. Lloyd's was the center for insurance and shipping matters and as such could get very noisy at times. Not today. Obviously, no large ships or cargoes were in dispute.

Russell stood as Max approached. He was smiling broadly, his round, apparently guileless face displaying nothing but bonhomie and pleasure. That was part of his danger. Max had been trying to work with Russell for years but had never before gathered the capital to make an investment of this size and importance. With this deal, Max would become an insurer in his own right. His fortune would expand beyond anything he'd achieved, his future secure. So much was balanced on this transaction that he was keyed up beyond the level he considered possible. Not that he allowed any of it to show.

Max went on guard at Russell's words. When Russell showed that untroubled, smiling face, he had something on his mind. A twist in the deal?

Mentally, Max went through the complicated contract he knew by heart. They'd made a few tiny amendments, none of which threatened to wreck this agreement, and that was all. Nothing. But this man was planning something. Russell hadn't climbed the tree to become one of the wealthiest men in the precious square mile known as the City of London by being pleasant to everyone.

Russell was in many ways the epitome of the City businessman. Dressed in sober, though excellent, clothes, today of russet brown with spotlessly clean linen and a simple bob-wig, he was neither this nor that, neither ostentatious nor puritanical. Keeping a steady course between all factions had gone a long way to his success. His shining face spoke both of his attention to cleanliness and the heat in this place. Whatever the temperature outside, it was never cold in Lloyd's, due to the huge fire kept burning well into April and the hot air rising from the discussions.

A waiting-woman approached him. Max gave her a friendly smile and asked for tea. No women were allowed here except for the serving girls and the lady sitting behind the desk by the door, where the customers paid before they left. Knowing the caliber of some of the women in the City, Max wondered that none of them had stormed the citadel before. Perhaps they disliked tobacco smoke. Or preferred to use agents, as many of the City's other investments did.

Max had always conducted his business for himself. Just as well, since he couldn't afford an agent when he first started to make deals at the tender age of seventeen. He'd had to use the estate trustees to commission the actual business and sign the documents until he came of age. Now, partly due to the man who took a seat at the table across from him, he could afford much more. He was as wealthy as anyone in this room, and that was saying something.

He waited on events. One thing Max had learned over the years was the value of silence.

"You were concerned about the quantity of barrels on the lower deck?" Russell queried.

Right to business. Max settled into the final discussions. "I thought we could get more in if we stacked them deeper into the hull."

Russell nodded. "It's possible, but not advisable, although when you brought the matter up, I did speak to the captain of the fleet. Apparently it would unbalance the disposition of the cargo."

Max agreed to let that part of the contract stay as it was. He dug in the inside pocket of his olive-green coat for his account book and flipped through the well-worn pages until he reached the one he needed.

The coffee house kept a bottle of ink and pens on every table for that purpose, the ink invariably gritty and the pens often blunt. It made a mark, and that was all Max required.

The girl delivered his tea. He picked it up and took a sip.

They worked through the other matters swiftly. This contract would involve a fleet of six ships with varied cargo. They'd insure them all, and Max had some investment in the cargo, too.

A failure at this stage wouldn't ruin him as it might have at the beginning of his City career, but it meant a great deal. Success would finally boost him to the heights he'd been aiming for right from the beginning.

Light at heart, he finished his tea and prepared to leave to sign the contracts. Probably in triplicate, at least.

"A moment," Russell murmured.

Max's mood plummeted to his well-shod feet. He hadn't been wrong then. Russell had suggested Lloyd's because he wanted to discuss something else. "You have another caveat?"

Russell shook his head. "Not precisely. Hear me out, if you please."

"I'm very happy with the business as it stands, sir." Would be happier after they'd signed. "Is this a fresh agreement?" His heart lifted at the prospect. More business would only prove better, especially with this man.

"This is, I hope, the first of many contracts between us. Our methods suit and our processes are similar. We work well together."

Max said nothing, but nodded. He agreed completely. Russell was so wealthy Max suspected even the man himself didn't know how much he was worth. Max had the prestige and the contacts to find new opportunities, which benefited everyone. The burgeoning wealth of the men in the City with the new worlds they were opening could only be good for the country. This association with Thomas Russell was the start of many such contracts. He didn't doubt that for a minute.

Was the man suggesting a more formal association? A jointly owned company? Despite his determination to remain focused, Max breathed deeply to quell his excitement at the prospect. His fingertips tingled.

Under the table, he pressed them together. He forced a slight smile to his lips. "I, too, look forward to the day when we may work together again."

"I'm gratified that you would think so." Russell waved, flicking his hand in a gesture of dismissal.

Max turned his head. The serving girl retreated. A private matter, then. His heart in his mouth, he waited to hear what Russell had in mind.

The wily man bent nearer, speaking lower. "I have worked hard to build a business my descendants can be proud of."

Russell was a widower with one child, a girl. Max had met Sophia Russell a time or two but taken little notice of the self-effacing, cool woman.

So Russell wanted a more permanent association. Perhaps a company that would give his daughter a good amount of money. Enough to net herself a husband.

Max needed Russell to speak clearer, but he didn't know the man well enough to demand clarification straight out. "You've done much. You have a great deal to be proud of."

"So do you." Russell fixed him with a clear gaze. "I've worked hard to make the business my father entrusted to my care even greater. When it became obvious I would have no more children of my own, I expected to find a youth I could train, who would take over when I was gone. I found one and set matters in place. I was also considering marrying him to Sophia. She liked him well enough. He was an intelligent young man, presentable and bright who would continue the business after I'm gone."

His face changed to heavy-jowled depression, his mouth turning hard and his eyes to chips of flint. "Unfortunately, the man I chose did not prove suitable after all." He paused. "He was—untrustworthy."

Had this person endangered Russell's business? Was it safe to invest with him any longer?

"He attempted to...seduce my daughter before I'd given him permission to approach her."

"*Seduce?*" Max snapped. Had the man offered violence to Sophia? Violence to any woman was anathema to any decent man. He glanced around. Nobody sat within listening distance, but still... "Why meet here to discuss such a personal matter?"

Russell rubbed his forehead. "Sophia is at home to visitors today. The house is full of her guests. Today at least, I have considerably more privacy here than at home. I need my daughter married, and soon."

No, oh no. Not that. Surely Russell wouldn't want that.

Russell spread his hands, indicating the company. Men chatted, busy about their own concerns, uninterested in the doings of two of the regular customers. Whereas, if he visited Russell's home during an at home day, gossip would spread.

If Russell took him to his office, showed him favor, he would be bound to go through with it to save face. However, if either of them walked away here, in the coffee house, nobody would consider it amiss. Gossip was the very devil.

If he wanted this business—and he did, so badly he could taste it— he'd have to take the daughter. His head whirled. He needed time to think this over. Time he didn't have, because this wily old fox had arranged it that way.

He could always ask more about the situation. "So tell me," he said, careful to keep his voice low. "What did you do with this man?"

"I sent him away." The older man's pale eyes sharpened. He lifted his coffee cup to his lips and then put it down, the rim rattling against the table. It was already empty. "Unfortunately he spread a rumor that Sophia had seduced *him.* And succeeded in persuading some. It has besmirched her reputation in certain circles."

So he was being asked to take on soiled goods. As long as the chit wasn't pregnant, he would at least consider the possibility. But for Russell, marrying his daughter to a peer of the realm was a leap up the social scale.

"I haven't heard it." But then, Max didn't move in the social milieu of the City. He attended dinners and other functions at the Guildhall, but no more than that.

"Good. I had considered leaving my business solely to Sophia when I die. She's a clever woman, and it's not unknown for women to run businesses."

The worm on the end of the hook. Take Sophia, take the business. A very juicy worm. Max would be an idiot if the prospect didn't tempt him.

Max quirked his lips. "I'm not unaware of that, sir. The company that provides much of my silverware is run by a woman." He had no objection to a female running a business. Max never denied the truth when it presented itself as such.

Russell heaved a sigh. "I could provide her with the structure she needs. A woman cannot come to a place like this, but her prestige would mean that they would go to her. My man of business is solidly reliable, as is my chief clerk, my shipping agent, and so on." He leaned back, touched his cup, glanced up, and leaned forward again. "The recent incident has convinced me that I'm placing her in a dangerous position. She will be a woman of considerable substance. Fortune hunters will abound. They do now, but she doesn't encourage them. Already, rumors are spreading, thanks to the despicable youth whose name I will not mention."

He sighed and spread his hands in a gesture of helplessness. "Despite the recent marriage laws, wealthy young women are still abducted and forcibly wed. The rumors have weakened Sophia's position, and the vultures are gathering. I need her married to a man I can trust, and it must happen quickly."

Max didn't like the way this conversation was going, but at least Russell seemed to be putting his cards on the table. But did he have an ace shoved up his sleeve? "Could you not find a good man for your daughter? One she could rely on to stay out of the way of the business?"

"A cipher you mean?" Russell shook his head. "Sophia would never stand for that. Neither would I. Once she marries, what is hers belongs to her husband, and what I have will come to her in the fullness of time. There are few men who would resist the challenge to take control."

Max breathed more easily. This was a business proposition like any other. "So who do you have in mind?" A notion occurred to him. "Do you wish Sophia introduced into society so she can find a husband of her own?"

Russell shook his head. "She did that once. She didn't take. You may not be aware of this, but my late wife was Lady Mary Howard of Lancashire. She had a certain cachet in several circles. But there was some dispute, and my wife preferred not to acknowledge her family."

Some dispute? What on earth did that mean? Sophia was still a cit, and some members of society were unreasonably prejudiced against men of the City of London. However Sophia could enter society, and her mother's connections would satisfy all but the highest sticklers. "I can certainly help you there. My mother, my sister, could introduce her."

"No need." Russell clamped his mouth shut and stared at Max.

How the hell did he get out of this? He ached to continue the association with Russell, but enough to marry his daughter? Marriage didn't figure in his plans, not for years yet. Or hadn't until just now.

A pair of crease lines appeared between Russell's brows. "While I appreciate your offer, the recent incident has disturbed me more than I'd like. Introducing her to society, finding her a husband would all take too long. In any case, I know my Sophia. Her charms aren't obvious to many, and she may not have the skills to shine." His lips tightened. "She tried. She had her come-out, her mother made sure of that, but Sophia doesn't have the... She's not accomplished."

"You told me that she was." What was Russell was trying to say? She wanted a teacher? Perhaps his cousin Helena could help. She had taken Alex Ripley's beloved under her wing, so successfully that the lady was now Lady Ripley. Or maybe his mother and his sister Poppea, known in the family as Poppy, would agree to take Sophia in hand. "You mean she needs some town bronze?"

The frown disappeared and Russell laughed outright. He glanced around as someone approached them, but their combined stares saw him off. The man quickly turned tail and turned around.

"No." Russell turned back to Max. "She's been on the town all her life. Here's my proposition, and it's as businesslike as any other we've undertaken or are likely to make. You're young, you're wealthy, and you're as honest as any businessman I've ever met. I observed you for some time before I agreed to work with you, and I've been very pleased with our dealings together so far. I want you for Sophia. Wait—"

As Max would have spoken, Russell held up his gnarled hand. Max remained silent.

"My Sophia deserves the best. You could take my company and make it the biggest in the City of London, which means in the world."

Staggered, Max was lost for words. He closed his mouth with a snap. Russell continued with his proposal.

"If you agree to do this, I'll make you my heir. It will be part of the marriage settlement." He leaned back, his attention fixed on Max. "It's a good offer."

Just as if he was offering another business deal, which, to all intents and purposes, he was. Except it involved far more personal relations than any other business deal would. Was Max ready to let a woman into his well-ordered life?

The sound of the coffee house continued as if Max's world hadn't spun on its axis. The buzz of conversation went on around them, punctuated by occasional shout or laugh. Normal life revolved around him as he fought to get his thoughts into some kind of order.

"Sophia will make you an excellent marchioness."

About to refuse outright, Max paused, staring at the man who had made such an outrageous offer. A cit to a marquess. But an extremely wealthy cit to a previously impoverished marquess. His title hadn't put food on the table; his business acumen had done that.

If he wanted a wife, Sophia was the kind of woman he'd be looking for, rather than a society maiden fresh out of the schoolroom. She had business acumen, and she was attractive enough, from what he'd seen of her.

And the inducement—mouthwatering. He could give his mother her life back and continue with his own. After all, he knew hardly anyone whose marriage hadn't been arranged. What was this but another one?

What was he thinking? Max had always sworn to avoid the arranged marriage. He wanted to choose his wife for himself. But if he agreed to this, he'd have everything he ever wanted, not just for himself, but for his mother and his sister, Poppy. Not such a sacrifice. And many married couples lived completely separate lives. His heart sank and his stomach hollowed. Above all things he wanted a harmonious home, someone he could build a life with. But love—he didn't want that. Bile rose to his throat. Not for him, never.

Russell tapped one finger on the table, bringing Max back to attention. "Walk back some of the way with me."

Max accompanied Russell to the offices of his man of business, where his own would be waiting in a very different frame of mind to the one he'd expected. Not happy with a job well done, but in complete turmoil. Marry? He tipped back his head, sucking down as much fresh air as this crowded part of London afforded, trying to shake some sense into it.

Russell remained mainly silent during the short journey, giving Max a chance to settle his whirling thoughts.

Without a husband and with the gossips busy circulating the stories spread by her erstwhile suitor, Sophia would be a target for every unscrupulous fortune-hunter in the country. But no respectable men. Her reputation would be wrecked by the man she'd refused.

Russell's wealth ensured that she'd find *someone*. Max could induce his mother to introduce her. But the kind of society his family moved in contained more fortune hunters than anywhere else, because it also contained some of the wealthiest and best connected people in the country. Mercenary and vicious, they'd quell Sophia, mistreat her, and waste her fortune. Several of that breed had attached themselves to Poppy, or tried to, before Max or another of his male relatives had seen them off. Without that protection, Sophia would be achingly vulnerable.

Max wasn't the only man left with little fortune and a huge monstrosity of a house to care for. Many men would be glad of Sophia's wealth to shore up their ailing finances. They'd care for her, too. Not all fortune hunters were heartless.

But that wouldn't help his business. Max could help Sophia find someone suitable, but that would distance him from the business he'd worked so hard to connect with.

They walked past other coffee houses with businesses as thriving as Lloyd's—Tom's with its clutch of men looking for women to pass the time with. A house that infuriated the magistrates at Bow Street because no actual illegal acts ever took place on the premises.

Then they passed the theater at Drury Lane, its doors currently closed pending the evening's performances, and turned the corner, away from Seven Dials. Nobody went that way unless they had some criminal business to pursue. They passed several tall buildings lining the narrow streets with columns of brass plaques outside, indicating the concerns based there.

Normally Max would be reveling in the place, in the variety and the exhibition of life in all its variations, but this time he only noted the familiar landmarks without thought. His mind was occupied with one thing. Sophia. A pretty girl, and one who answered sensibly when addressed, but not someone who quickened his heart or had attracted much of his attention. No sense of excitement or anticipation when he'd seen her, which was rarely.

Was she avoiding him? He didn't think so. Perhaps she was as reticent with everyone she met. That didn't augur well for Sophia as a society lady. Reticence would be considered bad breeding, nothing more.

Children of Max's station were bred to expect people to stare at them and single them out. They should not avoid that task. Otherwise it could be regarded as bad manners. Would Sophia make a good marchioness? The reticence didn't indicate that.

Before they reached their destination, Max recommenced discussing the problem with Russell. They were moving too fast and with too much purpose for anyone to catch more than a few words in passing, so they were as private here as at the discreet corner table at Lloyd's. "Do you intend Sophia to continue the business after she marries, or will you expect her to withdraw from commercial life?"

Russell laughed as he dodged a dark pool of something unpleasantly liquid. Since it hadn't rained for a day or so, it was unlikely to be water. "I'd consider any man who chose not to consult her an idiot. She knows the various enterprises as well as I do. It's sheer madness to ignore expertise in whatever guise it appears, male or female."

Relief flooded him. She was an intelligent woman, then. "Why the hurry to hand over your business? You, sir, are in your prime." He assumed Russell to be around fifty. His vigor and mental acuity pointed to a lack of extreme age.

Russell raised a brow. "Thank you for that. It's time I took life at a more leisurely pace."

Did he have a health problem? The lines of his face and the gnarled hands were probably from Russell's early years on board ship, where he made his first fortune. But perhaps the lines were deeper, the eyes a little less clear.

"My daughter is twenty-four. She needs a husband, one who will care for her and ensure she comes to no harm. And you are the best candidate. My lord," he added as if an afterthought.

In fact, Max's colleague was reminding him of his exalted title and station. True, he could enhance Russell's business merely by being a peer of the realm.

He could finally restore the house. His parents had spent all their money and lavished their love on the house in the country. Devereaux House had been a large establishment, suitable for a marquess's main residence, and his parents had enlarged it still further. Now it was packed with treasures, beautified, and redesigned.

His land steward had loftily informed Max that the house contained as many rooms as there were days in the year. The news appalled Max. How could anyone live in a monstrosity that size? Now the place belonged to him, or more precisely, had devolved to him with the entail on the land. He couldn't sell it. He never went there.

After his father's death, Max had closed and shuttered the place, retaining a skeleton staff to keep the house clear of the pests that might damage the treasures. Even that had cost him more than he could afford.

His mother had adored her husband, and therefore she adored the house, too. Not that she lived there. That was a constant needle in Max's side. His mother should have her house back.

With Russell's fortune, starting with the no doubt generous settlement that would come with Sophia, he could do it. Restore the parts that had suffered during his time as owner and give it back to her.

And he wanted to give his sister something more than she had now. Poppy deserved better. Because she was a single female, she had to live with her mother, which meant sharing the peripatetic life the dowager Lady Devereaux led these days.

Poppy should have a proper London season with the clothes to match. But when a lace petticoat cost more than a ship's captain could earn in half a year, that was difficult. Had been difficult.

Now Max could afford it, but he still needed a chaperone for Poppy. Somebody like—a wife.

He kept coming back to the inevitable topic. The walk only served to firm his resolve, which Russell probably knew since he kept quiet for most of it. A good businessman knew when to keep his tongue between his teeth.

They halted outside the office. Did he go in or not? Would he accept this agreement?

He had no choice.

Russell had dropped his daughter on Max like a woodcutter felling an oak tree.

"In principle, I agree to both your propositions," he said as calmly as he could. "Shall we?" Courteously he let the older man enter the building first and followed up the narrow stairway leading to the busy solicitor's office, the clerk with half a dozen quills stuck in his hair waving them on with only a small bow of acknowledgement.

All through the discussion of the various documents that put the agreement in place, Max's mind kept drifting elsewhere. Every time he hit upon an objection to the marriage, a reasonable solution popped into his mind.

Now he'd regained his fortune, women would start chasing him. He'd seen it happen to other men. Now his turn had arrived. Some mysterious scent, like trailing a corpse for the hounds affected men of title, wealth, and enough youth not to repel. No, forget the last one, Max had seen eighty-year-old dukes fall for the wiles of a twenty-year-old woman.

Hell and damnation, he'd never had this difficulty making up his mind.

Yes, damn it, he'd do it. He nodded when Mr. Fisk hesitated. "Go on. I daresay the marriage settlement is here?"

His own man of business shot him a startled look. Max gave him a beatific smile in return. The original contract agreed upon, they settled to discussing the marriage contract and its ramifications.

So Sophia was four-and-twenty? He had thought her younger. That changed his perspective on his colleague's proposal because he'd never been in favor of marrying chits straight out of the schoolroom. He'd never had the luxury of a childhood or the customary Grand Tour that young men of his status generally undertook before settling into what passed for ordinary life. Max had little in common with the brats he'd been introduced to and found more conducive conversation with older women, who'd seen a little more and expected a lot less.

He had to force himself to concentrate on the signing. He never signed a contract without reading it through just before he signed, in case the other party had tried to slip something in, hoping he wouldn't notice. He *always* noticed.

Today he could have been signing his soul away to the devil. He tried, but couldn't concentrate.

He hovered his pen over the other contract, the one binding him for life to a woman he hardly knew. And had a brainwave. "I cannot sign this without the other party present."

"Of course," Russell said smoothly. "But we can have it ready for Sophia to sign. You can sign your part now."

Max tested the proposal, considered the aspects of tying himself to someone for life. If the personal association didn't work, they would always have the business one.

When Max made a decision, he didn't delay. He preferred to see the matter through swiftly and efficiently. As far as he was concerned, the matter was set aside to be filed with a blue ribbon, his office code for "Done."

He signed the document in the requisite places with a few sure slashes of the pen. Then, with a smile, he returned them to their men of business to arrange the copies and the filing.

He'd leave telling his mother until tomorrow.

Chapter 2

Sophia was sick of fielding questions about the young men she might consider marrying. Her father, his good mood flowing over to the dinner they held that night, kept the gentlemen in the dining room longer than usual, and Sophia, perforce, had to entertain the ladies in the drawing-room.

One lady suggested that John Hayes would be growing impatient.

He could get as impatient as he liked, but he wasn't coming anywhere near her again. She forced a smile and gave a non-committal, "Really?" with a touch of aspersion.

She'd trusted a man who had traduced and despised her. He'd only wanted her for her money, nothing else, but she'd believed every lying honeyed word that had dropped from his lips. Until that afternoon when he'd taken matters too far. Her father had ejected him from her life. She was surprised she hadn't felt a jot of regret, not even recalling the times John was so charming to her. She didn't miss him one bit.

"But I daresay we'll be hearing an announcement soon?" Mrs. Cleverly said.

If Sophia said anything other than, "I don't know," the news would be all over London, at least the part of it that mattered most to her. She gave a wan smile. "We found we didn't suit. I believe he has found a position elsewhere."

Enough of a hint to suggest the fault was on his side. As much as she dared, anyway.

Mrs. Cleverly's carefully penciled brows rose a fraction. "I thought you were almost declaring for each other."

Sophia shook her head. "We never took matters that far."

Another lady, a younger one, and the wife of one of London's most daring investors, said, "But what about that handsome marquess?"

Immediately Sophia's thoughts flew to the Marquess of Devereaux, and inwardly she groaned. He barely noticed her, probably didn't know her name. "He is my father's business associate. I admit he is handsome, but City and County don't mix, do they? More tea?" She lifted the pot, shaking it a little to make sure there was enough left.

She'd noticed him from the moment his tall, lean form entered the banqueting hall at the Guildhall, at the formal dinner she was attending with her father. He'd made her feel underdressed and inconspicuous, but not from anything he did. He was punctiliously polite. He had exchanged a few innocuous words with her and moved on, leaving her gaping at his sheer masculine beauty and his elegance.

He probably wouldn't remember her name if she met him again. Or perhaps his impeccable manners had led him to commit it to memory. Sophia wasn't fooled, though. He'd only spoken to her because he was courting her father. No gleam of interest sparked his astonishing green eyes, no warm words or a request to visit her home. Not that he could, because Sophia had done away with chaperones a year ago and firmly declared herself perfectly able to run her own affairs.

More fool she. If she'd allowed her tedious aunt to stay, she wouldn't have got into the pickle with John.

Half an hour later, she closed the door on the last guest with a weary sigh.

She picked up the silver snuffers, extinguished the candles in the sconces, crossed to the table, and extinguished the others. The fire and the moonlight glimmering through the gap in the window shutters produced the only remaining light. Unearthly, it streaked across the room to cast the portrait of her mother in a silvery glimmer.

If Sophia were superstitious, the ethereal light would worry her, but she'd seen that effect more than once. Merely a product of the situation of the portrait and the way the moonlight hit it. Instead of running screaming, she stared at the painting of the lovely woman who'd died six years ago.

She smiled up at her mother. Lady Mary Howard was depicted at the height of her beauty, holding a fan in her satin-clad lap. Although Sophia shared her mother's coloring, she didn't otherwise resemble her much. Nor her father. Perhaps she looked like her grandparents, but since both her mother and her father's parents had died before she could properly remember them, she could only speculate.

The door opened. A figure stood shadowed against the light from the hall. "Sophia, are you all right in here with no lights?"

"I was just putting them out, Papa. The servants will bring their own once they come to clear up. No sense wasting best beeswax when there's nobody in here."

"Ever the housekeeper. Sophia my dear, come and talk to me. I have some news for you."

She couldn't see his smile, but she could hear it in his voice. She couldn't pull her watch from her pocket to check the time in this light, but she was tempted to depress the repeater to hear it chime the hour. Her father would hear it too, so she resisted. "Father, it must be ten o'clock. I thought you'd gone up to bed."

"I have some news for you, and I don't wish to wait. Come."

Unusual for him to be so uncharacteristically impatient. Sophia followed her father out of the dining room and downstairs to his study. Her father conducted some of his business from here.

She knew it well, from the legal documents tied with red tape to the tall account books he kept here. With fire a constant threat, her father always had two copies of every important document written out. The original for the office, one for here, and another for the house in the country. Somehow Sophia doubted London would see another Great Fire, but as he often said, "You never know."

The familiarity gave her assurance. Wait—he'd left to sign the agreement with the marquess earlier today. Had the deal gone awry?

Her heart in her mouth, she waited for him to say that the contract was null. She'd labored long hours copying out that document. She'd hate it to go to waste.

He took a seat, leaned back in his chair, and motioned to the one on the other side of his huge desk, the one she customarily used.

Sophia smoothed her skirts and sat, finding it mildly uncomfortable to be here in her evening silks and not her daytime wool and linen.

He didn't appear put out, no trace of a frown between his brows. "My daughter, you are well?"

That was more than a courteous inquiry after her health. John's behavior had distressed her, and although she'd tried not to reveal the level of her distress, her father had discerned it. "Very, thank you, Father."

"I am extremely pleased to hear it." He glanced down at the papers before him, picked up his gold-rimmed glasses, and propped them on the high bridge of his nose. "I have some news that affects you directly. You recall I was signing the contract with the Marquess of Devereaux today?"

"Yes, sir."

"That went without a hitch. We discussed a few small matters, which I would request you add to our copy tomorrow, but nothing that materially alters the agreement."

A sigh of relief escaped her lips. "I'm glad. That will benefit us considerably." And the employees of her father's company.

"Indeed. I'm glad to have it done. But we discussed another matter." He regarded her in silence for a moment before speaking again. "You are four and twenty and a considerable heiress."

"I am aware of that, Papa."

The ghost of a smile crossed his lips. "Until recently, I had ignored the implications of those simple facts. However, it was borne on me recently that I should pay serious attention to the matter."

Sophia repressed a shudder. "I am fine, Papa."

"A society lady would have had a companion or a chaperone."

With a curl of her lip, she replied, "I am not a society lady. You provide me with a footman to protect me outside the house, and indoors I need nobody. Neither am I a girl fresh from the schoolroom." Her father had seen that she learned what she needed, but her training in account-keeping went far beyond maintaining the household records.

He harrumphed. "You are not. But you are ready to wed."

What was this? Although startled, Sophia knew better than to deny his assertion. Opposing her father wasn't the best way to make him see reason. He would dig his feet in and insist, and then there'd be no budging him. She would find another way to avoid her father's concerns.

He had meant for her to marry John, and she'd been happy to comply, especially after John's careful courtship, but that had of course come to nothing. She had thought herself safe for a year or two at least.

Distracting him with business usually worked best. Preparing to listen, she folded her hands in her lap and pasted an expression of mild interest on to her face. "Some women don't marry until they're nearly thirty, Papa."

"I spoke with the marquess at some length today and offered him a new contract to accompany the other."

"Oh?" The implications of what he was leading to struck her after her mild expression of interest. Her father had spoken before of her going back into society. Perhaps he wanted the marquess to sponsor her re-entry, under the aegis of a suitable female relative.

She didn't want that. Her debut had been a disaster. Nobody had taken any notice of her, until they learned how rich she would be, and she left the ballrooms of Mayfair with nothing but relief, vowing never to return.

Her mother had been disappointed, but shortly after that first season, she had died, so Sophia had never returned. And she'd never been missed.

A light approach would work best. "Does the marquess know a suitable candidate?" Her heart beat faster, and she tried to breathe normally. Her laces were tighter than usual, so her bosom would reveal her state of agitation if she didn't take care.

"He does." Her father's sly smile sent chills running through her.

"Papa, I am of a mind not to marry for some time yet. Do we really need to consider it now?"

"What? Yes, we do. I was deeply deceived in Hayes, and I would not have that happen again. It must not."

Because it diminished her reputation, came close to destroying it? Sophia had worked hard to rebuild her reputation, and she was nearly there. Without compromising and allowing another chaperone into the house. What was she, some society miss who couldn't go outdoors without a footman?

Sophia had a cordial relationship with her father, one that didn't lead either of them to vouchsafe their most intimate emotions. Even after John's attack, her father had been more concerned with her physical condition. In other words, was she still a virgin? She could assure him on that point, although had a few more moments passed, she might not have been.

She would never forget that feeling of utter helplessness as John pinned her legs open and held her hands above her head. That had been the worst, even more than his gloating expression as he loomed above her, his breeches open.

Her heart beat faster, and the breath caught in her throat. With an effort, she forced her mind off that track. Reliving that scene never did any good.

Now her father was talking, and unusually for him, avoiding getting to the point. He was discussing the incident with John as if it were the topic of the conversation. But that was done, and she didn't want to think about it any longer. As soon as she had controlled her breathing she broke into his monologue. "Papa, I appreciate your concern. I will never allow myself to be in a room alone with a man again." She offered a smile. "Except for you, of course."

He shook his head. "No, that will not do. Your potential fortune will increase with this new venture and others I have in mind. So much that few men will find themselves able to resist you."

She hadn't thought of that. He was right. The greater her potential fortune grew, the greater temptation she became to fortune hunters. She might have to let Aunt Jane back after all.

"If your mother and I had had more children, that would have helped to dissipate the effect, but we did not." He regarded her steadily.

She was forced to glance down, using the pretext of tidying a pile of papers. She didn't understand why he hadn't remarried. Perhaps he would yet. But after her mother's death, he'd immersed himself in work. Then they had become comfortable with each other and settled into a routine that did not include another woman. He'd seemed content enough, and so was she.

"As well as signing the original contract, we agreed another. Your marriage contract with Lord Devereaux. You will sign it on Friday, when it has been drawn up properly, and marry on Monday." He smiled broadly. "Daughter, I saw how you looked at him at the Guildhall dinner. You wanted him. I got him for you."

No, oh no.

What she didn't want, what she feared more than anything else, was being married as an object, someone unimportant in herself, whose fortune was more important. She'd so nearly succumbed to that with John. For all his protestations of love he had never wanted her, only what she represented. Every day she remained unmarried was another when she didn't have to face that fate—to be a thing. Now, with the Marquess of Devereaux, she was confronted with it again.

The world knew how hard his lordship had worked to restore his fortunes after his father had spent it. Of course he'd take her money, even if she went with it. He barely noticed her. He would continue the same way, wife or not.

That gave her an idea. She got up and hurried to the bookshelves ranged against one wall, finding what she needed almost immediately— the book that detailed the peers of Britain, the one she and her father used when some aristocrat came to them, cap in hand. Over the years, she and her father had made notes that they might find useful. Such details could prove immensely useful in negotiations.

Flipping through the pages quickly, she came to the one she wanted.

"Papa, listen to this. If this doesn't persuade you that I'm unsuitable, nothing will." She began to read.

"The Devereaux title dates back to the Elizabethan era, and the present holder of the title can trace his ancestry back directly to the courtier who took to the High Seas and brought the queen a fortune. The family's

fortunes have gone up and down, and are currently flourishing. Lord Devereaux owns one of the largest houses in the country, Devereaux Place, which might as well be termed Palace. It is reported to have one room for each day of the year. Despite the magnificent pile, his lordship prefers to spend his time in town. He is unmarried and has one sister. 1753." She'd made the extra notes last year, after the fateful meeting at the Guildhall.

"I can't marry someone like that, Papa. What do I know about houses in the country?"

Her father regarded her closely, but said nothing for a moment. When he did speak, it was in that quiet, determined voice that told her she would win nothing by arguing. "You will learn, if necessary. The deal is made, and you should spend your time preparing yourself."

With another man, she might make something—a relationship, a friendship—but with him, she doubted it. Her feet itched with the desire to leave the room, but if she left now, she'd concede defeat.

Her father's cold statement filled Sophia with pure rage. Never, ever had she felt so furious with anyone. That it was with her father didn't surprise her, because he was one of the few people in the world who could affect her mood. Arguing reasonably be damned. At least she'd say what she thought.

Her heart pounded, and heat rose to her cheeks. "Do I have no say in this agreement?" In the circumstances she considered her words calm and collected, but she couldn't make them warm or prevent the telling tremble in her voice.

Her father watched her. An old trick to use silence against her, but he'd taught her that tactic himself, so she was not affected by it. She waited until she had swallowed down some of her betraying emotion.

"I have nothing but consideration for you," he said eventually. "You need a husband, and I have obtained the best possible candidate. You should be grateful."

"Grateful?" However hard she tried, Sophia couldn't control her trembling. "Should you not have consulted with me first?"

"Since we were at the lawyer's office, I took the opportunity to request the contract signed with the other. It's a standard marriage contract. You will not find yourself disadvantaged by it."

"Not financially," she snapped. "What about my personal happiness?"

He looked at her. Just looked, until she shook her head.

"I cannot marry him, Papa."

"Why not? Has he shown you a lack of respect? Or worse?"

"He hardly notices me," she said bitterly. "We spoke once only."

"Then it's your pride that's hurt?"

He was too perceptive, but she'd always known that. "No. But I would like my future husband to show some preference for me."

He brushed aside her protests with a careless wave of his hand. "Pooh! You will no doubt have preference to spare once you are wed. This is not a romantic association, but it will make you part of an alliance that will affect society. Perhaps history. Do you not want that?"

"All I ever wanted was to do my best. I have no desire to make history." Even though her father wasn't exaggerating.

He lost any semblance of geniality, his mouth tightening into a thin line. She was in deep trouble. He had made up his mind and there was no changing it. "Do you deny that your emotions get you into trouble?"

She said nothing.

"This is an association, an alliance. The marquess is a sensible man; he will listen to your advice. And I will leave certain matters in your hands. Your erstwhile inamorato has been spreading rumors about you and your so-called wanton behavior. You know how badly that will go down in some quarters of the City."

By "City," he didn't mean the geographical area. He meant the men who ran the financial matters that spread worldwide. Yes, John's malicious lies had some people doubting her morality, and thus her veracity. Consequently her father's too, however unfair that judgment was in reality.

He wasn't finished. "And children, do you not want them?"

She refused to answer any more. She knew what her father was doing; he would drag her into paths she couldn't win, place arguments against her that would force her to agree with him. So she would make her statement and then leave with all the dignity she could muster. Perhaps he would consider her objections, perhaps not. It remained to be seen how much stake he'd put on this deal.

"Papa, I respect your views, and I owe you obedience as my parent. However, I also have a life that will continue for some time, and I have no wish to spend it with someone I hardly know. I would like at least the pretense of courtship. He is marrying a fortune, not me. I'm marrying a marquisate, not him."

"You cannot deny you took a fancy to him. You must be married, my child. You are too much of a temptation to those who would take advantage of you. You will obey me in this," he continued softly.

Her father rarely raised his voice; he didn't have to. "You have three days to change your mind. I don't expect to see you until you are ready to sign the contract."

She left the room.

He called after her, "And that is on Saturday."

He ordered her to stay in her room and had her fed on bread and water. That hadn't happened since Sophia's childhood.

He also had her maid remove her books and writing materials, except a copy of the Bible. "*To give you a chance to reflect on your decision and pray for the correct outcome,*" the note he sent told her.

Why was her father was so determined that she marry Lord Devereaux? She hadn't considered her papa so intractable before, and unafraid of his temper, she could usually talk him around to her way of thinking. Not this time. He refused to consider anything but acceptance. A marchioness? Worse, *his* marchioness? She couldn't do it.

Then her father sent his ultimatum. On Friday afternoon she stared at the note in horror. "*The Marquess or the country. Your choice, my child.*"

If she continued to refuse, he would send her to the country, leave her to molder away without the opportunity to return to the life she loved. He could destroy everything she had worked for and reduce her to utter tedium, and that would drive her mad. Her father had complete jurisdiction over her, and if she didn't obey, he'd do it. The notes he'd sent over the past three days gave her no doubt.

She drifted over to the window and gazed out at the street she'd seen all her life.

Carriages went by below, the constant sound of trotting horses a background she hardly noticed. But no more, if her father had his way, and he would. She couldn't stop him.

She had to do something. Obviously her life was about to change, and she'd prefer some say in how it did so. Time to take action.

Leaving her room, Sophia called for her maid. Her father was out of the house and she had a call to make. Bedamned his stricture to keep her in his room. She'd go anyway, and he'd be glad she did. Damn her reputation, too. If she destroyed it utterly, the aspirants to her hand might finally leave her alone. Including the marquess.

Chapter 3

"My lord, there's a young lady to see you."

He had wanted a few hours' uninterrupted concentration. Sitting at his desk bent over a set of papers, Max gave his butler a fulminating glance. Rayne never showed an iota of emotion when on duty, but Max could have sworn the man's eyebrows were a fraction higher than usual.

Was one of his lady loves creating a scene? Surely not. He hadn't had one for some time, and Rayne could cope with a woman of that ilk with one hand tied behind his back. "Well, what's the problem?"

"She's alone, sir, and she appears respectable."

"Do you by any chance have a name?"

Rayne's lip gained a distinct curl. "Miss Russell."

"Ah." That came as a surprise, to say the least. "And does she have what is generally known as a respectable female with her?"

"She does, my lord. But in my opinion, the respectable female appears more in the nature of a maid."

What the devil did she want? He was seeing her tomorrow at the lawyer's office. Was that not soon enough?

"Show her into the parlor, if you please."

The choice seemed to mollify Rayne, as he bowed, his usual demeanor of a frozen sheep restored. "Yes, my lord. Should I serve refreshments?"

"Tea, please. And some of those little sweet things ladies like."

"I shall have it brought to you directly, sir."

Max had hoped for a quiet hour or two sorting through his invoices before he had to leave for an evening affair. Already dressed in his eveningwear of satin breeches and heavily embroidered waistcoat—although, this being a mild day, he wouldn't put on his coat until he had to—he got to his feet. He gave Rayne time to show her to the parlor before he got to his feet.

Perhaps he should have received her in the salon upstairs, but in truth, Max preferred the smaller, less grand room, the morning parlor at the front of the house where he received more informal guests and spent his evenings, when he had the chance. His voice didn't echo so much, and he could keep an eye on the world outside. The furniture was less…spindly.

He went in prepared to send her away. But at the sight of her, something echoed inside him—something he couldn't define—that defied description. Not pity. Sympathy was the nearest he could get to it.

A young, slender woman with dark hair sat staring into the empty fire grate. Since he was planning to go out, Max hadn't ordered a fire set there today. Now he wished he had. Despite the warm weather she looked cold. Her body hunched over, her hands tightly clasped.

Her hair gleamed in the candlelight, and Max wanted to test it with his fingers to discover if it was as silky as it appeared. Odd, since he'd never felt that way toward her before. Inconvenient. He didn't wish for anything but a business partnership from his upcoming marriage.

She should not be here. "Ma'am, I'm afraid you find my mother away from home. I will have you escorted back to your house." Disturbed by her presence, he turned to leave the room. She was alone. She'd left the respectable female in the hall. Nothing about this situation was right.

"No, please. I have to talk to you."

He'd considered his future bride a biddable female, quiet and unassuming. But a woman who came to visit him, risking wrecking her reputation all over again? She was anything but quiet and unassuming.

He stayed by the door. "Madam, I cannot receive you alone. It would compromise you beyond recovery."

"If it becomes known"—her voice was charmingly musical. Why had he not noticed that before?—"the woman I brought will swear she was with me all the time."

He nodded, deciding to trust her. He wouldn't get rid of her until she'd had her say. "In that case, perhaps you should remove your outer garments. It's a warm evening." Why the hell had he said that? Only that he wanted to see more of her than he could. At the moment, she was shrouded in a hat, gloves, and an enveloping cloak, perhaps more in an attempt to disguise her appearance than to keep warm.

Ah well, he'd said it now.

She stood and serenely drew out the long pins holding her hat in place before sticking them carefully back into the straw. She removed it and looked around, eventually hanging it on the back post of her chair. She did the same with her cloak.

Her hands trembled. If he hadn't been watching so closely, he'd never have noticed. He lifted his gaze to her face, and their eyes locked. Hers were dark. Blue or brown? He couldn't tell from this distance, a matter of ten feet or so. He took a step closer and then another, went forward and held out his hand to take her cloak. She laid it over his arm. He didn't remove his attention from her face.

"Sir, I—I would rather you were not so close."

His lips relaxed in a smile. "After Monday, I will be much closer."

"It is one of the matters I wish to discuss." Her voice deepened, grew throaty. Her lips were full, and he caught a flash of sharp, white teeth.

Frowning, he moved back and laid her cloak across the nearby chair. She began to remove her gloves. She gave tiny tugs to the tip of each finger, and then pulled the glove off, slowly revealing soft, pale skin. Her fingernails were neatly trimmed, not the carefully manicured and polished shells of the society lady. She used those hands, worked with them. A tiny ink mark stained the base of her thumb.

She performed the same office for the other glove, carefully easing off the thin kid, revealing her fingers slowly, carefully, as if unearthing a secret personal treasure.

Max had rarely seen anything so erotic in his life. He longed to know what those hands could do if he placed them on his body and told her to make free with them.

She kept her gloves in one hand. She caught her lower lip in her teeth, worrying it for a bare second before she stopped. Those lips parted as she took a deep breath and firmed her chin. A pretty chin, one he'd love to touch as he held her steady for his kiss. He would have at least that before she left. It would serve her right for coming here on her own.

"Where *is* your maid?"

She grimaced. "She is my chaperone for this visit. I don't have a companion or a respectable female, so I brought her. I did my best to make her appear a companion. What did I do wrong?"

"My butler, Rayne," he said, his eyes warming. "He can spot domestics at a glance. But fear not, we won't betray your secret. What is so urgent that won't wait?"

She took another deep breath, her bosom shifting enticingly beneath her thick practical linen fichu. He would enjoy revealing her body. He had never taken much notice of it before, but now it would be his, he decided he liked it. Liked her.

She was slender, but with curves that hinted at the pleasing shape beneath.

"I wanted to discuss this marriage with you. I don't want to have my life arranged for me."

"Did your father not consult you first? I thought you willing." Regretfully, he pondered the possibility of not marrying her. Once he'd made up his mind, he'd considered the matter settled. In this case, it seemed not.

"I wasn't asked, I was *told*. Sir, I don't know you very well. I need some assurances."

"Please, take a seat," he said, belatedly recalling his manners.

She shook her head, dark curls bouncing against the white column of her neck. "I'll stand, thank you. I must not stay long. My father is at a guild dinner, but he won't be long tonight. I left him a note so he wouldn't worry, but I'd rather he never saw it."

Thus the ink spot.

"You'd no doubt prefer to be back before him."

She shrugged, but he didn't miss her hesitation, the way her eyes flicked to one side before she returned her attention to him. "I am willing to marry you, but I don't wish for…r-relations."

He suppressed his smile. "In what way?" He knew what she meant, but he was curious to know why she asked for this. Besides, he wanted to see more of that pretty flush.

"In the bedroom, you know. We will have separate bedrooms?"

"Of course. I have no wish to intrude on your levées or your dressing rituals." That left her to assume he intended to intrude at other times.

"I don't wish us to visit each other at all."

He took pity on her. "You desire a white marriage?" He used the French term, meaning a union without consummation. "My dear, I hate to disappoint you, but I do need heirs. I have only a sister, no brother to inherit. The duty of providing heirs is mine. And yours, once we marry."

Her eyes widened. Stricken, she stared at him. "You can't make a will—"

"For my fortune, yes. But not the estate. That's entailed. As is the title."

She bit her lip again, a fleeting movement, as if she were aware it wasn't allowed. "Of course. I'm sorry. No male relatives?"

He shook his head, taking it as no male relatives he wanted to inherit. A pity his mother's relatives couldn't inherit, but there it was.

She wrung her hands together. "Then may I request more time to accustom myself to the idea? If you ask for it, my father will surely grant it."

He moved closer, observing her carefully. She seemed jumpy to the point of panic. "Is there something wrong?"

"No, why should there be?" Her response came too quickly. The little pulse at the base of her throat beat erratically and she wouldn't meet his eyes.

She'd shown great courage coming here by herself, although he would wager her maid remained within screaming distance. Not that he meant to make her scream. Not tonight, at any rate, and never from fear. "Then I advise you to let it happen. Is there nothing else? Your concern is personal?"

She jerked a nod. "I will ensure that my portion is fair, and I would request that I oversee where it's invested, but I know you can do it as well as I."

"Yes, that's true. But I have no objection in you overseeing your own investments. Or in taking an interest in my concerns."

She brightened, her mouth relaxing. "That's very enlightened of you."

"If half of what your father says about your expertise in commerce is true, I'd be a fool to ignore such an asset." Business was the last thing on his mind, but he understood her concerns. That demand sounded reasonable to him. But not the other.

"Thank you."

"No doubt we'll arrange financial matters later, when we meet to sign the contract. So do you wish to discuss the personal aspect now?"

Swallowing, her throat tight, she nodded.

He had to go gently here, but she must know the truth. "I have no intention of staying away from your bedroom."

He hated the expression that returned now. Tight lips, wide eyes, tiny creases at the corners of her mouth, and her pulse didn't so much beat as flutter, it was going so fast. But he wouldn't let her build barriers between their bedrooms. On impulse he reached out and took her hands.

They were cold. When she tugged, he tightened his hold. Before it turned into an undignified tussle, she stopped and let her hands rest passively in his. "Your name is Sophia, is it not? Do you prefer that, or Sophie, or something else?"

She shrugged. "It doesn't matter."

Then he would choose. "I like your full name. It suits you. You have an innate elegance that I find pleasing. Well, then, Sophia, we are to be close. You will be the mother of my heirs. Of our heirs." She had a considerable fortune of her own, thanks to her father.

Blinking, she said, "Does it take long to make heirs?"

That naiveté shocked him and forced a laugh out of him. He'd never considered intimate relations with anyone other than ladies of the night or willing widows looking for a dalliance. Certainly not inexperienced women.

Even females paid to act as innocent virgins for the delectation of their clientele weren't this jumpy. "It takes as long as it takes. Some women fall pregnant the first time, and with others, it takes years."

He pulled gently on her hands. Silk rustled when she moved closer. This was like taming a wild animal, drawing it closer with kindness. *No sudden moves.* "The act can be extremely pleasurable."

"No!" She said it quickly, as if unconsidered. Too fast, a visceral response.

He frowned. Did she know? Should he ask about the incident with John Hayes?

If he did he might receive information he didn't want to know. Like she was no longer a virgin. Was she in fact fond of the man her father had caught her with?

"Is there someone else you would rather marry?" he asked. "I won't wed a woman who is thinking of someone else in the marriage bed. I am no man's substitute." That, at least, he was sure of.

Vigorously, she shook her head. "No, no, truly." At least her hands had stopped trembling. "There is no one."

He'd had enough. He wanted her close, badly. Her scent, the feel of her hands in his, and her charming figure had had its predictable effect on him. While his agile mind tried to process the information, his body was rising to the occasion. He couldn't reason this need away.

Why had he never noticed her in this way before? Because she had never spoken to him directly, or because she had avoided attracting his attention? He had no idea, but he certainly noticed her now.

When he drew her even closer, she came, so he could release her hands and hold her waist instead. "Put your hands on my shoulders."

Eyes wide—they were brown—she did so. "You will not—"

Whatever she was about to say he muffled with his mouth.

Her lips were soft, with an underlying firmness that pleased him. Although she'd been speaking, when he touched her she clamped her lips together. He was in no mind to force her.

Her body stiffened so much, he felt it under the unforgiving bones of her stays, but he wanted to taste her. Sweet, so sweet, that even a closed-mouth kiss pushed his arousal up another notch.

On Monday, he would have her. Anything else was unthinkable. He finished the kiss, but kept her close. Her breath came in fast pants, making her bosom swell enticingly in an erratic fashion. He would do that again.

But her hands lay unmoving on his shoulders, her body still but rigid. Shyness, or something else?

If she were concealing a lover and wasn't a virgin, Max didn't care as much as he should. As long as she wasn't pregnant. But if she had lost her virginity to violence, he'd hunt down the man who did it and personally run him through with his sword. Several times.

He moved his mouth over hers, touching her lips with his tongue, tracing the lines with the tip.

With a sigh, she opened very slightly, enough for him to slip his tongue between her teeth and enter her mouth.

She jerked away, covering her rosy lips with her hand, her eyes wide with shock. "I—I'm sorry."

He wasn't. "Has nobody done that before?"

"No."

The man who'd approached her before, Hayes, had frightened her, because not even a reticent maiden would be this skittish. She wouldn't have come to visit him, risked her reputation three days before the wedding were she not very disturbed by the notion of marriage.

Unfortunately, he needed to make sure of his suspicion. She would hardly allow him to lift her skirts and discover it for himself, not after that travesty of a kiss.

He stepped back, smiled at her, giving her a moment to collect herself. Only one more thing remained.

He was hard and aching, but he couldn't allow that to control what he must ask her. "I'm sorry, but I have to know. Are you pregnant?" Did the scene with John Hayes have more consequences than her father had imagined?

The possibility nagged at him. However much he wanted her, he couldn't allow that to happen. He couldn't pass his title and estate on to another man's child. Although he didn't hold either in high esteem, he owed his ancestors that much. "Be sure that if you are, I swear not to tell anyone. And I'll render all the help I can, but I can't marry you in those circumstances."

"No!" Coloring, she snatched up her hat. "How could you think such a thing?"

"Forgive me. But your father has stressed haste in this. He said that his dispute with a former employee had caused the man to spread rumors about you that could prove extremely damaging both to you and your business."

"But I didn't! It didn't go that far, I swear!" Her eyes glistened with unshed tears and her face was so red she looked as if he'd slapped her.

Regret swept away his other concerns. She didn't manufacture that look, but he had considered that she had come to tell him and didn't know how to say it. "Hush, be still. I'm sorry." And he would take her at her word. "I believe you." He would accept it. After all, what did it matter who fathered a child? Some of his compatriots, titleholders, were not the biological children of their parents. He'd asked, and he'd abide by his decision now.

Abruptly, he turned away and picked up her cloak. "Come, you must go." He held it open for her to put on.

She turned her back to him, and he wrapped her securely in the folds. Surprised by a powerful urge to enclose her in his arms and keep her safe, he nevertheless kept his touch light.

"I will see you tomorrow at the solicitor's office." Deliberately he bent and touched his mouth to the spot beneath her ear where most women were sensitive.

She shuddered, but was it reticence or suppressed desire? He would find out. "On Monday we marry, and on Monday night I'll come to your room. Don't try to stop me. We need to do that, to make the marriage complete." And he wanted her. Of course divorce and annulment weren't possible. Non-consummation was not fair grounds for divorce, and a marriage was valid whether the couple had engaged in intimate relations or not. But he wanted that heir, and he would ensure she didn't start building walls between them from the start.

He had to trust his own judgment on this and make the commitment, but if he discovered anything amiss, he'd have the truth out of her. "After that, we'll see."

Suspicions were the very devil. If left, they would fester and multiply. Rather than that, he'd do what he had to and take the consequences.

Chapter 4

Sophia reached home before her father and destroyed the note she'd left for him. If the servants didn't talk, she'd be fine. If they did, she'd tell him where she'd gone and suffer his opprobrium. He wouldn't be too harsh on her, because she was about to accede to his will.

She told him as soon as he came home. He embraced her warmly.

"He's a good man," he said. "The marquess will be an excellent husband for you."

Sophia wondered about that. His very presence excited her in a way she didn't know how to cope with. Even when she'd considered John a suitor and not a threat, he'd never raised the hairs on her skin merely by looking at her. But when the marquess—Max—had fixed his emerald-green gaze on her face, every hair on her body prickled with awareness. It had excited her and scared her in equal measure.

She hadn't found the sensation unpleasant. But his proximity, and when he'd held her around her waist, that was something else. His touch had burned right through to her bare flesh.

Perhaps what John had intended to do was what all men did. That notion terrified her, and during the last few months the fear had only grown. That they would throw her down and ignore her protests, rip her skirts out of the way, and then gloat. The knowledge that men could do that, that they were strong enough to accomplish the feat even if she protested, froze her with dread.

No, she wouldn't think of it. Every time the memory of that scene intruded, she pushed it away. Eventually it would become less vivid. It had to.

* * * *

The next day was a bright morning that augured well for the marriage, or so her father said. At the solicitor's office Sophia carefully read through the marriage contract, ignoring the "tut" noises coming from the clerk, before she signed. It was fair. Her father and her…fiancé…waited patiently for her. Today she was able to concentrate, to think more clearly.

She was her father's heir. When he died, his property would become her husband's, but the men had agreed certain caveats. Even if she chose to live apart from her husband, she would have ample means to do so. Property and money were left in trust for her with no way for Devereaux to get hold of them. She couldn't even sign it over to him, as several of her father's colleagues would have to agree first and countersign.

Her father had chosen the most puritanical of his friends for this task, together with two men who regarded her fondly. They would only do what they considered best for her. Financially, she was as protected as her father could make her.

Personally, though, she was wide open.

She clamped her lips together, stilling their trembling. She would have to learn, that was all.

When Max had kissed her, she'd had a strong urge to move closer, to see where that one kiss would lead. At the same time, panic rose, shortening her breath and making her heart pound double-time until she'd feared he'd feel it against his chest. Only his loose hold had given her the strength to stay where she was because he'd given her the choice to stay or to move away.

Nobody knew what John had done, the names he'd called her. The things he'd said. It would remain that way. Her father had seen enough to know John wasn't trustworthy. She'd been lying on the floor in John's arms, her clothes disarrayed, but that was after she'd fought off his first foray and he was heading towards another skirmish. He'd been in the process of telling her so.

He'd called her missish, said she'd learn to like it. But he'd forced himself on her, made her touch his…shaft, she supposed, from the way it felt, although he'd called it something else.

Sophia had never seen her father so angry. However, he didn't know it all. He never would, if she could help it. She'd led him on, John said, and she'd determined not to do that anymore. Ever, with anyone. Not if the consequences led to…that.

Including the man who'd just signed the papers promising to become her husband. He would never know everything; she couldn't afford for him to. If either of them broke that contract, they'd be subject to awful penalties in law, and the resultant court cases could ruin them both. So this was it, and they were committed.

Max took her hand and lifted it to his lips. "I need to visit my mother now." He grimaced. "I haven't told her yet. I doubt she'll object, though."

"You said—" She gulped when she recalled when he'd said his mother wasn't at home.

"She's acting as temporary chaperone for my cousin, Helena Vernon."

"Lady Helena Vernon," her father prompted. "Sister to the Earl of Winterton. Heir to the Duke of Kirkburton."

"Really. On your mother's side of the family." She recalled the book in her father's study with all the details of the most important families in the nation.

Max gave her a small bow. "Indeed so. I'm closer to my maternal relations. Most of my father's family is dead."

And so the need to provide an heir reared its ugly head yet again. *She would endure.*

"I would ask you to accompany me, but I pray your indulgence. I think I'm better telling her on my own. You will wish to arrange your packing, I daresay."

Although they weren't supposed to work on Sundays, that wouldn't stop Sophia ensuring her most precious personal belongings were packed ready for the move across London on Monday. "Will your mother be living in the house?"

Max's expression shuttered. "Some of the time. I hope to prepare the house in the country for her, so she may reside there. It has always been her dearest wish."

"I see." Should she be happy or sad that they would have the London house to themselves? Presumably with Max's mother came his sister. Sophia could excuse herself her marital duties, avoid spending too much time with this disconcerting man. At least until she'd learned to control her emotions better when she was near him. "Then I shall see you on Monday. Do you go to St. George's tomorrow?"

"I think not. I'll attend St. Margaret's, where we're to wed." A smaller church, almost a private chapel, where many of the aristocracy married.

"Should I go?"

"There's no need," he assured her, and after lifting her hand to his lips once more, he took his leave.

* * * *

Max wasn't looking forward to facing his mother. To tell the truth, he hadn't known how to tell her. And the arrangements happened so quickly he'd hardly had time to consider his actions.

Until yesterday she'd been in the country with Helena on a brief visit to a cousin, but now they were back and Max had no more excuses. He had to get this done, or she'd be so hurt he hadn't informed her of his wedding that she'd never speak to him again.

Accordingly he set out for the home of his cousin Julius, Earl of Winterton, half hoping he'd find them away from home. Then he couldn't be blamed, could he?

Unfortunately they were all in. Worse, they were *en famille.* If they'd had guests, he could have managed with a quiet private word before he left. But oh, no, they were in the elegantly appointed salon on the first floor of the house, even Julius's daughter Caroline, an adorable blond child of five—or was it six now?

Julius was seated on a sofa with her, reading from a book, and they laughed together as Max entered the room.

Anyone not knowing Julius well would be shocked by his relaxed, easy manner here. In society he was haughty and cold. Very few people understood why he behaved that way. Max did.

He glanced up at Max and paused, his sapphire blue gaze fixed on Max's face.

Max shrugged, and then greeted his mother, sister, and Julius's sister Helena. Helena vastly preferred living here than in the household of their father, the stiff and formal Duke of Kirkburton, who was also Max's uncle.

Interesting that his mother didn't notice the strain on Max's features, but the far more perceptive Julius did.

"Out with it," Julius said.

Max's mother, in the process of pouring her son a dish of tea, glanced at him. "Out with what?" She handed him the tea-dish in its deep saucer.

Max murmured his thanks. He held the delicate porcelain, wondering if Sophia would like something similar. He supposed he'd have to fill his house with feminine folderols.

He forced a smile and looked up. "I'm getting married."

His mother's dish hardly trembled in its saucer. She arched a finely-plucked brow. "Do we know her?"

Oh no, that "We" told him she was on her highest horse. "We" meant, "Is she one of us?"

"Sophia Russell," he said. "The daughter of one of my colleagues."

Julius pursed his lips in a soundless whistle. "Goldenbags," he murmured.

Thomas Russell's vulgar nickname, one he never answered to and Max pretended he didn't know when in the man's company.

"Yes. His daughter." For something to do, Max took a sip of tea. It tasted bitter on his tongue.

"One of the Bedfordshire Russells?" His mother's haughtiness came straight from court.

"One of the London Russells," he replied.

Helena was smiling. Max didn't trust that expression. She knew who he was talking about, too.

His sister, Poppy, on the other hand, seemed to have no idea. She was watching the conversation carefully, but from her sparkling eyes, Max knew she'd begin a volley of questions too. Poppy, to his jaundiced eyes, was the prettiest girl in the room, although Helena's serene loveliness drew attention from a multitude of admirers. The family resemblance between them wasn't marked, however. Poppy had a liveliness that often betrayed her into inappropriate but highly amusing comments. Helena measured everything she said and did. Her grace and elegance were renowned. Only the family knew the reason for that. If she took a wrong turn, did anything wrong, her mother would snatch her back.

Helena was the subject of a tug-of-war between Julius and his mother, the diminutive but redoubtable Duchess of Kirkburton. His mother wanted a companion, someone to fetch and carry and keep her company. Julius wanted Helena to have a life of her own.

By agreeing to act as Helena's chaperone in this house instead of her mother's, Max's mother had stepped between them. Max had to give his parent credit for that.

Now he addressed his sister before she made one of her unfortunate comments. He had no idea what it would be; that was one of Poppy's charms. But not in this instance. "Thomas Russell, Sophia's father, is reputed to be one of the wealthiest men in the country. I've known him for a while. His daughter is charming."

Max had no idea anyone could sniff so loudly before his mother did it. "A cit! You can't marry a cit, Devereaux!" She couldn't have been more shocked had he told her he was marrying a courtesan. "Upstarts. How will she go on?"

"Most creditably, I imagine." Should he pretend he was in love with her? No, because his mother would label that as vulgar. Love was for the lower classes, and it had no place in a proper marriage. He'd heard her say that so many times and ignored it just as many. He could mention her mother, but he'd do that in his own good time. "You should meet Russell, Mama."

"I cannot imagine what I would say to him."

It became Max's new ambition to bring the two together. "You may discuss your views with him on Monday." He answered her unspoken question. "That's when I'm marrying. The special license is in my possession, and we've signed the contracts."

"Without my agreement?"

He forbore to tell her that he didn't need her permission. Or agreement. But he'd rather have her approval, however grudging, if only to smooth Sophia's entry into his world. "Mama, I would appreciate your blessing. You'll like Sophia. She's a modest girl and a sweet one." And too easily biddable by someone as forcible as his mother.

For once, Max was glad his mama didn't live in his house. "She is a competent manager and prettily behaved."

"I cannot imagine how a woman of that background will manage in society. Will she expect me to sponsor her?" She sighed. "I suppose it is my duty."

"Mama, I will give you your house back." Expecting his mother's opinion to change, he continued, warming to his subject. "I can reopen Devereaux Place, restore the parts we had to close down, and complete the others. Finally you can have the house you spent do long creating."

She gave him a long unsmiling look. "I hope you haven't entered into this bargain just for that."

"No, Mama." Not the response he'd hoped for.

All his mother needed to set off on a diatribe on the modern way of life that looked as if it might continue for some time.

Ten minutes in, Max had had enough. He recalled another factor. He hated appealing to his mother's innate sense of superiority, but needs must, and he wanted her on Sophia's side. "Sophia came out six years ago. Her mother was Lady Mary Howard of Lancashire, but the lady unfortunately died shortly after Sophia's debut, and Sophia chose not to return to society."

At least that nugget won a pause from her ladyship. "Nevertheless, how will she cope with court mantuas?" And she was off again.

Murmuring that he needed to make arrangements for his bride, Max excused himself and quit the room, but by then, Lady Devereaux barely noticed. She was well into a story about Lady Mary Wortley Montagu's husband, who was a mere mister, and the marriage ultimately failed, and set fair to move on to others. He'd wager she'd almost forgotten his news but was enjoying reciting the choices pieces of gossip.

Footsteps behind him told him that Julius had also beaten a hasty retreat.

"A moment," his cousin said in that clear, penetrating voice of his. "In here, if you can spare me a little time."

He opened a door to one of the smaller rooms on this floor. Elegantly furnished for all its size, with gilded furniture and light blue upholstery. The walls held paintings, set in panels, of the four seasons. A room to make a person smile with pleasure. Max did not smile and followed Julius inside.

"Do you know of a man called John Hayes?" Julius asked.

A chill went through Max. What was this? "John Hayes is the man who used to work for my future father-in-law."

"I know." Julius folded his arms. "And something else, maybe?"

Max glared at him, thin-lipped, anger seeping through him. "He offered my betrothed an insult."

"By which you mean he forced himself on her?"

If anyone but Julius had brought up this subject, Max would have denied everything and left. Julius wouldn't have introduced the subject if he didn't have a reason. "Where the hell did you hear that?"

Max quelled his anger and, with an effort, concentrated on what Julius was saying. "You know I hear them all. What actually happened is your concern and yours alone. If asked, I will of course deny it. But you don't know everything about Hayes. You need to see something."

His cousin strolled across to a bonheur du jour set by one paneled wall, shook back the lace at his wrists and opened a marquetry drawer, pulling out a piece of paper. He handed it to Max. "What do you make of this?"

Max glanced at the document, then, when he reached the signature at the bottom, his attention sharpened. He read it again. "A letter from Hayes to the Duke of Northwich," he said. "What of it? It appears to be a standard business letter."

"Did you know Russell had dealings with Northwich?"

Max shrugged. "I didn't ask."

He glanced at the letter again. Read it. Frowned. "I don't know all his concerns but I'd be very surprised if Russell were doing business with these people."

He was reading about a consortium led by the Duke of Northwich, more political than anything else. "He wouldn't ally himself to a cause. Apart from all other concerns, it's not good business."

"I thought so." Julius returned the document to the bureau and turned the key. "From my research into Russell, I believe he's as honest as a businessman can be."

Max chose to take offence. After all, he was a businessman himself. He raised a haughty brow. "By which you are implying…?"

Julius barked a laugh. "That he has more integrity than the average politician. You can't go through life without getting a little dirty. Some are dirtier than others, that's all."

"Russell was grooming Hayes as his heir, but after Hayes's attack on Sophia, Russell dismissed him. Was the letter dated?"

Julius shook his head regretfully. "Unfortunately not."

"So he could have written it before or after his association with Thomas Russell." Max's frown deepened. "I'll speak to him about it."

Julius's chin jutted out. "Can you trust him?"

"Absolutely." He paused. "Treason isn't profitable, and it doesn't work with Russell's character."

"He would be a useful ally."

Max knew that tone. Julius's special area of business concerned the feud with the Dankworths and the connotations opposing the highly political family held. Julius was the conduit for the rest of the family, collecting information about the family that had plagued the Emperors of London for so long.

Their support for the Jacobites had nearly finished the powerful family of the Duke of Northwich. The Dankworths had been slowly rebuilding their fortunes after sacrificing a few of their number to justice after the Forty-five had dashed their hopes of a Stuart monarchy and power. After working slowly and surely for a decade, Northwich had become a power to be reckoned with once more.

Although nominally at least Protestant and loyal to the Crown, the Dankworths were still Jacobite to the last one of them. That was where their power lay. They would not give that up easily.

Max swore. Then used a few more words for good measure. "So what can I do about it? I'm as sure as I can be without seeing absolute proof that Russell isn't involved. But Hayes has connected with Dankworth at some point, either with or without his then master's permission. What does that mean?"

Julius bit his lip. And then took a quick breath. "You know war is coming. The Peace of Aix was a breathing-space, that's all." He shot Max a perceptive glance, his blue eyes sharp. "War is good for the economy, is it not?"

"Sometimes." Max hated to admit it, but he was a realist and he couldn't deny the truth. Commercially, war meant a full-time army and the supplies it needed, a national sense of optimism and patriotism, among other things. "Not that that's any reason to promote it."

"True, but some unscrupulous people might do so." Julius paused. "You know what happened to Alex?"

Another cousin, another Emperor. "I know he's blissfully happy with his new bride."

"But not without interference from the Dankworths." Julius grimaced and took a few paces from the window to the fireplace and back. Behind him the clock tinkled the half-hour. "The trouble with his wife, the brothel, the auction, that was all financed by Northwich. He was the mystery backer of the place that nearly proved Connie's downfall. I believe that was an opening salvo. A test, if you like, of how strong we are. Dankworth discovered we will hold together if we need to. He would have picked us off singly otherwise."

"Why would he set himself against us?" Max asked, genuinely perplexed. He shoved his hands into his breeches' pockets. "Surely our political opposition is old news. We ally ourselves with the winners. Always have. They can't bear a grudge, can they?" Although Julius dressed in the highest of high fashion and Max rarely bothered with his brocades and satins unless he had to, he felt more comfortable with Julius than with most men he knew. They thought alike, and neither had to bow to the other's intelligence. They could keep up with each other.

Julius frowned. "Think again. Northwich bears grudges that last a lifetime. But there are other reasons for him opposing the Emperors. Between us, we control, or have considerable influence in, most spheres of interest. Look at you, in the City. You could prove useful to Northwich, should he turn you to his cause. So could I, and Alex, and Nic. Everyone. I don't doubt he's testing us on a few fronts, but a wise soldier concentrates on one campaign at a time. And I fear we, the Emperors, are that campaign." He paused. "Your father-in-law-to-be is immensely influential. He has fingers in pies we cannot reach. He could be a useful addition to our party, if we need help. Or his."

"I see." Yes, he could. "Russell is loyal to the Crown, always has been, but he doesn't dabble in politics."

"He doesn't have to."

Max considered Julius's request and nodded. "I'll talk to him. Apprise him of the situation." It would be a prudent move.

Julius took a turn around the room, his coat skirt swinging. He paused to give the clock on the mantelpiece an infinitesimal adjustment. "Russell should know that allying himself to us would make him unacceptable in some quarters. The duke would do anything to bring us down." He turned back to face Max. The corner of his mouth quirked in a cynical half-smile. "Who knows? If we'd been on the losing side at Culloden, maybe we'd feel the same."

Max took half a second to consider his opinion on that issue. "My father threw away his fortune on that huge monstrosity in Buckinghamshire rather than fight renegade Jacobites."

"It's very beautiful," Julius, the lover of fine art protested.

"Some of it is. But who wants a palace? Especially one I can't do anything with. I'd love to sell the thing. Would you buy it?"

Julius gave a hard laugh. "Not a chance. We have our own palace, and one is more than enough. At least it keeps my father busy."

"Is your mother becoming a problem again?" Julius's mother made concerted attempts to reclaim Helena, but now Julius had brought his aunt, Max's mother, into the scene, Max wondered how matters would progress.

"No more than yours."

Both men laughed.

"Maybe we should start a book at White's," Max said. "On the winner and how long it will take." His mood sobered. "But seriously, now I'm marrying, we can offer Helena a haven, if she wishes it. Even at the mausoleum."

"I appreciate it." Julius crossed the room to Max and held out his hand. "I haven't said congratulations."

Max shook his hand briskly. "Thank you. Not something I expected to happen anytime soon, but I have to admit, I couldn't have done better from my personal point of view."

Julius frowned. "You love her?"

Max would have laughed, but Julius appeared too serious for him to mock. Then Max remembered what he should never have forgotten; Julius's own doomed love. He'd adored the woman he married—wild, bad, troubled Lady Caroline Foster. Julius had fallen completely for the delicate but beautiful woman, and when she'd died, many of the family had heaved sighs, very quietly so nobody would hear. Julius had frozen since her death five years ago, become the icicle some claimed.

That would make little Caroline six. Yes, the child was six. Sad that he could remember when Caro had died, but not when Caroline was born. If not for the child, Julius would have become completely sealed off, but he adored his daughter. The rest of the family loved her for helping him, however unwittingly, to keep part of himself alive.

Max thought of an appropriate answer. "Sophia's attractive, intelligent, and I like her." More than that he'd keep to himself. He couldn't admit how much the idea of having her in his bed excited him because he didn't understand or trust it.

"It's a good start," Julius said. "Better than many people have."

Chapter 5

Sophia went through her wedding with an air of disbelief.

She met her groom at the altar, but in one way he hadn't left her since she'd visited his house on Friday. She'd tried shopping to get his face out of her mind. She'd stopped at the Royal Exchange and purchased a new fan and gloves. But when she got home she wondered what she'd been thinking to buy a fan in such a lurid shade of pink. How could people produce such a violent color, and why would they? It was a poor impulse purchase like the gown of blue silk that had seemed so pretty on the bolt but once made up, didn't suit her at all.

She wasn't considering purchases or practical matters. All she recalled was his kiss. It kept replaying in her mind, the way their lips had met and melded. The way their bodies had pressed together and her heart had leaped, just once, as if it wanted to join his. More of those, and she'd be good for nothing.

She didn't use the fan or the gown for her wedding, but she did wear the gloves, which she had to take off at the altar when Max slid the ring on her finger. He'd chosen a single emerald with diamonds either side. Although she was no expert, Sophia knew a beautiful gem when she saw it. Clear, with color as true and pure as his eyes, the ring would remind her of him when he wasn't with her.

She'd never escape him, even if she wanted to.

She'd never seen Max so carefully dressed. When he was in the City, he wore plain clothes of excellent quality, as most merchants did, and if he attended a City function, he dressed soberly but finely. Not in shimmering scarlet with gold embroidery as he did today. He wore a wig, too, even though he'd grown his natural hair long and normally wore it tied it back with a black velvet ribbon. At least he didn't wear full maquillage, unlike his cousin Julius, Lord Winterton, who appeared unearthly in his magnificence.

Lord Winterton made Sophia fear him in this guise. Truthfully, she suspected he'd intimidate her anyway. He carried an aristocratic hauteur she had no idea how to counter.

At least she wasn't marrying him. A mere marquess, not a duke's heir. Not that the notion made her feel much better.

Most of Max's cousins attended the wedding breakfast, the panoply of the Emperors of London with outlandish names like Nicephorus and Marcus Aurelius. They held the breakfast at Max's town house, now her home. Her belongings would arrive, if they hadn't already, together with her maid. Even the ugly fan and the blue gown.

Apart from that clandestine visit last Friday, Sophia had never visited the house before. She knew the main rooms because all modern town houses had similar layouts. The ground floor contained smaller parlors and bookrooms or studies, the first, up the sweeping, elegant staircase, the drawing-rooms, music rooms, and farther up the grand bedrooms. She moved around the large salon with feigned confidence she was far from feeling inside. Reminding herself that this house was merely her father's house writ large, she went upstairs on her husband's arm and took charge of her domain.

The furniture was upholstered in pale ivory, and the wood polished to within an inch of its life. She'd be afraid to touch it, lest she leave fingerprints. Or to sit on the sofas, in case she left dust or dropped crumbs on the surface. Extravagance had a price.

Today she wore her best pale green with a white embroidered petticoat and stomacher, with her mother's pearls, a set so fine few could equal it. She'd felt well dressed until she saw some of the Emperors, and the Empresses, sisters and wives both. Still, the pearls could match anything they had to offer.

Her new mother-in-law approached her, smiling graciously. The title suited this lady much more than it did Sophia.

The dowager presented her hand as if she meant Sophia to bow over it, but she knew better. She touched it with her gloved fingers and lowered her eyes for a second, indicating respect but not deference. Respect for age and a prior holder of the title. The one she now held.

Lady Devereaux was a few inches shorter than Sophia, but that didn't give Sophia the advantage. Rather the opposite, as her ladyship had the bearing of a queen. And this was the lady who traveled from relative to relative acting as unpaid companion? Sophia found it hard to believe. Her ladyship's gown of cream watered silk was as fine as her own, and her diamonds gleamed in the light of the bright spring day.

"I am delighted to make your ladyship's acquaintance," she ventured. Any show of shyness, and the woman would eat her up like a crocodile savoring a little fish.

"The feeling is mutual, I vow." The aristocratic drawl she affected was completely absent in her son. He wouldn't have lasted long in the City had he used that. They'd have laughed at him while they took his money. But the older lady's speech made her appear even more daunting. "A little odd to marry this early in the season."

"I'm no debutante," Sophia said and felt obliged to add, "But my mother was."

Her ladyship's gaze focused on something in the far distance, and then returned to Sophia. "Ah yes. Lady Mary Howard. She was a taking little thing in her day, but somewhat wild, they always said. We thought it very strange when she married…your father."

A man from the City. One in Trade, or at least servicing it, for her father's main concerns were shipping and insurance. Would it have been better had he been a country squire? It could have been worse.

Sophia had no way of assessing the nuances of the way society judged people outside its purview. "My father was a perfectly suitable husband for her." She glanced at Max, busy in conversation with an older man she didn't recognize.

With only a slight glance to one side, the dowager swept up a glass of wine held on a tray by a servant who was heading past her. Sophia would have tumbled the whole tray had she tried that. She took a sip of her own wine, the cut glass winking in the sunshine coming in through the window.

"I daresay you wish me to introduce you to society?" the dowager said.

Sophia hated that she had to say this, but if she wanted peace between Max and his mother, she would have to. "I would consider it a great favor, my lady."

"Indeed." The dowager accepted the tribute as her due. "I will view my invitations and arrange matters."

"Will you move back to the house?" Sophia said.

Immediately the dowager shook her head. "I shall remain with dear Helena, and naturally Poppea will remain with me. They need me. Julius is interviewing suitable candidates for the post of governess to his daughter and companion for his sister, but it will take some time. He will be hard put to find one who fits his exacting standards, but I'm hopeful that he'll find success. However, I will not be far away."

This house was close to Grosvenor Square, set on one of the gracious streets nearby, the exterior white stucco, the interior all fashionable elegance. Sophia had not seen the room she was to occupy as the Marchioness of Devereaux, but she feared it already. If it was white or ivory, she'd have it changed tomorrow. If she dared. She needed *one* room to be comfortable in. Surely someone could be comfortable and fashionable at the same time?

Lost, adrift, Sophia planted her feet on the Aubusson carpet and waited on events, smiling and pretending to drink from her glass. Until the glass was empty and pretense had become reality. She took another one.

"Welcome to the family," a soft, feminine voice said.

When she spun around, Sophia nearly lost her drink. As it was, she had to contain the sloshing by holding it aside. Another black mark for her. She wasn't usually this gauche but then, she wasn't usually facing a wedding night with a man she barely knew, fighting impulses she didn't know what to do with.

She smiled at the lovely golden-haired woman standing before her and searched her memory for names. "Lady Ripley," she said eventually. "Thank you."

"Connie, please," the lady said. "I'm a relative by marriage, still getting used to the great Emperors. I'm a countrywoman at heart."

Married to the dark handsome man laughing with his cousin across the room. Lord Ripley, heir to the Earl of Leverton. Goodness, all these titles made Sophia's head spin. As bad as remembering which guild the man her father wanted her to meet belonged to and which coffee houses he frequented to conduct his business. Her problem was she had to commit both those spheres of influence to her memory now.

"I've never lived in the country," she confessed. "Unusual for an Englishwoman, I know, but not in the City. Most of us reside there all year round. We have a small house in the country, but we rarely go there." At Connie's arched brow, she gave a shamefaced laugh. "That is, my father and I. I'm sorry, I'm still trying to get accustomed to my new status."

"One step at a time," Connie said. "Take it slowly, and it will come to you. Remember when people say 'My lady,' they're referring to you. That took some getting used to. I keep turning around to look for Lady Ripley."

Sophia was surprised to discover she could smile. Even laugh.

Connie added, "Of course, I'm only a baroness. Alex's title is a courtesy one, but you married straight into the aristocracy." She lowered her voice. "Devereaux tends to intimidate me, although I don't think he knows he's doing it. He's so clever! Please don't tell him, because he is always so kind. But I have never been comfortable in the presence of people who can add a column of figures three times and get the same answer."

Sophia wouldn't tell her she could do it too, because this was the first person in this room to show her friendship.

Connie had clear blue eyes, and her lovely complexion was a thing of pellucid beauty. Everything Sophia had prayed for in her blemish-ridden, fluffy-hair days when she was supposed to be serene. Even this morning, she'd discovered a freckle on the upper slopes of her bosom and despaired all over again. Too high to cover with her fichu, which in any case was a gauzy silk affair and not her usual practical linen.

Connie's husband glanced across the room, and his attention fixed and held on his wife. Slowly he smiled, and it was a wonderful sight. It demonstrated all his love and devotion with no excuses and no concessions to anyone watching.

In that instant, Sophia's ambitions crystallized. She wanted her husband to look at her that way. As if the world revolved around her.

If only she'd known she wanted that before she married Devereaux! He was never likely to give her that kind of regard. He'd be considerate, in his way, and in time she could hope for an equitable relationship with him, but love? She doubted that. They'd agreed to marry for separate reasons of their own, but love didn't feature in any of them. Nobody would ever adore her like that.

Loneliness seized her in a tidal wave of despair. She had to fight to prevent any trace of it appearing on her face.

After a word to Sophia's husband, Lord Ripley set off across the room to join his wife. Devereaux accompanied him, and they arrived to claim their ladies, but Devereaux offered his arm for Sophia to lay her hand on and Ripley shamelessly ogled his lovely wife. Her response was to laugh.

Devereaux regarded them with indulgence, but when he turned to Sophia, his expression was coolly polite. But that expression the Ripleys exchanged had reminded her painfully of that kiss last Friday. For once, everything except the moment fell away.

She'd hoped to—what? Panic had driven her as much as any plan. She'd wanted to see him, try to understand what lay behind the handsome, controlled exterior, but she was no nearer that than before, when he'd been merely another of her father's business colleagues. "We will be going in to the dining room soon," he murmured to her. "Are you familiar with precedence?"

The rigid rules by which society conducted itself on formal occasions demanded that the hostess was aware of who went in with whom. At last something she could do. She knew all the ranks present today, and firmly putting personal considerations aside, she went about arranging people into the correct groupings.

* * * *

"That will please your mother," Alex said to Max as they watched Sophia efficiently and graciously go about her duties.

Max grunted. "Nothing about Sophia pleases her at the moment. She's not moving back home. She's staying with Helena."

Alex raised a dark brow. "Your mother could make Sophia's entrance into society easier."

"I believe she knows that." Max had no illusions about his mother. "Sophia has to prove to her that she's a worthy cause."

Alex hummed. "It could be worse."

As one of the few people who knew Connie's difficult path to love, Max understood what he meant. Alex had determinedly forced his wife on society, and now they had little choice, since she had the backing of the rest of the family. The Emperors would not be denied.

"Be bold," Alex said. "It's the only way."

"She has the strength to do it." Max knew that much about his new wife. "I have faith in her abilities to win society over."

"How about you?" Alex asked quietly.

Max shot him a puzzled glance. "I have no idea what you mean."

"Will she win you over? Has she done it already?"

Max raised a brow, giving his cousin a quizzical smile. "I am not unhappy, if that's what you mean. Don't expect everyone to find the kind of bliss you and Connie share."

"At least we proved it's possible, even in this family."

"Even? Nic's mother found true love."

"At the second attempt. You know her husband well, don't you?"

"He's a City man, and yes, I do meet him from time to time." Max recalled Thaddeus Beaumont, who was in a different line of business, but their paths crossed occasionally. "Aunt Frederica seems happy with him." Like the rest of the family, he'd breathed a sigh of relief when his aunt remarried a man who gave her the tranquility she needed after the turbulent first attempt.

"I like her." Julius had joined them.

He had two ways of moving. One was the flamboyant one, accompanied by the click of heels, the rustle of expensive fabric and waves of subtle but distinctive scent. The second was silent as a cat. This was the cat. Max had no idea how he did it, but he'd have paid dearly to know.

"My wife?"

"Yes, dear boy, your wife." Julius stood behind them, speaking low so only they could hear. "She has grace and poise. And a determination that I don't think you'll find it easy to overcome. I'd advise you not to."

What was this familial love for Sophia? She was winning over his family effortlessly. "I should have done this years ago, then. From what you say, I've married a saint."

Sophia, in the process of linking the people to go in to dinner, glanced at him. Had she heard him? He hoped not. He hadn't meant his comment to be as waspish as it sounded, but he was finding this day somewhat of a strain. Social occasions could be a trial, not to mention tedious, and this was no exception.

"Take care, Devereaux," Julius murmured. "Your lady has teeth."

* * * *

After dinner, they returned to the drawing room where Sophia set them working. One sang; another played the harpsichord. Since they were now joined by a stream of guests who arrived to wish the married couple well, this worked. At about ten, the company began to drift away.

Sophia kept her expression firmly in place, despite feeling like a doll tricked out for the amusement of the visitors. More would arrive in the days to come. How would she bear it? Whatever happened, she must. First impressions counted, and her acceptance into society was important to her husband.

Lady Devereaux mentioned her appearance at court during dinner. "For of course I will sponsor your appearance. I believe we should arrange a date for next month. Do you have a court mantua?"

Sophia shook her head. She'd never needed one. King George was old and a widower. Since the death of the Prince of Wales, Prince Frederick, the Duke of Cumberland and his wife had usually done the honors. Sophia knew that much because she read the newspapers. But before last week, she had no notion she would have to undergo the ordeal. With the gown.

Court dresses were hideous affairs that gave the wearer the appearance of a walking sofa. A huge flat hooped petticoat, the likes of the ones worn by the previous generation, and the mantua, long superseded in normal life by more modern styles.

"I'll visit a mantua-maker next week." Her usual dressmaker would probably not serve. Although she liked Mrs. Dormer's work as it was neat and fast, the fashioning of a mantua would take an expert.

"I can take you to mine," the dowager said. "You will probably find yourself in need of other items."

A slow tide of anger rose inside Sophia. How dare her ladyship assume, as if Sophia had come to this house in sackcloth? She wasn't without fashionable clothes, but she'd been aware she might need more. Armor. But to have her mother-in-law state the fact baldly made Sophia appear rustic and ignorant. Two things she was far from being.

"I appreciate the offer, ma'am, but I am not without resources of my own."

"Still," the dowager said, spreading her hands wide, "I would help you if you wish it."

"Thank you. I don't think that will be necessary."

Without meaning to, Sophia had drawn battle lines. Her lamentable temper! What was worse, Devereaux glared at her, his green gaze cold enough to send a breeze down her spine.

She spent the rest of the day in a miserable mood, but that at least enabled her to assess what was needed after dinner and to ensure it took place. All the time she was aware of her ladyship's icy regard, silent but deadly as a dagger between her ribs.

Girding her spirits, she decided to face this as she did everything, with serenity and dignity. Nobody should know her heart was quaking and her knees knocking under her elegant pale blue skirts.

She'd learned that lesson a long time ago; if she didn't show it, nobody knew. She had the kind of face that would conceal her anxieties, such that many people assumed she was cool and in control. It helped, but it didn't mean she hadn't vomited in private before public functions. As she had this morning, for instance.

So now she lifted her head and offered her ladyship the baked mushrooms, secretly hoping that they didn't agree with her and feeling guilty about the puerile wish.

Then finally, when the guests had departed, came her worst trial.

Predictably, Sophia lost most of her dinner before she left the powder room to take her place in the impossibly grand bed in the terrifyingly elegant room that would be hers. She had to rinse her mouth and clean her teeth all over again, but at least that deferred the moment.

The décor in her room was fresh and new, and as she'd feared, cream brocade predominated. For someone of her coloring—dark hair and skin some called creamy and others called sallow—it was the worst possible choice. But very elegant, nonetheless.

Her maid, French, helped her disrobe in near-silence. After all, what was there to say?

Sophia ordered tea. Always her first line of defense. She drank two dishes while French brushed out her hair and plaited it into its night-time braids.

Without her grand gown, Sophia felt smaller and without shields. Open, in a strange way. Nobody except her maid had ever seen her in her night clothes before, even though she wore a voluminous night rail and a robe over the top. But without her stays and hoop she felt raw, naked, and she disliked the vulnerability such a lack of garments brought to her.

Devereaux's deep voice shocked her. She hadn't heard him or seen him come in from her vantage point in front of the draped dressing table.

His first words were for French. "You may go. I'll see to her ladyship's needs."

He wore a robe too, and the white folds of a male nightshirt were visible above the deep crimson brocade. Sophia swallowed and pressed her fingertips on the table to still their trembling.

She'd known matters would come to this, but she couldn't still her shaking hands. Or put completely out of her mind what had happened when she'd last allowed a man this close. He'd hurt her, enough that she'd borne the marks for weeks and had to stop French helping her undress at night for fear she'd gossip. All servants gossiped. What they didn't know wasn't worth knowing.

John had damaged her pride, destroyed her confidence in her body. She recognized that, but it didn't help her overcome it.

She pushed the memories aside. That happened, and it was gone. Max wouldn't do that to her. Would he?

He smiled gently as the door closed behind French and held his hand out to her. "Come, my wife. Let's to bed."

Sophia ensured she locked her knees as she stood, or she might have fallen to the floor. She hated herself for this weakness, but she couldn't control it.

Concentrating on the face before her, she stepped forward and placed her hand in his. He drew her closer, slowly urging rather than dragging her, and gazed into her face.

"How long since that man put his hands on you?" he asked.

Shocked that he was thinking about the same thing, she gasped, the sound echoing around the room. "John, you mean?"

"Yes. Him." He sounded rough, but perhaps that was his way. Or he was concerned about her. She could trust him, tell him everything that had happened, but would he react in the same way her father would have? She'd never told her father for his own protection. If she'd told him the whole, he would have caused serious damage to John. While her father wasn't demonstrative, he did care for his own. Fear for her parent, not for her would-be lover, had driven her actions then.

In law, she belonged to *this* man now. Not something she liked, but she was never one to shy away from the facts. By signing the marriage contract and the marriage lines, she'd given herself to the Marquess of Devereaux. Willingly.

"Three months," she said. Should she tell Max it was a trivial event, that she'd exaggerated it out of proportion? No, because that would be to deny herself.

In a swift, decisive movement, he lowered his head and kissed her.

Totally shocked, unable to respond, she stood still and let him kiss her. She tried pursing her lips. He made a small sound, half gasp, half moan, and kissed her harder.

Her mind flashed back to that other experience. She frowned and pushed it away. Not here, not now. Not her.

Concentrating, she remained where she was, still, but she stiffened and her arms clamped her thighs. Reaching down, he touched her knuckles, eased them away, and guided her hands to his shoulders.

He was strong, his muscles flexing under her hands. When he drew his lips away from hers, he opened his eyes. "We must do this," he said. "You understand?"

She smiled, afraid it was more than a grimace.

"I won't hurt you. By all that's holy, I swear it. Come, then." He slid his arm around her waist and walked her to the bed. It was a grand construction, fashioned from mahogany with elaborate cream brocade drapery. By drawing back the covers, he revealed crisp white sheets. The sight seemed far too intimate for her liking. Would he want her naked? John had wanted it, although he hadn't succeeded.

No, she wouldn't think of that man. Absolutely not. Just that—she was afraid she didn't know if what John did was usual, normal for a man.

She was about to find out.

The bed was high and she needed to use the footstool to climb up. But before she did, he loosened the sash on her robe. The garment fell open, revealing her ankle-length white night-rail. It fastened with tapes at her neck, the sleeves came down to the middle of her forearms and the hem halfway down her calves, but for all the fullness, she felt bare. The fact that she was naked underneath made her fidgety.

Heat rushed through her body and she gazed at his feet, his shoulders, but not his face.

He undid the frogged fastenings at the neck and chest of his robe. When he held out his hand, she gave him hers. He took them to a chair set before fire.

Taking the opportunity of his turned back, Sophia scrambled into bed. By the time he turned back to her, she was sitting up with the candles in the inner sconces snuffed and the covers up to her neck.

He said nothing, but strolled across the room as if he had all the time in the world, and this was merely another social event. She hated that he seemed so at ease and she was eaten up, her breath short, her heart beating as if trying to find its way out of her chest. He showed no sign of agitation or excitement.

John had wide eyes, the pupil large, and his cheeks had flushed red as he tried to persuade her to do more than she wanted.

She swallowed, and did her best to control her rising panic.

Chapter 6

Max appeared perfectly calm. Those green eyes were bright, and he breathed in a steady rhythm that moved his chest under his nightshirt. Sophia had seen bare male legs before. She told herself she was seeing no more than she should.

But these legs belonged to a man who was about to get into bed next to her. And stay there, for she didn't know how long. Perhaps all night.

He might want to do it more than once. Was that possible? Not for the first time she cursed that she didn't know more, that she had no idea how to discover what she wanted to know. If she had, would she be so damnably afraid?

Probably. It might make this ordeal worse.

The mattress depressed when he got into bed, urging her to move toward him. Sophia fought to stay upright and keep her position straight. But when he reached for her, she didn't resist.

Gazing at her face, he seemed close to kissing her again, but then he sighed. "I'll make this as easy for us both as I can. I want heirs, Sophia. You understand?"

"Yes." She wet her lips and tried again. "Of course."

Gently he laid her down and watched her as he slid his arm to one side of her waist. "I must ensure you're ready for me. But before I do, know this. At any time if you are uncomfortable or you don't want me to do something, say so. I have never imposed myself on a woman without her agreement, and I won't start with my own wife."

During the service, they'd promised to worship each other with their bodies. That meant they had to undertake this act. She wanted this marriage to continue. She'd taken oaths and signed contracts, and to Sophia, that meant she had to go forward and fulfil her part of the agreement.

He stilled and gazed at her face. "Should we leave this for another time?"

Vigorously, she shook her head. She wouldn't be able to face this uncertainty any longer. She had to get it done now. "It's just anxiety."

He smoothed one hand over her waist. "I understand. Tell me if you're uncomfortable. I'm guessing you'll be easier in your mind if I explain what I'm going to do. Am I right?"

She nodded.

When he eased her down she did as he urged and lay on her back. Watching her face, he slid up her night-rail, right up to mid-thigh, and then touched her bare skin.

She flinched. He stopped, but she forced a smile. "I'm not used to it, that's all."

He paused, examined her face with a look that said he could see through to her soul with little effort. "I should stop."

"No, please."

With a sigh, he moved his hand, and a pleasurable shiver followed. "Your skin is soft. Warm."

Wasn't all skin? But he was trying to relax her, so she concentrated on his face and watched him as he touched her.

Nobody had touched her *there*. When she bathed or washed she treated the area exactly the same as she did the rest of her body, rinsing it thoroughly but not lingering. French helped her by washing her hair and her back, but she never allowed any intimate touching, although she knew some women didn't care. Sometimes she'd experienced strange feelings, stronger than usual sensations, but she hadn't lingered to discover.

Max's strong fingers grazed her most sensitive flesh, but he didn't stop there. He slid a finger between her folds and stroked down toward the opening. She swallowed but remained still for him.

Bringing his fingers to his mouth he wet them.

Had he really done that? Her moisture must be on his fingers. Was that what men did?

It was what this man did.

Then he slid his hand back *there* and touched her, stroked up and down. He moved easier now, and he hadn't pushed her night-rail up all the way, exposing her to his gaze. If he kept it like this, he wouldn't open her completely. She could pretend it was happening to somebody else. That way she could cope.

He touched her more intimately, deeper, and slid a finger inside her body. She gasped and bit her lip.

He paused. "Try to relax. It won't hurt as much."

"It will hurt?" Her alarm rose, and she must have tightened, because he withdrew.

"Yes, it will hurt a little. It usually does the first time, or so I'm told."

"You've never done this before?"

He shook his head. "Not with a virgin." At the word he stilled, gazed at her face. "You are a virgin, aren't you?"

She nodded, but she couldn't be certain. How could she know? John had hurt and frightened her, and made her furious with herself for not making him stop sooner. Had he taken her virginity? She hadn't bled much, more as if he'd scratched her. And she hadn't felt so stretched as she did when her husband moved his finger inside her.

"Of course you are," he said grimly. She kept her attention on his face as he adjusted his own clothing, but thank God, didn't take anything off. Then he moved over her.

He kept his weight off her, but his thighs nestled next to hers, straddling her. Sophia concentrated on keeping her breathing steady. Slowly he lowered his body until he—*that*—touched her. He was dry but soft, silky. His breathing deepened. Hers quickened.

With an abrupt movement untypical for him, he lifted himself off her. "No," he said. He dragged her night-rail back down her legs and pulled the covers over her before he took her hand. "You're tired. It's been a stressful day and you're not ready."

Afraid, uncertain, she grasped his hand. "I'm fine, truly. Please do this."

"Get it over with?" he said with a wry twist of his lips.

"Yes. I can't bear not knowing. Not—I don't want you to stop." So afraid that if he left now she'd never let him back.

He gazed at her, his face so serious but closed-off. She couldn't tell what he was thinking. "You're unwilling."

"I'm not." Tears nestled in her eyes but she ignored them. They were only a reaction, nothing of importance. But she would not allow them to fall. She hadn't cried since—no, she wouldn't think of it. "Please, Max." She'd used his name. The word dropped from her lips without conscious thought. A spark of courage returned.

He searched her face again as if he could read the truth there. Perhaps he could. "You promise to tell me if you're uncomfortable or you want me to stop."

She swallowed again and clutched his sleeve. "Do this. I want to be a proper wife to you." Whatever it took.

His face relaxed a little, enough to allow him to smile. "We're both novices at this."

"But you've...done it before."

The smile broadened. "Yes, I have. But not with you."

When he straddled her again, she knew what he'd do, and she could relax until he was once more settled between her thighs. This time he grasped his member and guided it closer. Then he touched her opening.

Sophia was proud of herself. She didn't flinch and kept her expression steady. Dry-eyed, she met his green gaze. His eyes were almost uniformly green, the lighter sparks unnoticeable, a darker ring surrounding the iris, but the shade was as remarkable close-up as it was at a distance.

"Ready?"

"As I'll ever be."

He withdrew his hand. Then pushed.

He grunted low in his throat but he didn't press harder. That would definitely have hurt.

"Lift your knees."

She did. He moved a little farther inside. Not far, she could tell, but enough to lodge the very tip at her entrance. Was that enough?

He nudged again. This time the resistance gave slightly. His next move was to rotate his hips. His member shifted. Sophia bit her lip, but lifted her hands to hold on to his upper arms. Under the fine cloth of his nightshirt, his muscles were hard as iron, which surprised her. To know her husband was stronger than she'd imagined should have given her pause, but it reassured her. He could have used that strength to take her as he wanted, but he chose to introduce her to this as carefully as possible.

Keeping his weight off her, he raised his body and straightened his arms. "Hold on," he said, and he thrust hard.

Right inside. A sharp pang tore through her, sending agony shooting through her whole body.

After one shocked cry Sophia forced herself to quieten, afraid he would leave. She wanted this over now, to complete the act so she could rest, so she knew what to expect in future.

The pain receded, and she could once more assess how she responded. Still here, still Sophia, and with part of a man's body inside her own. Strange but not unbearable. In relief, she smiled.

He smiled back. "Better now?"

"Much."

Now, with a man closer, more intimate than anyone had ever been before, she felt strangely content. "Is that it?"

"This? Oh no, my sweet. There is the matter of satisfaction. I have to… Wait and see."

But her anxiety didn't rise again to swamp her, because she trusted him to take care. This was his right, and he could do what he liked in the marital chamber. Instead of hurting her or taking her quickly, he'd taken every care to give her the least discomfort.

He moved, working his shaft partly out, and then in again.

"I never imagined a woman could be this tight," he said, and then, "Are you all right?"

She'd never imagined she could talk while he was doing this, but she found it quite easy. Except she doubted she could concentrate on anything but him and what he was doing to her. "This is…fine."

His smile turned wry. "I'm glad to hear it," was all he said.

His movements turned into a steady rhythm. She counted, opened her legs to allow him as much access as he needed. It wasn't unpleasant once she'd recovered from her initial shock. He slid easier as time passed, around the sixth stroke. By the tenth, warmth heated her body, and his face had flushed. Not all over, but just his cheekbones. His eyes darkened, but intelligence remained there, and he watched her for signs that she was uncomfortable. They were making a sound now, the steady slap of flesh meeting flesh, and a wet sound she should have been ashamed to make, but was not.

She couldn't claim she was uncomfortable, and wouldn't have told him in any case. A residue of fear remained, but not unreasoning. More acceptable, something that was a natural reaction to a situation that was completely new to her. An intimacy she'd never known before, and one she wasn't entirely sure she liked. But she didn't find the experience so terrifying.

By the tenth stroke, his breath was coming shorter and she watched him, waited.

Then, on the sixteenth, he grunted low in his throat, such a masculine sound that she almost smiled. He gritted his teeth as heat gushed into her below, wet heat that dampened the tops of her thighs.

He hung over her, his head dropped forward, breaking eye contact, and his chest heaved with deep breaths. She hadn't thought he'd exerted himself too much. But perhaps she'd concentrated so hard on keeping herself still for him, receiving his attentions and not alarming him in any way, that she'd missed it.

After a few minutes, his breathing steadied, and he lifted his gaze to meet hers once more. Without warning, he dipped his head and planted a swift kiss on her lips, not pausing to explore as he'd tried to do before. Then he pushed off her.

Wetness flooded out of her, but before she could turn away, embarrassed, he turned over and swung out of bed.

"Stay there," he said.

Bemused, Sophia watched him cross the room to her washstand. After wringing out a fresh cloth in the water in the basin he returned to her. "Let me make you more comfortable." He applied the cloth to her nether regions.

The water was cool, but it she welcomed the way it soothed her heated flesh. She'd never have considered doing such a thing, but he was right. It did help.

Reaching down, she took the cloth from him and did it herself, careful to keep her night-rail as a modest cover. While not afraid of what he'd do any more, she still didn't want him staring at her, especially in such an undignified situation. "Thank you," she said. "That is better."

His lips quirked. "I wondered what you were thanking me for. How do you feel?"

Relieved. "Fine," she said, wondering how she could tell him that he'd eased her concerns. But she couldn't discuss her previous experience while she was in bed with him. It didn't seem right. "Will I fall pregnant now?"

"You might," he said, "But it usually takes more than once."

Apprehension tightened her chest once more. "Tonight?"

"No." His tones were firm. "Perhaps not for a few days. I'm told that virgins need time to recover."

"Where did you find these things out?" Perhaps she could find out more too. At present, she found it difficult to understand why people would choose to do this for pleasure, or why so many problems stemmed from this act. It wasn't something she couldn't live without. Surely there had to be more to it.

"There are places. Not ones where you may go, my lady. We won't repeat this for a while, until you've recovered."

Yes, that was a good word for it. She would need time to recover. Like an invalid resting after an illness. Not that she wanted to think of it that way, but when she shifted experimentally, she winced.

He grimaced. He was sitting on the side of the bed, not fully in it. "You're sore. Don't deny it. I expected you would be. I tried to lessen it for you. Are you feeling better now?"

Lynne Connolly

She nodded. Yes, she'd be fine. She could do this. Relief swept through her. The idea of being treated as John had treated her for the rest of her life, perhaps every night, had worried her beyond reason. But her new husband had shown her that it didn't have to be that way. It would work. They might even become friends.

In her youth, she had read accounts of undying love, but she'd never aspired to it. Romeo and Juliet got nothing but death from it, and other couples had seen love as the symbol of their destruction. Anthony and Cleopatra, Francesca and Paolo. No, she could easily survive without that. But a friend with whom she made children and shared her life—yes, she could do that. They had a mutual interest in figures and in business, and that would help, too.

Her mind clicked back into action, beginning to run along its usual course. Business, household, and now she could add children. If and when they came.

Max refreshed the cloth once more and, when she was done, took it away and helped her put her nightwear into a modest arrangement. Then he covered her up and bade her lie down.

"Get some sleep," he said kindly. "It's been a very long day. Stay in bed tomorrow if you wish to. Nobody will consider it unusual."

He didn't kiss her again but patted her shoulder in an awkward gesture before he turned and left the room. Not by the main door, but by the one on the side wall that connected her room with the boudoir and then with his suite.

* * * *

What the hell had gone wrong? Max hadn't meant his wedding night to take the course it had. He'd done the best he could, but he still felt like the greatest beast in nature.

Returning to his room, he'd stripped off his robe and nightshirt and dropped them on the floor. He never wanted to see them again.

How could he have treated her that way? Striding naked across the floor, he reached for the brandy decanter and poured a healthy libation. The decanter rattled against the glass, demonstrating his agitation in a light clatter.

Sophia had borne it bravely, but she'd been terrified. He swallowed the brandy without tasting it, savoring the heat as the liquor trickled down to his stomach. He poured another.

He'd taken her like a rutting bull. Once he'd entered her and made her his, he couldn't stop. She'd felt like heaven.

True, he hadn't had a woman for some time. Six months or thereabouts, but he'd been too busy working, preparing the ground for the deal he'd finally inked with Russell.

But Sophia, his wife, had welcomed him with a sweetness he didn't deserve and a fortitude that made him want to weep.

What had that bastard done to her? Even given her virginal state, Sophia was unreasonably terrified. He'd had to use all his concentration to work his way inside without causing her too much hurt, because she'd clamped around him like a mantrap.

He winced at the notion. Ugly, painful things. He didn't allow them on his estates.

But she'd made him into one. Her reaction had rocked him. He'd planned to stay with her, to gentle her into accepting him lying next to her, holding her, but he couldn't do it. He'd wanted her badly, taken with a primitive need to claim her.

He'd never forget her expression. When he'd entered her, her eyes were wide and her mouth drawn back. He never, ever wanted to see that expression again.

Better to let his wife get used to her new station and then return, see if she could accept him more willingly. But he'd give her time.

He took his third drink to bed with him and sat up, sipping slowly. Time. Perhaps they both needed it.

Chapter 7

Ranelagh Gardens wasn't a new place to Sophia, although her hosts appeared to think so. Julius and Helena had brought her here to celebrate her recovery from the ordeal of being presented at court. Sophia felt far more comfortable in these raffish gardens, not because she was raffishly inclined, but because of her familiarity with them.

Julius and his sister had been more than kind to her. Now she called them by their given names, and she wondered how she could ever have considered Julius intimidating. She'd seen him with his little girl, and with his sister, Helena, teasing him, and because he'd allowed her to share his more human side, Sophia liked him. Even better, she had none of the feelings that made her tongue-tied and stupid, as with Max.

Julius had acquired a booth by the Octagon, where they could watch the world go by, eat an elegant supper, and listen to the orchestra, who tonight were defiantly playing Italian music. Defiantly, because Ranelagh's main rival, Vauxhall, was a strong supporter of Handel's music.

Due to the huge chandelier above, one of the marvels of London, and the lights in the booths, the light was almost as bright as day in this part of the Gardens. People promenaded, watching each other with avid or curious eyes, and Sophia drank in the vista from her new perspective of one of the highest in the land. Or rather, the wife of one of them.

Most people acknowledged her, and the few who didn't obviously didn't realize that repercussions from the Emperors could be societal death.

If the Pretender ever set foot on England's shores, as rumor had it he did, he'd come here rather than Vauxhall. Probably feel quite at home. Not that Sophia expected to meet him tonight. Or any other, come to that.

Julius had gathered a convivial but select group of his friends who welcomed Sophia warmly into their midst. That came as a welcome change. In the three weeks since her marriage, Sophia had attended balls, routs, and Venetian breakfasts, and had her stultifying, agonizing presentation at court that day.

She was now officially a member of society, with the most expensive hideous gown she'd ever owned taking up space in her clothes press.

Tonight she wore apple green, the triple ruffles of pure white lace at her elbows a testament to the skill of the Frenchman who'd had made it. She'd chosen her pearls as jewelry, but she had more gems at her command these days, thanks to Max's careless generosity. Almost as if he were trying to make up for his constant absences from her side and total absence from her bed.

At court, the Duke of Cumberland had been kind but distant. The duchess kind and vague. Sophia had managed to walk backward without falling over her train, so she'd counted that day a success. And for a change, Max had been there. To her chagrin, she craved his touch, longed for him to join her in bed once more. But he never had, and she hadn't yet built the courage to visit him in his bed. If he rejected her, she feared she'd never recover the ground lost.

"More wine?"

Shaking her head, she covered her glass. "I still have some."

Julius raised a brow. "You're slowing down."

She laughed. "I don't drink a great deal."

Max's cousin had shown her a great deal of kindness and attention. At first, she'd thought he was interested in more than her friendship, and she'd shied off, but he'd put her at ease. In fact, for a man with such a fearsome reputation, he'd behaved perfectly honorably. Sophia had to admit she'd been disappointed at first, as well as relieved that he didn't see her as one of his conquests. But she feared she wasn't bait for the roués and rakes of this world. Not even for her own husband.

Julius had a reputation as a heartbreaker, a man who moved from woman to woman as the fancy took him, keeping his own heart intact. He had no heart to lose since the death of his wife, or so gossip had it. Where Max had left her to her own devices, Julius had been as attentive as he could without raising gossip.

"Do you expect Max tonight?" he asked, his tone indifferent.

She shook her head. "He has a great deal of work to do, so I gave him the evening off. My father has a new scheme in mind and they are discussing it tonight."

"You know your father's business well." Julius toasted her, the red wine in his glass gleaming in the candlelight. "A clever woman."

"Oh no, I'm no bluestocking." She could never hold her own with the intellectuals in the literary salons. Not that anyone had asked. Leaning back, she watched the spectacle of a man who seemed to be laced tighter than she was struggling to dance.

Julius followed her gaze. "Indeed," he said thoughtfully. "I don't like to speak ill of anyone, but he does appear to have overdone the stays."

The man in question bulged top and bottom. Although nobody would consider him overweight, a slender waist and hips were aspirations of men of fashion, and this one seemed determined to enhance his assets.

"I didn't realize men laced," she said.

"Some do it for reasons other than vanity," Julius drawled.

She turned her head and stared at him in astonishment. His sapphire eyes twinkled in the low light of the candles set in the sconces at the back of the booth. She caught a whiff of his cologne, something citrus. Oranges. He was exquisitely dressed, but nonetheless as masculine as a man could be, yet he didn't arouse anything but amusement in her. "What can you mean?"

He raised a brow and leaned forward, lowering his voice to a confidential undertone. "I'm only telling you this because you're a married woman. I couldn't possibly tell my sister, so you must promise not to let her know."

Sophia would guess that the worldly Helena knew whatever Julius was about to tell her already. But she went along with the game and willingly gave her word. "She won't hear it from me."

He lowered his voice to a near-whisper. "I hear tight lacing enhances pleasure under certain circumstances." He leaned back, smiling. "Of course, you'd know that better than I. I don't lace."

Stricken, she stared at him. Her one experience of intimate relations had told her nothing of pleasure. Only discomfort and respect. Someone drew her attention, a man dancing at the opposite side of the Rotunda from their booth. A familiar movement, a turn of his body, and he'd gone again.

Quickly, she flicked open her fan and passed it before her face, but he took it from her and performed that office.

His expression had turned grave. "Is something wrong?"

"No, nothing." She prayed her heated face wasn't resulting in a fiery blush, but she feared the worst.

"Can it be...?" He searched her visually, his sharp gaze missing nothing. "I won't ask," he said eventually. "I don't need to."

She needed to leave. On her own. Rising, she held out her hand, palm out to prevent him getting to his feet. "I'll be back soon. I need some air."

That was often a euphemism for needing to use the necessary, and the excuse would stop him coming with her.

He inclined his head and shot a glance at her maid. French, sitting quietly at the back of the booth, stood and followed Sophia out.

"I'm hot," Sophia said, strolling along the path that led to the groves. They were designed for a certain amount of privacy, so she wouldn't enter one. Julius had drawn too close to her secret shame. Her husband hadn't been near her bedroom since their wedding night. Hadn't shown any desire to do so. When she'd caught him looking at her, it had been with a speculative air, not desire.

One time she'd seen pure animal lust, and it had frightened her out of her mind.

She'd had an admittedly limited experience of intimate relations, so she couldn't be sure. All she knew was that she never wanted that to happen again.

So much that she thought she'd seen John Hayes by the Rotunda, dancing with a lady in pink. But after he'd attacked her, she'd seen him everywhere in her imagination, so it was probably a result of that.

She took deep breaths of the crisp, late spring air and forced calm into herself. Since she'd glimpsed that man who'd looked like John her breath had shortened and her heart beat faster, while panic threatened to overwhelm her. For no reason.

This was foolish and she hated it. Hated feeling helpless and fluttery when she saw someone who vaguely resembled him. And when she thought back, the experience hadn't been too bad.

"Sophia."

She spun around. No, no mistake. John Hayes in person. Wildly, her heart pounding, she looked about her. A few people wandered within screaming distance, but that was all. If she ran he'd catch her. But he didn't look as if he was going to attack her. No, he was at ease, confident.

He was wearing his green coat, the best he owned, and a new waistcoat which glinted with silver and brilliants. He'd swept off his cocked hat but didn't take his attention from her face as he bowed to her.

The air caught in her throat once more as if she'd never recovered from the initial ordeal. She would not give in, not allow him to see how much he'd hurt her.

He smiled, that self-confident grin she remembered. Strangely, that helped. It reminded her of the time when he was courting her, behaving like a gentleman. Civilized, almost.

Still, she kept her distance. She gave him a chilly nod. "Mr. Hayes."

"Do I not merit a 'John'? We are old friends, after all."

If she succumbed to that, it gave him permission to use her first name. It would give him tacit permission to call a marchioness "Sophia," and he could take advantage of that. She'd ignored his earlier use of her name, as to object would have been undignified and petty, but she wouldn't give him explicit permission. She didn't reply, and tilted her head. He stood between her and the booths, as no doubt he knew.

Breathe.

She forced a breath in, and then another. "I'm not Sophia Russell any more. As no doubt you know."

A tinge of sadness entered his bright eyes. They were blue, not as deep and rich as Julius's, but with an icy touch that chilled. Even now, when they were filled with warmth, that edge of coldness remained. "Of course." He executed a low, graceful bow. "My lady."

She inclined her head graciously, praying the pulse frantically beating in her throat didn't show in the soft light. Flambeaux—flaming torches set in sconces—lit these paths, but the effect was deliberately limited to give lovers the privacy they craved. He was standing between her and escape.

"I have to congratulate you on your good fortune," he said. "But to my demerit."

Rising from his bow, he took a step toward her. If he leaped at her, French would have to run to the booths. Could she get there and back in time?

Sophia fought not to retreat. "Thank you," she murmured. She'd have to walk toward him to get away, so she stayed where she was and recalled her father's training. She removed her emotions and observed him. Studied him.

He was handsome, shorter in height than Max, with less…vitality, somehow. Max had an energy that was apparent in everything he did. John kept his thoughts to himself, so she had never been sure what he was about to do or say.

He wasn't a monster, after all. Slowly his image had grown and developed in her mind until he became everything that was evil. As she breathed easier, her reason started working again, as if a blossom opened deep in her heart.

She would stay and exchange a few cold words with him, making it clear she didn't want to know him anymore.

He watched her and he broke into a smile, as sweet as she remembered. Before that day, he'd amused her, persuaded her that she loved him. "I have missed you, Sophia. More than I can say. And yet I feel responsible for your…hasty marriage."

He'd used her name anyway. She wouldn't encourage it.

Now she'd forced rationality back into her head, she could assess his thoughts and she could almost see them, as if he'd written them down. Had she married Max because she couldn't have John?

"I'm not unhappy." Yes, she was, but he didn't need to know that. Would never know it if she could prevent it.

"I see. And of course, the chance of becoming a marchioness is not to be sniffed at."

She frowned at that gentle hint of…what? Did John want something? Patronage?

He gave her a small bow. "I'm currently working as a political secretary to a man of rank. I do hear more than I used to, and I wasn't uninformed then."

A shadow crossed his eyes, or was that because he'd tilted his head farther to the left? He glanced at French, but the maid stood her ground, watching him warily. Sophia had put off the clothes she'd worn the day John had attacked her and told French to get rid of them, not wanting to see them again.

"May we have a moment's privacy?"

Sophia glanced at French and nodded. That gave her maid the opportunity to move past John, on the right side, ready to run for help should she need to. Fortunately, French seemed to have some sense and did exactly that.

John lowered his voice to an intimate level, but Sophia refused to venture any closer, as his tones invited. "What passed between us the last time we met… Sophia, I'm sorry. I can't tell you how sorry I am. I cannot undo what I did. I can only pray I didn't do too much."

He flicked a glance up at her face. She kept her expression steady and waited for him to continue.

"I was carried away, and I thought you wanted what I did. I would have stopped before your father interrupted us, I swear, but nothing has affected me that deeply before."

She didn't believe him. He had shown no intention of slowing down, had resisted her when she fought him. She repressed her shudder.

"I regret so much what I did. It placed you out of reach, ensured that I would never win you." Not to mention losing his lucrative place in her father's company. "More than anything in the world, I wanted you. I still do, but believe me, I will only act as your friend. I'll never behave inappropriately again, I swear."

"I doubt our paths will meet." Her heart pounded harder. An apology at last, but did he mean it?

"I fear they might." His mouth turned down. "My new position puts me in places where it's possible we'll see each other. I wanted to speak to you in private to assure you that I will never, ever, behave like that again."

A spark flickered in the depths of his eyes and then was gone, leaving Sophia wondering if she'd imagined it.

"Uninvited, unwanted. I frightened you and I'm more sorry for that than for everything else."

She found her voice. "Shocked."

John's words sounded like a true apology, and after all, they'd only completed the act once. Out of all the times they'd spent alone together, only once had he attempted to go too far. She'd enjoyed his kisses and caresses before that last time, and he'd always stopped when she'd asked him to.

Already she was halfway to forgiving him, but she couldn't be sorry she hadn't married him. John's persuasiveness could carry him far. She appreciated his thoughtfulness in speaking to her before she met him in public. If that was all he wanted.

So far her marriage hadn't proved an unmitigated success. John had been kind, thoughtful, respectful, even, until that last time.

Why had he done it? Had he thought she wanted him to take her by force? Or was she so repellent that men had to force themselves to take her?

Probably, she thought with an inward sigh. So far the two men who had shown any interest in her were either too enthusiastic or not enthusiastic at all. One had terrified her, the other bewildered her. Max had made her want him, had eased her fears, and then left her completely alone.

"I was shocked," she repeated, more firmly this time. "What made you do it?"

"A demon," he growled and put his hand to his head, giving his wig a twitch. "I wanted you, but I lost all sense of propriety. It was my fault entirely. Hotheaded youth, that was all. I was foolish."

She could accept that, intellectually. With her head she understood, but her body still screamed at her to run, to get away. "And your reason for approaching me tonight was…?"

"Because I have burned to apologize to you, but events separated us. I believe your father arranged your marriage to keep you away from me, and I bitterly regret that."

"And the rumors?" The ones that had nearly destroyed her reputation, brought her down, and put her father's business in danger. If he couldn't control her, why would people assume he could manage their investments?

"That was not me, I swear it. I would never spread such scurrilous gossip."

If John had obtained a political secretary's position, that spoke to his discretion. What if it wasn't he who'd told her friends that she'd let him seduce her?

"So I have you to thank that I'm now a marchioness." She gave him a slight smile, one she hoped appeared condescending and aristocratic. "Thank you."

"You're welcome." His smile was broader. "I didn't want you to meet me somewhere you didn't expect and have a fit or something. Like Lady Danvers's ball next week." He shrugged. "I should be attending that, and other events too."

My, he had come up in the world. He didn't sound sorry for that. She presumed political secretaries would go to some of the larger gatherings, if only to collect information for their employers.

Lifting her skirts, as if to take care not to touch him, she gave him what she hoped was a gracious nod and stepped forward, her heart working double-time. "I doubt you'd have given me an apoplexy. What happened between us may be termed unfortunate. Nothing more. Let us forget it, pray."

Not that she ever would, but he didn't have to know that.

He moved out of the way, and she sailed back to the booth where Julius and Helena were waiting. Julius gave her a raised brow and a, "Better now?" to which she nodded. She could even drink her wine.

Chapter 8

When she came down the stairs one evening a week after meeting John at Ranelagh, Sophia found her husband waiting.

She was attending yet another ball and not looking forward to it one bit, but she'd manage. This endless succession of routs, balls, and entertainments meant she spent the days replenishing her wardrobe and the evenings attending the functions. Sometimes she read about herself in the newspapers the next day. After the first time, she learned to accept it, if not like it.

The constant round of activity bewildered her. Before, she had a purpose, but now she wasn't sure what she was doing. And that was what she said to Max when she saw him in the hall, ignoring his broad-shouldered handsomeness as best she could.

"Why do we do this?"

"What?" He brushed a fleck of dust off his sleeve and glanced at her. Then stilled, his hand not moving and his gaze fixed on her. He perused her, head to toe and then back again, and for some reason she shivered. It wasn't a cold night.

She groped for the banister rail and went down the remaining steps with caution, until she reached him.

His handsome face broke into a smile. "You look lovely tonight. I like you in green."

"I match your eyes," was all she could think of saying. Stupid, but it came out so quickly she couldn't stop it. She'd chosen the fabric for this gown because it reminded her of his eyes. Like it or not, her husband attracted her as no other man.

He flicked a glance over her head to the pier glass on the opposite wall. "So it does. Although that wasn't the first thing I thought of when I saw you." He put his hands on her waist, drew her closer, and lowered his head.

His lips met hers. She'd assumed he wanted to kiss her cheek, as he had in the past weeks from time to time. But he didn't. He took her mouth.

They couldn't nestle close. Her hooped petticoat wouldn't allow it, but she stretched up to meet him and opened her hand on his cheek, the bristles prickling her palm.

His lips moved as they kissed. Bliss. He tasted her when she opened her mouth shyly against his, slid his tongue around her lips and moaned a little, the sound vibrating against her skin, deliciously teasing.

The kiss finished slowly, and he drew away from her slowly, gazing at her. "You're beautiful," he said.

That moment was so perfect, Sophia had forgotten the presence of the servants, something that usually inhibited her behavior. At home with her father, although the house was much smaller, they had fewer servants, and Sophia always had them knock before they entered a room. But Max had the aristocratic way of ignoring the domestics, unless he wanted something.

With a flourish, he held out his arm. She placed her gloved hand on it in the approved manner. He liked her. He thought she looked attractive. So why wasn't he coming to her bed?

Sophia had no idea why, but perhaps the way to entice him back was to make friends. Men disliked disturbance. Her father hated it. So undertake her duties cheerfully, support him, deal with her problems, and smile through it.

Not that she'd beg. She did that as much for her own pride as she did for him. She had her standards, and they didn't include spending the day in idleness.

Max helped her into the carriage. "Is there anyone we should be talking to tonight?" she asked him, once she'd settled her skirts.

He was gazing at her. She shifted as her body heated uncomfortably.

"Ah...in what way?"

"You're a businessman," she reminded him.

He leaned back opposite her and crossed his legs. "So I am. No, there is nobody in particular. But it's a big event, and there could be all manner of people there." His attention sharpened. "One of the things I like about you is your intelligence."

And here she was enjoying his powerful body and handsome features. Ah well, it was a start.

After seeing John at Ranelagh, Sophia had finally managed to get her experience with him into perspective. It had been the most unpleasant time of her life, but it had ended with no harm. Somehow she'd become stuck on it, made it more important than it should be, but now she could see it for what it was. A minor incident that had no bearing on whatever she chose to do with the rest of her life. Time to move on, to look forward to her new life.

"Thank you. I'll bear that in mind."

The dim light of the carriage revealed no more than the glitter of his eyes. "Perhaps we may continue what we started in the hall tonight when we get home."

Shock and pleasure held her frozen for a minute. As she opened her mouth to reply, the carriage drew up outside the house in Grosvenor Square where they were due to attend the ball.

Torchères were lit outside the houses on this side of the square, and as they descended, link boys rushed over to light their way. As if they had more than half a dozen steps to take. Sophia laid her hand on her husband's arm, feeling a fraudster. She shouldn't be here, with people treating her like a princess, wearing clothes that would keep a governess in funds for years. Not only did she have a maid, but her maid had an assistant.

Did anyone else here feel that way? As they went through to the brightly-illuminated hall, she glanced at the others present, who appeared nonchalant and careless. They would toss those exquisitely fashioned garments and fans at their servants and say they were tired of them. Sophia would be more likely to wear them until she'd worn them out. Not that she could, because after one season they were out of style. A waste, but as she knew only too well, a boon to the silk weavers of Spitalfields.

So many guests made the spacious hall appear small. Candles guttered in the sconces, filling the air with the aroma of hot beeswax and perfumes blended to a mixture of sweet and musky.

Max took the whole scene in at a glance. He assessed the people and put them into neat categories as she did when she sorted her papers into regulated stacks.

She had to release his arm to remove her hat and cloak, but she performed the office quickly, afraid he'd leave her to her own devices. He'd probably assumed she could cope perfectly, since she attended grand dinners and balls at the Mansion House or the Guildhall, but while the functions appeared similar, she found one big difference. She knew few people here well enough to chat to as she did those she'd grown up with. The people who worked in the City of London, that precious square mile that had held her whole life up to now.

This time he waited for her, finding someone to chat to while she disposed of her outer wear, and then came back to her, all attention.

Maybe tonight they would begin their marriage properly. Anticipation filled her stomach with flutters. Pleasurable ones. Suddenly she couldn't wait for the evening to end.

Upstairs the quartet was striking up for a minuet, and after sweeping her an exaggerated bow that made her smile, Max led her on to the floor.

The murmur of conversation surrounded them, and a hundred candles twinkled overhead. The floor was polished wood, and she wore a lovely gown. Cinderella she was not, but the magic of the occasion wasn't lost on her.

Nobody paid them particular attention. The couples around them swayed gently like a field of flowers. The quartet played a tune Sophia had learned in the schoolroom, and she was hard put not to hum, as was her habit when she was happy.

Her husband gazed at her as they danced, and she had eyes only for him. She was being too fond, but she didn't care. She'd had too few times like this in her life, when a man paid her so much attention, and that after a toe-melting kiss.

However long this lasted, she'd commit it to memory.

The dance was stately and graceful. Although she wasn't the best dancer, she didn't care, because in her eyes, her partner was the finest male on the floor. His mouth curled in a half-smile, and when, finally, the quartet drew the music to a close, she sank into a curtsey as deep as was decently allowable. His bow was sweet.

But her dream had to end, as all dreams did. For a husband to spend an evening at his wife's side was to invite condemnation for behaving like a provincial.

Someone waited for them at the edge of the floor, a man, dark-eyed, watching them intently. Discomfort stirred inside her.

Max merely grinned and gave the man a short bow. "Allow me to introduce you, my dear. This is yet another of my reprehensible cousins. Antoninus Beaumont, only son of Thaddeus Beaumont. Thaddeus is married to my aunt Frederica."

Another of the Duke of Kirkwood's cousins. "Oh, I know Mr. Beaumont! He's a colleague of my father's. I'm delighted to meet you at last, sir."

Antoninus Beaumont bowed. "If I'd met you before Max did, you might be Mrs. Beaumont by now. I'm sorry for the omission. I've been abroad far too long."

A charmer, then.

"And do you return to the army?"

Antoninus shook his head. "No, I fear not. My father has finally prevailed on me to come home. Although I confess I had enough of the army in peace time. I may join again once the government finally stops prevaricating."

"If the government didn't prevaricate, we'd be sending the army to war with ploughshares for swords," Max said dryly. "Have patience, Tony."

Tony shot his cousin a cynical glance. "Me? My mother will tell you I was the first to walk and the first to talk. My brother waited until he was good and ready, apparently."

His brother was the son of Mrs. Beaumont's first marriage to Viscount Westwood. Max's family was extensive and had a complicated history. She'd learn them all in time. Knowing their history from her father's book helped. Tony was tall and lean, but with a no-nonsense air about him that reminded Sophia of his father.

Now he grimaced. "I do much to please my mother, including not attending City dinners with my father. I deeply regret that now." He bowed over her hand while she laughed.

"It appears that all I have to do is get married to become the most desirable woman in London."

Tony exchanged a smile with Max. "I've heard women say that before, but never with such untruth."

Sophia enjoyed foolish compliments, playful ones. She added one of her own. "If you had remained in the army, you'd have rivalled the greatest general."

Tony raised a dark brow. "Can you name one?"

"The Duke of Cumberland?"

He had a merry laugh. "Indeed. But he's at the Court of St. James's these days. I confess I've been avoiding a similar fate and looking for something interesting to do. Do you know anything? Ah, no, you come from the City. Not my idea of interesting."

Sophia refused to make a stupid joke out of "Interest" and "Business," although this man made her want to. So when the quartet began again, she gladly agreed to dance with him.

Only when they were half way through the piece did she realize that this was the first time she'd ever danced without a pause. Two men, one after the other. As if she were a debutante or the daughter of a duke.

Tony took her to meet other people then, including his mother, who she knew from the City. Lady Beaumont had a sharp, no-nonsense attitude

Sophia appreciated, and she was happy to sit by her side and listen to her trenchant comments on the company. At last she was beginning to fit in. All she wanted was that, to be a part of this company and not avoided for no reason than that she wasn't brought up with these people. That she was a merchant's daughter.

If the family stood together, as Max had assured her they would, society would accept her.

Except when she stood to collect a glass of wine for her ladyship and one for herself, the same thing happened as always. People glanced at her, gave her considering stares, and turned away. They didn't acknowledge her, but they didn't ignore her either. A cold numbness invaded her.

On her walk to the supper room, her happy spirits evaporated into nothing. She hated dealing with this kind of smoke. If they turned their backs or cut her when she approached them, she'd recognize the shunning as a tangible thing and handle it. Go forward fighting. But this way she had nothing to fight against, like punching a wall of silk gauze. She could do nothing, and it angered her.

Persistence would win through. That and producing an heir for Max, someone who would be part of this. Part of *them*. Max had disappeared, no doubt using the opportunity to develop some deal or other. He never stopped working.

At least, that was what Sophia told herself. In truth, she had no idea, because their relationship hadn't yet developed beyond the polite. It would, she promised herself. She wouldn't allow him to keep her at arm's length forever.

A single word heralded John's presence at the ball tonight. "Sophia!"

A voice she knew but didn't welcome. But she couldn't afford to make a scene.

John bowed low. "I beg your pardon, *Lady Devereaux*. Our old acquaintance encouraged me presume too much."

She didn't make the same mistake, which was no mistake at all, and use his first name. "Mr. Hayes." She would not yield and reveal her jittery nerves. "I trust you are well?" She couldn't say it was good to see him, because it wasn't.

"Extremely, thank you." He dressed finer than he used to, a necessity in this company, but not nearly as grandly as some of the men there.

Max, for instance, had his emerald signet ring on tonight because it matched his coat, but the size of the engraved gem only emphasized the slenderness of his fingers. At the memory of their shielded strength she almost smiled. But not quite, because John would probably think her mad, laughing at nothing.

"My lady, your presence improves my health. I rejoice to see you so well."

Sophia suppressed her embarrassed squirm at the flowery compliment. Over-flowery, neither truthful nor outrageous enough to amuse her. Where Tony had amused her with his pleasantries, John made her want to move away.

She inclined her head in what she hoped was gracious acceptance. "Thank you." She was just taking a breath in preparation to excuse herself, when a voice broke in to their conversation.

"Why, Mr. Hayes, well met!"

Another man blocked her way into the refreshment room. Sophia didn't know him. She thought about turning around, but that would be to admit defeat, so she stood her ground. He would step aside in a moment.

"Lady Devereaux, may I present Lord Alconbury?"

The man, dressed finely in dark brown velvet, bowed low as Sophia offered her hand for him to kiss. Devilishly dark and severely handsome. Also so tall she had to tilt her head to look up at him. His smile promised wicked delights.

He took it gently and kissed the air an inch above the back of her hand in the approved manner. "I'm honored, my lady."

So relieved to meet someone who seemed genuinely pleased to see her, Sophia allowed the gentleman to accompany her to the refreshment room. "I've had some dealings with your husband," he said, his low voice almost too quiet to hear. But he moved with confidence and let her place her hand on his arm.

"I'm afraid I'm not familiar—"

He paused and turned to her. "Lord Devereaux knows many people. Our paths have crossed a time or two. How are you finding the season, my lady? Your come-out was some time ago, so much of this must be new to you."

She didn't object to his practical statement. "I wish more people would see it as such, my lord. I have no desire to force myself on anyone."

"Indeed never think that way. They'll respect you more if you disdain them and ignore them. You should be cruel to your servants and insist they work all the hours of the day. Build a reputation for carelessness. Never rise until noon, and never go to bed before two."

He had a charming smile. Although not exactly handsome, he had an attractive countenance and a pleasant disposition. She laughed with him. "I'm afraid I'm too carefully brought up for that."

"Then try." He bent closer, but not so close that it disturbed her. But he could lower his voice. "Lady Devereaux, if you ever need a friend, I'll stand for you."

She blinked up at him, startled. He was exceedingly tall. "Why should you say that, sir?"

"Recently I heard information that might make it possible that you'll need a friend."

Giving a practiced smile, she refused to listen to such enigmatic pronouncements. "Truly sir, I have a husband and a father. Not to mention many other people I can rely on. I am not friendless."

"If ever you are, come to me."

He guided her to the tables and handed her a glass of wine.

"You're very kind, sir, but I've only just met you."

Her husband's voice came from behind her. "Sophia, I wondered where you were. Are you ready to leave?" He sounded hard, unreachable once more. Totally unlike the soft voice he'd used earlier, after they'd kissed and in the carriage.

She turned around to face him. "We've only been here an hour. Are we promised anywhere else tonight?" They weren't, but perhaps he'd received an invitation. Or surely they would stay longer.

"No."

No question, no request, no excuse. Sometimes he'd go somewhere else and she'd return home, or she'd accompany Poppy or Helena to a different ball. But as Max glared at her, she knew he was making that option impossible.

What had happened? Her heart ached. The progress they'd made earlier in the evening had dissipated like smoke in the wind. Nothing left.

When she turned to take her leave of Lord Alconbury, he'd gone. Max hadn't bothered to conceal his sudden frostiness.

Rather than create a fuss, she mustered what dignity she could and left with her head held high.

She had to use every bit of her self-control not to refuse Max's help into the carriage. Of course his touch had its usual predictable outcome, triggering those now unwanted emotions of yearning and need.

He didn't speak to her but observed her, tight-lipped, on the short journey back to their town house.

He helped her out with due punctiliousness and led her in. They went past a clearly startled footman who had probably not expected them back so early and straight into the breakfast parlor at the rear of the house.

The room was cold and unlit. Max paused to find the tinder box and light a branch of candles before he turned to her. The relatively dim light didn't help to dispel his stern mien.

"You are not to talk to that man again."

"What man? John Hayes? Believe me, I have no wish to talk to him, but if society sees me shunning him, it will add to the gossip."

"No, not him. Alconbury."

She glared at him. Alconbury's arrival had come as a relief, breaking any presumptions John might have. "Why not? Is he a notorious flirt? Are you by any chance jealous, Max? I found him amusing and respectful. I will most certainly speak to him again if he wishes it."

"I forbid it."

Astonished, she dropped her mouth open. She closed it with a snap of her teeth and found her voice. "I beg your pardon?"

Max wasn't the only person who could make his voice drip ice if they chose. She had had enough. "You cannot preserve me in aspic and then scold me for talking to men who at least have the courtesy of taking care of me. You are, Max, the most complete hand. I do not mean that as a compliment."

"I am aware of that." He came close enough for her to see the sparks in his eyes, enhanced by the flickering candles and the lighter flecks of color. But he looked dangerous and, with his ascetic features, almost otherworldly. An angry god. The emerald at his throat gleamed with malicious intent. If an emerald could be said to have intent. "However it is my wish that you do not speak to him again."

Why should she? If he'd given her an explanation, then yes, she'd have considered it. But to present it as an order and to give no reason?

"Max, I'm asking you one more time. Why don't you want me to speak with him? Give me a cause, rephrase your command, and I might consider it. But I am not the kind of wife who will meekly obey without question. Respect creates respect, and I've had precious little from you recently."

He glared at her and then spun away, the skirts of his coat catching her gown and forcing her to take a step back. She firmly stepped forward, but kept close to the door. If she exited, she wanted the exercise dignified, not with him in the way. He took a few paces into the room and back again before he turned to face her.

"He's a Dankworth."

"What?"

"He's the son of the Duke of Northwich. A Dankworth. They're dangerous, and they would do anything to put the Emperors in a bad light."

She hadn't realized that. Her father's book only concerned itself with the people they were likely to do business with. Northwich never struck either of them as a good prospect.

Then Lord Alconbury was the son of John's new employer. But he was perfectly respectable, or he seemed so. "Why?" That sounded like Shakespearian tragedy rather than real life. She needed more than that.

"They're Jacobites."

She snorted. "Pooh, everybody knows that!" The Dankworths were long-established Jacobites, but since the rebellion had been put down so decisively, the Stuart faction hadn't counted for much. "They're a spent force. Not even welcome in France these days."

"That could change." He took a deep breath through his nose, like a dragon about to belch fire. His nostrils flared. "We don't wish to be associated with them."

"We? Do I not have an identity of my own, then?"

"Not in law."

Fury filled her. If he'd asked, if he'd reasoned with her, she'd have listened, but he had not. He ordered, and Sophia never obeyed orders blindly. "My lord, I am not the meek and mild wife you imagine. I will not be commanded, and I will not accept your word without good reason. So far you've given me none. Ten years ago I might have listened to you, but that's not enough. Jacobites!"

Time to leave. A family feud didn't sound like anything she wanted any part of. Destructive and stupid. No merit at all. No profit in it.

With a flounce, she spun around and showed him what skirts really looked like when they were flared. Then she stalked out of the room and went to bed.

She dampened her pillow that night, but her tears were as much fury as frustration. She'd longed to get closer to her husband, but not at the expense of her independent spirit. Tonight he'd made advances that had given her hope, only to dash it later.

She would not let him or anyone else trample her into the dust. After years of defying and proving to her father that she was as good as any son, she wasn't about to lose the battle to another man.

Chapter 9

John Hayes approached Sophia in the park the next day, when she was taking the air with only her maid and a footman for company. Sophia showed him a serene face. More to demonstrate to Max that she wouldn't obey his strictures than because she was glad to see John.

Still not in charity with Hayes and angry with the way her body reacted by tightening in fear whenever she saw him, she understood she would have to conquer that emotion. The best way to do it was with familiarity. Only the social kind, naturally, but it would do.

Although the last thing she wanted to do was rest her fingertips on his arm, she did it, glad she was wearing gloves. That layer of fabric gave her another piece of distance. At least he couldn't attack her here, in the fashionable hour at the park with much of society looking on.

"I'm pleased I found you in private," John said. "I'm sorry, however, that we can't speak somewhere quieter."

She stared at him incredulously. "There is no chance of that. You've apologized for what you did, but I'm not sure I totally forgive you. It's obvious you want to seek out my presence. After this, I'd appreciate it if you did not. Too much familiarity is as bad as too little."

"We will meet, though."

"I daresay, and give each other courteous nods. That will do. If you want to get back into my father's graces, I have to tell you that you're a lost cause with him. Give it up."

"I know," he said sadly. "I wouldn't have upset him for the world."

What about her? "Nevertheless, you have."

He heaved a dramatic sigh. "I will never cease to regret that day. I found you irresistible, and I offered you behavior I should never have allowed in myself. It was unthinking and instinctive."

"Plenty of people seem able to resist me." That, at least, was obvious.

She nodded to Lady Carter, currently driving past in her carriage. The lady nodded back.

Good. The initial doubts at her entry into society were dispelling. The longer she behaved as she should, the more they would accept her.

"Sophia, I need to tell you something. In my current position I heard some disturbing rumors, and I went to my employer for confirmation. He said it was so, and he wanted to see you."

"Does this concern me, or is it society gossip?"

"It certainly concerns you. It also explains why the Marquess of Devereaux wished to marry you, and so quickly, too."

Because he desired the arrangement with the Russells made formal without delay. Although now he didn't appear too enthusiastic to further the relationship.

"I can't tell you everything because I don't know it. Have you heard the rumors?"

"Which particular rumors?" There were always rumors.

"That you're not your father's daughter." His words dropped like a stone into a frozen pond, shards of awareness smashing the surface.

Hearing the words and absorbing them proved two very different things. At first she laughed. Then she stared at him. "What on earth are you talking about?"

"That's why some people don't talk to you. Don't bother to deny it. I know it's true." His blue gaze compassionate, John waited for her to respond.

Somehow she kept walking. "That is idiocy. I'm my father's heir, his only..." She cleared her throat and began again. "My mother was the daughter of an earl, and my father is one of the wealthiest men in London. That is who I am. They are my acknowledged parents."

She hadn't realized how tightly she was gripping his coat. Deliberately she eased her hold.

He patted her hand. "That's what I thought, and it's certainly the legal case, although your father may leave his fortune where he wishes."

She knew that, but she didn't care. Once she'd thought he'd leave it to John, as long as he married her. But that one day changed everything, and now here she was, a marchioness. With an unknown father, if what John said were true.

Of course it was not. Gravel scuffed under her feet, the sound unnaturally loud.

"When I first heard the rumor, I scoffed too," he continued.

They walked at a steady pace. At least she could glance away and angle her head so the broad brim of her hat concealed her hurt.

"But they are strong. I asked my employer about it, knowing him for a discreet man, and he gave me advice. He said to bring you to see him. He says he knows the truth, but he wishes to speak to you about it face to face."

She dug her heels in to the path. John had to come to a halt or walk on without her. He stopped. With deliberate intent, she removed her hand from his arm and gave him a frosty smile.

"What kind of fool do you take me for? Do you think to force me into a private conversation with you?" And more, no doubt. Had he never given up wanting her? She couldn't doubt that this was a ruse to take her somewhere private yet again.

"You are much mistaken, Mr. Hayes. I'm not such a gullible idiot. You had your chance, and you failed so miserably that I should have listened to my heart when I saw you at Ranelagh. I wish I'd walked the other way. Now you tell me some ridiculous rumor?"

If not for the gossip she'd inevitably cause if she walked away from him, she'd do so. But the rumors about them made clear that people would watch them closely. Any offence, or on the opposite side, any particular warmth, would only fuel the fire. A cordiality engendered by their previous acquaintances seemed to be the safest path to take. But she hated it. She would have far rather had nothing to do with him.

He shook his head. "It's true. When I saw the evidence, I had to believe it."

"Until I see absolute proof I won't believe it. I will reject it. What's more, I'll ensure people know it's a lie. Rumors are stupid and not worth listening to." This rumor was another, probably put about by people jealous of her success. Or jealous that she'd snared Max. He was a catch, she knew that, but as far as she was concerned, they could have him back and keep him. "So who is your employer?" She might as well know the name of the man who was helping to spread malicious rumors about her.

"His Grace the Duke of Northwich."

The man Max had warned her about. Everything came back to him. She refused to listen to any more. "Don't try to speak to me again."

Sophia turned her back on John. She'd had enough of John Hayes and his schemes. She needed to know more, but not from him. Perhaps he'd stumbled on a germ of truth. After her early morning stroll she discovered she was quite hungry and decided to go home for breakfast.

* * * *

After a breakfast in which the atmosphere was silent and frozen, Sophia ordered the carriage brought around. She had no idea if her husband stayed at home or was out, nor did she care. Anyone who used such bullying tactics as to order her to do something without explaining himself wasn't worth thinking about, much less crying over. Not that she'd done that last night. Oh no, not one bit.

In the carriage she sat perfectly still, watching the fashionable squares as they gave way to the familiar, narrower streets of the City. She still loved the square mile. More than anywhere else in the world, it was her home.

The streets teemed with life. From children dodging between people— some pickpockets, some merely mischievous—to street sellers shouting their wares to City businessmen, dapper and serious for the most part. They passed her favorite print shop, which had a slew of new caricatures in the windows. She wanted to stop and stare, but she was afraid that now she had joined the great and the not-so-good, she might feature there.

Someone would recognize her and she'd never get to see her father. He was the person who would give her the confidence to deny the stupid rumors.

If he wasn't in his office at home, she'd order some tea and send a footman to find him. He'd be in one of the coffee houses, probably Lloyd's, or the Exchange, or at his own office. Easy to find him.

Not so easy to find her husband. He disappeared, and she never asked where he went. Did he have a mistress? Was she pretty?

To her chagrin, Sophia still cared about that. Even when he'd treated her with disdain, she yearned for his approval. What kind of idiot did that make her?

Her mood eased when she saw the house, with the black paint on the front door that had dulled with time. Her father should have it redone.

The windows were set lower, closer to the street, so living there was to share life with the people outside, not stare loftily down on it. Her new home was beautiful, but she'd put no mark on it.

She would. That was her first decision of the day. She'd change her bedroom with that lovely, though inappropriate, cream upholstery and drapes. That would be a good place to start.

And give her something to do, instead of worrying about the state of her marriage. It would either come right or it would not. Her resolve firm in her mind, she felt better as she stepped down from the carriage and went to the front door.

The footman informed her that her father was at home, working in his study. As she often did during the day, she had tea brought to the back parlor to give him a break from his work. And some of those little cakes he liked. She was glad to note that the cook was still looking after him properly, and Nina the cat, lounging in a spot of sunlight in the hall, was still plump and happy.

She served her father a large dish of the dark brown brew, He took it and leaned back with a sigh.

He straightened his back, which was no doubt aching from hours of bending over columns of figures. "I can't deny I'm glad to see you, daughter, but is this an impulsive call? You should have sent a note."

She stared at him over the rim of her tea-dish. "I needed to come to you, Papa. Something's happened that I need to discuss with you."

He lifted his eyes and met her gaze. His were blue, so unlike her own, but she looked more like her mother, he'd always told her.

"It's too soon to declare your marriage a failure, child."

Startled she blinked at him, not sure what to say. "What do you mean?" Was it that obvious that she and Max weren't getting along? Who else knew?

"Or is this advice on business?" He studied her a moment longer. "No, I don't think so. This is personal. You're distressed. You are holding your jaw too rigidly, and you have those little creases by your eyes." He grinned. "What, you think I don't know, that I haven't studied my child over the years?" He took a long draught of tea before he spoke next. "If it's a matter between you and your husband, it is for you to sort out your problems. If it is business, I don't want to hear anything that is confidential."

"I wouldn't do that, Papa." Although Max's business interlinked with her father's, both men had interests outside their joint concerns.

"No, I don't believe you would. First, you must tell me if you're well and content with the bargain you made."

Although from his lips it sounded like a business matter, Sophia knew better. The words *well* and *content* didn't mean solely a business agreement. "Yes, Papa, I am."

Because he was right. What was happening in her marriage was for nobody's ears but hers and her husband's. But her father deserved some kind of warning. "It's very early days as yet, and we do not know each other very well, but we get along happily enough."

Or had, until he'd closed down the other night.

"I'm glad to hear it. I can't deny the arrangement was extremely advantageous for me, but I would not have my only child unhappy."

All the time he drank, he was watching her, clear eyes fixed on her face. She could hide nothing.

"I heard a rumor," she said. "I wish to deny it absolutely, so I came to warn you. It may become known or it may not. I have no idea where the person who told me received his information, or if it's true. It's not something I've ever heard before." Aware she was prevaricating, she allowed herself a sip of the reviving brew before she placed her dish carefully on its saucer. She turned the pattern so it showed to its best advantage. She'd always like the twining vines. As a child she'd imagined letters in the intricate decoration.

"There are always rumors."

But he was interested, she could see that. She'd piqued his interest.

"Are these financial?"

"No, Papa, they are about me." As calmly as possible, even knowing that her father could read her face as well as he could an account-book, she still tried to keep her demeanor steady. "Someone informed me that you were not my real father. Not the man who fathered me." She added the last because in every way the man before her had been her father, and would continue in that regard.

Shock ringed his eyes, set his hands to claws around his tea-dish. He never took his gaze from her while he put his dish down. It rattled in the saucer. "Who told you that?"

Not wanting to tell him, she yet bowed to the inevitable. "John Hayes."

"I thought so." He closed his eyes and sighed heavily. "That man must have discovered more than he should have in this house. I fear I trusted him with far too much."

Opening his eyes again, he gazed at her soulfully. Not an expression she was used to in her surviving parent. "I blame myself for allowing him into my life. But he had a quick mind and was amenable to learning about my business. Too amenable, I fear. And he must have helped himself to information he was not entitled to."

"What information?"

He paused. "Daughter, I had hoped never to tell you this."

For the first time since she'd asked him, he looked away, down at the well-worn surface of his desk. She'd sat on his knee while he taught her how to add columns of figures, practiced her handwriting here. That desk was part of her life.

"Let me tell this as a story. As it happened. Perhaps then you'll understand."

Cold fingers clutched her heart. It was true, then. What would this mean to her husband? Would Max understand? Probably not, but he couldn't divorce her because of this, though he might wish to separate from her. He needed his heir, he said. She'd find it unbearable to perform her duties as coldly as she had on their one night together. Thoughts rattled around her head, all of them centering on Max.

Why did everything always come back to him?

Her father took a few moments to collect his thoughts, as he always did when about to embark on something important. Then he looked up again, and hurt lay in his eyes. "Years ago I was starting my business. My parents had been hard-working tradespeople. Artisans." Mercers, they'd had a business close by this very house.

"I know that, Papa."

"Don't interrupt," he snapped.

She nodded and kept her mouth closed.

"When they died, taken by fever within a month of each other, I was working on my first insurance contract. A safe cargo with a relatively safe passage. But the ship didn't return. Others that limped back to port made it clear that an unexpected storm had taken many unsuspecting vessels on their way to the Spice Islands. Add to that my first, tentative investments in the stock market. You remember what happened in 1728?"

She shook her head.

"Not as bad as the collapse of the South Sea company, but the market dipped. Lack of confidence. People began to panic, but I had no choice. I could not sell out. At that time, a man approached me. Lord Morningside, a Scottish peer who had lost most of his fortune in the '15. The first Jacobite rebellion."

She knew about the dip in her father's fortunes and his meeting with the Earl of Morningside, her maternal grandfather.

"He wished his daughter safe from the troubles and from scandal," her father said. "Because of their association with the Stuarts, she would be unlikely to find a husband in London society. He offered me a great sum of money to care for his child. All he had left. He told me that if he didn't, the Pretender would probably have it off him, and if there was one person he loved more than his king, it was his daughter. A foolish man." He shook his head. "No king is worth that much."

Sophia glanced at her tea-dish, and then decided against it. She didn't trust the steadiness of her hands. Instead, she gripped them hard together in her lap. Her knuckles turned white while her stomach churned.

"My stipulations included cutting relations with her father. I didn't think she would do it, but she agreed. I couldn't afford any links with the Stuarts, you see. That would have been disastrous." He reached out and covered her hand.

She looked up, into a face wreathed with sorrow.

"She brought a baby with her. You."

Shock held her rigid, stopped her breath. "How can this be?"

"Her season was brief, but not brief enough. I never knew who the father was, but she swore it had only happened once, and you were the result. You were a girl. At the time, I thought I would have other children, but as matters turned out, you were the only child I would ever have." He reached out at the same time she did.

His hand, warm over hers, felt as it always had. His face looked the same. But they were not the features of the man who fathered her.

"I took you anyway." The corner of his mouth twitched. "How could I turn such an innocent away? I persuaded myself it was my Christian duty, but the truth is that I took one look at you and fell in love."

"H-How did you manage?" How could they cover up such a thing?

He smiled gently. "I went away for a while. Abroad, I said, to attend to business. Indeed, I did so. But I returned after a year with a wife and a child. You know that part, that your mother and I married on the continent, that I met her during a business trip."

With a sudden movement, he withdrew his hand, dropped his head, and groaned. His neat bob-wig drooped forward, forcing him to lift his head or lose it. He twitched the wig into place with a movement that spoke of long habit.

"We put back the date of the wedding. In those days, marriages were more irregular, so nobody suspected. Nobody cared enough about us to check. After all, what did it matter to anyone?"

He shook his head mournfully. "I don't deserve your forgiveness, but I ask for it now."

"No!" How could anyone turn her taciturn, cool father into this unhappy man? She hated John and his machinations, hated to hear a secret nobody need have known. What difference did it make?

She was the result of the mechanical act. That made nobody a father, not in truth. It meant nothing. "You are my father. You know that, Papa. I am your daughter."

"It heartens me to hear you say so," he said, getting to his feet. "The secret has been here all along. That tea set, for instance. Your mother brought it with her when she came here. Did you know it has the initials of the Old Pretender twined into the pattern? I didn't until a few years ago, and then we kept using the set because you liked them. It was you who pointed it out to me when you were a child. Do you remember?"

She recalled him telling her not to be so fanciful. A sharp reprimand to keep her attention on her work, adding up figures instead of tracing patterns on her tea-dish.

Once, he'd told her she could make out the letters more clearly than before. *JFES* for James Francis Edward Stuart. "A Jacobite." Strange how that lost cause had reared up in her life so much recently.

"I remember. Was my mother happy to renounce the cause?"

"It wasn't her cause," he said. "She was born into it, that was all. Did you never wonder why we had no more children?"

Strangely, she had not, although her parents had shared a bed until her mother took ill. She had accepted the situation as normal, thought her mother had perhaps suffered an injury at her birth. But neither had repined.

Once her mother had said although she would have preferred more children, at least they didn't have a houseful to provide for and she could devote her time to her one child and her husband. Come to think of it, she never referred to him as "Your father."

"And nobody suspected?"

"Why should they? Your mother was the daughter of a peer and brought a fortune with her. That was all most of my colleagues needed to know. They would have done the same."

He rose and took a step toward her. "Knowing you, I would not have had matters any different. You are my daughter and will always be so in my heart."

Tears sprang to her eyes. Her father had never been so demonstrative before. He'd always held himself apart, so she was used to the lack of emotion in her life. She despised the kind of person who wept at a moment's notice. Now she was in danger of turning into a watering-pot.

"Papa, you are the best of fathers." Even in arranging her marriage to someone when he feared she'd been compromised. Now she understood his harshness. The prospect of his daughter suffering the same fate as his wife must have galled him. Appalled him.

"At least I found you the right husband. I will never ask, but finding you with that man was a shock. I thought history was repeating itself."

She shook her head. That was why he had reacted so violently, forced her to marry Max.

"It was not." She had gone to her marriage bed a virgin. A sad smile wreathed her lips. "Perhaps, but it turned out for the best. I have a husband you can approve of, sir. A man to be proud of." Whatever his coldness in private, Max was a man of the utmost integrity in business, and she was a daughter of the City. Such virtues were to be celebrated.

A carriage went past outside, rattling the windows.

He grimaced. "The worst of it was that my reversal of fortune was temporary. My ship returned with a healthy profit, and the market regained its nerve within six months."

"But by then I was born."

"I can't be sorry for that." His voice softened in a way she hadn't heard for years. "I will always be proud of you."

"That's why I don't look like you." Now he'd told her, she wanted to know everything, absorb this truth. Only one portrait of her mother existed, the one at her father's house.

"You have your mother's coloring." He paused. "I fear you must tell your husband. Will he accept it?"

So much information made Sophia dizzy. She badly needed time to process this, to accept it and let it settle in her mind. Telling Max was imperative. "I will, but not immediately." Pausing, she thought of an excuse. "Business is keeping him occupied at the moment. I want his mind fully on the subject when I broach it with him."

He could easily repudiate her. While divorce would be difficult and expensive, almost impossible, separation was achievable. How would Max take the information that his wife could be the daughter of his enemy? The country's enemy?

Badly, that was how. Sophia was tempted, briefly, to tell Julius who had always treated her with respect and kindness. But Julius could be as formidable as Max. And it wasn't right to tell Julius before she told Max, who had a right to know the origin of the prospective mother of his children.

Although her father was dry-eyed and his demeanor steady, she could tell he was distressed by telling her this news. A haunted expression in his eyes, a jerky way of movement. Damn John! Without his intervention, she would never have known, might have lived her life in blissful ignorance of the fact that she wasn't her father's daughter. And yet she was.

"You had the making of me, Papa. You taught me, and you reared me. This information does not make you any less of a father to me."

If Max demanded she cut off relations with her father, she would refuse. He had a right to do so, but such cruelty didn't deserve reward. The trouble was, as matters lay between them, Max might jump on the excuse. He had distanced himself so effectively, it was like sharing a house with a stranger, and her bedroom was anathema to him. He hadn't set foot on the Aubusson since that fateful night.

Chapter 10

"You are happy in your marriage, my son?"

His mother would choose a ball to ask that, where he couldn't get emotional even if he wanted to. Which he didn't. With the greatest in society capering on the dance floor and sauntering around the perimeter, she gave him little choice. Not that he ever discussed his personal feelings with her. She'd never encouraged it. Her question was more of a polite enquiry than a real search for the truth.

"I am indeed," he said. "Sophia suits me well."

Even if he hadn't visited her bed since that disastrous wedding night. Giving Sophia a chance to recover had changed to giving her some privacy when she had her courses, and by that time they had a habit set up. At least, that was what he told himself. Until Julius had completed his research, Max was better staying away. This wife of his was too dangerous to his peace of mind.

He glanced to the dance floor where Sophia was tripping a measure with Tony. She danced competently and appeared to advantage in her favorite blue. She must favor the shade, since she wore a deal of it. She'd never told him so. They didn't have that kind of relationship.

His marriage was everything he'd wanted from the union. Except now he had it, he found he wanted something else.

"Besides, there is nothing we can do about it now." She sniffed, lifting her chin in an arrogant gesture. "You're married, and that's all there is to it."

He shot his attention back to his mother. Did she think he would change? The marriage had brought him everything he wanted. Nearly everything. "Why would we want to change it?"

Sophia was smiling at Tony. An urge seized Max to cross the room to her. Despite his determination to keep away, she still drew him. Her quiet beauty appealed to him at a visceral level, not a part of himself he was familiar with. He found it best to ignore those urges, at least for now. Before he married, he'd kept a convenient mistress or two to fulfil his carnal needs. He treated them like a business transaction, neat and clean. Done and gone. Now he had other factors to cope with. Emotions. He'd never been good with those.

One thing at a time. He shouldn't force his presence on his wife until she'd made a place for herself in society. At least she hadn't quickened from their one time together. Then she'd have more to deal with. Better to stay away until she'd settled into her new life and he heard from Julius about the other matter.

Not for anybody would he admit how much she drew his attention, his desire. He couldn't give way to that.

His mother placed her hand on his arm, and they took a gentle stroll, mainly so that nobody would interrupt them. She waved her fan, smiled at her acquaintances.

"You should come home, Mother," he said.

"Ah, but if I do, I will force Helena to return to her mother's ungentle embrace." The dowager shrugged. "Why my brother chose to marry such a woman...but we'll leave that discussion for another time."

She was getting remarkably indiscreet, which probably meant she had a feud currently waging with the dowager Duchess of Kirkburton. Nothing like the serious problems the family had always had with the Dankworths, but his family usually had one member at odds with another. They'd make it up. Was it this that prevented her from helping Sophia more?

"Helena could stay with us," Max offered.

"It isn't her home," his mother said promptly. She always had an answer. "Julius is interviewing suitable women to be a companion to her and a governess for sweet little Caroline. He was considering asking someone from the family, although I think this time an employee would prove more reliable." She laid a hand on his arm. "I can join you then."

"You're probably right." And then he'd get his mother back. A companion would be someone from a respectable family or from a minor branch of theirs who couldn't afford to support herself. As well as an income and a roof over her head, she'd have the advantage of entering society. Maybe even finding a husband, although not at the highest level. As Max already knew, marriages at his level occurred more for alliances and advantage than for personal reasons.

The dowager wafted her fan lazily, releasing an aroma of lavender. "I am doing my best to find Helena a husband. It's time, and that would solve our problems. But she is being stubborn. Says she wants love." She gave a "Tcha!" of derision. "She'll find someone. I am determined on it."

Max nodded, although he privately considered that at least one of the family should find happiness in marriage. Apart from Alex, that was.

On the other side of the dance floor, Tony bowed over Sophia's hand and led her to a sofa, where several ladies already perched. They presented a charming picture in delicately colored silks and satins, chattering, their fans fluttering to emphasize a point or draw attention to an attractive feature.

Before they reached the area, two of the ladies glanced up, and then at each other, and then left. Poppy and Helena, who were already there, did not.

Vaguely disturbed by the scene, Max turned back to his mother. "Sophia could use some help."

The dowager turned her shoulder elegantly. "She's coping well, from what I've been seeing. It's true she seems to prefer her own company, but she will learn."

"She's an only child." That might be the reason she hadn't received as many bride-visits as he'd expected. But she needed the support of his mother. "If you should like to take an airing on the park with her, I can put the carriage at your disposal."

"I have the landau," she said.

Max nearly snorted. Of course she did. Low-bodied, the thing went at a crawl. Not his kind of vehicle at all. He'd considered having the coat of arms on the door repainted to include the widow's lozenge. Sophia hadn't used it. She preferred to take a chair or go on foot, although he never allowed her out without at least one footman and her maid. Truthfully, he liked her independence of spirit, but he preferred to keep her safe. London was never safe, even for someone who knew it well.

They headed toward Helena and Poppy. Max firmly steered his mother around the edge of the dance floor. A flurry, a light scattering of people, impeded their progress as dancers began to assemble for the next set. The quartet of musicians in the corner sorted their music, ready for the next tune. Insipid, most likely.

"A word."

But for his society manners he'd have leaped three feet. "Dammit, Julius, you're a silent as a cat when you want to be!"

"I apologize."

Like hell he did. His cousin's blue eyes glinted with something that looked like anger. Here? What had happened? Intrigued, Max raised a brow. "A problem?"

"Not mine."

Oh, that was terse. Something had put him out. He turned to his mother. "May I escort you to Poppy?"

The dowager glanced at the sofa where Helena was talking to Sophia. "It appears Poppy has decided to dance. I'll pay a visit to the card room. It's been an age since I had a good hand of piquet, and I saw Lady Cooper there earlier. I will see if she's free."

"Just don't let her rook you, Mama," he said with a grin.

She laughed in derision. "We've been playing together for many years, and on or off the gaming table I can beat her best."

Max followed Julius out of the room to a narrower passageway. It led to a set of stairs at the end that were not the main stairway. The treads were padded with drugget, and the walls sported improving pictures and lists of instructions that Max didn't bother to peruse.

"The servants' way?"

"More discreet."

"So what are we doing here?"

"I don't want to be disturbed," Julius said sharply.

Someone had really upset him. Had he discovered something about the Dankworths and Sophia?

Once upstairs, Julius strolled along a wider hallway and then opened a door that led to a small, obviously unoccupied bedroom. Not a servants' room, but the dressing table was clear of accoutrements and the open door to the powder room showed everything in neat order. A guest room.

As soon as Max had closed the door, Julius whirled to face him. "What the *hell* are you doing?"

Taken aback, Max blinked at him. "What are you talking about?" He considered putting a chair between them. He didn't wish to get into a confrontation with his cousin here. Or anywhere else, come to that.

"Your wife!" He spat the word.

Bewildered, he faced his cousin, balancing on the balls of his feet, ready for anything. "What has she done?"

"Nothing!" Julius's eyes sparked fire. He shoved back his coat and put his hand on his hip, where he would normally wear his sword. This being a ball, he'd either left it at home or at the door. The perfect gentleman.

Just as well, because Max might have died without knowing what had angered Julius. Or killed him, and that wasn't something he wanted to do either.

"That is part of the problem. Isn't it?"

Max frowned. "I beg your pardon?"

Julius took a turn about the room, his shoes tapping on the parquet. "In the four weeks since your marriage, you haven't made a push to support her at all. Haven't demonstrated your loyalty."

Put like that, it sounded decidedly unpleasant. "You know why."

Julius shook his head. "Tell me."

"How can I support her when she might be a spy for the Dankworths?" he demanded. "How can I trust her?" How could he trust himself, when every time he saw her he wanted her more than ever?

He'd seen the evidence, heard it too. She wasn't to be trusted. Sophia hadn't told him her erstwhile lover, the man Russell had caught her *in flagrante delicto* with, was in the pocket of the Dankworths. Enemies of the Emperors. Traitors to the country. He desperately needed to hear that she was innocent. Longed for it. But he had moved all the most sensitive documents out of the house and into his office as a precaution. He hated himself for it, but more than his fate was at risk here. He couldn't place his investors in peril because of his own softer feelings.

And yet every time he came near her, he wanted her. So he didn't go near her. Waited for some evidence for or against.

"Have you discovered something about Sophia and the Dankworths?" he asked eagerly.

"No." Julius shook his head. "No progress on that. Forget it. That's not what I wanted to talk to you about." He brushed the matter aside as if it meant nothing. "That isn't the point tonight. The point is your behavior with your *wife*."

Max had never seen Julius so angry. His eyes sparked pure blue fire, his posture, clenched fists at his sides, suggested he was holding himself back from committing an act of violence.

If Julius was referring to Max and Sophia's lack of progress in bed, Max would have to have a word with her. Because the only way he would know that was if she'd gone blabbing to him. He couldn't imagine her doing that. The trouble was, what he saw in her didn't tally with the reports he was hearing. "She's a woman who is capable of asking for what she wants."

"Who is hardly ever seen with you in public."

"I accompany her to these affairs." He waved a hand impatiently. "She is accepted."

"And you do not *see*?" Julius waved a hand, his sapphire ring glittering fit to rival his eyes. "You can't tell that people move away from her when she approaches them? That they avoid talking to her?"

A slow fire kindled in Max's belly. "What are you talking about?" On the rare occasion that he accompanied her to balls, he danced once with her and excused himself to the card room or left her in the care of his mother or one of his aunts. She'd never complained. His behavior wasn't unusual. Many husbands did the same.

"Nobody is giving her the cut direct. While she has our family's support, they wouldn't dare. But they are shunning her. Avoiding her." Julius's mouth curled in a sneer. "It's society's way. The practice disgusts me."

"Isn't this a kind of baptism of fire?" A ritual before society accepted her?

"No it is not. The point is, why don't you know?"

Julius was right, damn him. Max whirled around, turning his back to his cousin, his heavy brocaded coat tangling around his thighs. "I've been very busy," he said, but even to his own ears that sounded foolish. "She hasn't complained." Even worse. "I thought she was coping." He did. "I thought it would pass in time. We only had to wait it out."

"She would not complain. Can it be that I know her better than you do?"

Max hated Julius at his most sarcastic. But he was right, and that made matters worse. "Yes, you probably do." He dropped his head. His epiphany rocked through him. Of course she wouldn't complain. Sophia wasn't the complaining type. She would never seek help.

But now Julius had mentioned it, he began to add things up. She had few visitors, and when she went out, it was to visit her father or to accompany Poppy or Helena or another of his cousins. Nobody else. *Hell*, nobody else. Julius was right.

He opened his arms, spread his hands. "I'm a man. What can I do? These women won't let us dictate how they run their lives. You know that as well as I do."

"Dictate?" Julius gave a harsh laugh. "True enough. But it's telling that you didn't realize."

A barbed comment to which he wouldn't respond with anger. "And how exactly am I supposed to do that? I'm in new country here. I've never been married before."

"I have."

Max turned around and faced his cousin at that quiet statement. Julius had never appeared so cold, so lacking in emotion, which meant he was still angry. "Are you telling me that Caro was shunned?"

Julius cracked a grin, but it wasn't an amused one. His eyes were steel-hard. "Caro was the daughter of one of the country's wealthiest peers. She belonged right from childhood. One of us, one of them, part of the club. We married, madly in love, but I found her difficult. As time went by, we found our own paths. Instead of talking to her and showing her what she meant to me, I tried to control her. Caro wasn't the type of woman who took kindly to control." His face shuttered, and his eyes were pinpoints of intense blue. "As her behavior became wilder, people began to avoid her. Nothing definite, they'd just move away when she was near or not invite her to the smaller, more select functions."

"So you noticed when it happened to Sophia."

Julius inclined his head. "Indeed. And like you, I did nothing. I thought Caro would settle down in time, when our child was born perhaps. She did not. She found the birth a trial, and while she loved Caroline, the baby was in the nature of a toy, a doll she could play with and then abandon. That angered me, and I spoke to her, something that only forced us farther apart. My reprimands only made Caro wilder. She undertook dares she should never have considered to spite me."

"Like the one that killed her."

Six years ago, Caro had died in what the charitable called a driving accident, although the best whip in the country couldn't have controlled the four horses she'd set to her carriage. When Julius had discovered her escapade, he'd raced *ventre á terre* to the location, but he'd arrived too late.

Although Sophia and Caro were very different women, they'd suffered the same ordeal in society. Sophia would never scandalize society. Couldn't afford to. If she did, that would give the biddies reason to ostracize her for good.

"Yes, like that."

The lack of emotion in Julius's voice didn't surprise Max. His cousin had never said a word, not even immediately after Caro's death. He'd taken control of his emotions and his life. For his daughter's sake, everyone thought.

But Max knew better. Julius was adept at hiding his emotions, at pushing them beneath the surface. Max had seen his cousin's despair before he'd locked it away.

Now Julius was trying to stop Max doing the same thing, and he should be grateful. Not now, when excoriating shame scraped his insides dry, but perhaps later.

"Your wife is cut from a different cloth. But Max, you're not supporting her. If you did, she would find this less difficult. I know your loyalty is strained, but you can't let her carry on this way. I made a mistake. I don't want you to do the same thing. You'll regret not standing by her side. Believe in yourself, Max, as I did not. Believe in your own judgment. What's in your heart. Trust her. Trust your feelings for her." Julius took a deep breath. "Sophia needs to know the world isn't against her. Trust your feelings, Max."

That advice went straight to his heart. Yes, that was what he should do. Though he couldn't understand why he couldn't see that for himself.

Without another word, shame scraping his insides raw, he left the room and went to find his wife.

* * * *

Sophia was becoming more aware that people, while not cutting her, were not seeking her presence. It had happened solidly for the last month and wasn't getting any better. Max needed their approval to pursue his many interests, and she was letting him down, but she couldn't break through. If she spoke to someone, the person would answer her politely but distantly and move away as soon as he or she could. How did she fight that? They'd judged her before they even knew her and found her wanting. Not everyone, of course. But even her husband—

Was the man who broke into her thoughts now, giving her a smooth smile and a short bow. "Would you care to dance, my love?"

What had he called her? In public? She blinked at him, taken aback, and then got to her feet, almost in a dream. He held out his hand, smiling in a way she hadn't seen before. As if he meant it. What could she do but smile back and place her hand on the back of his?

Had he really said that? "My love"?

That was something she'd never expected to hear, but, she told herself, men called their wives that all the time and they didn't mean it. He couldn't. But something inside her thawed when he came to her. He'd danced with her before, of course he had, but usually at the start of a ball. Then he'd disappeared to the card room or strolled around chatting to people.

He led her on to the floor, and they joined the others in the next set. Max was a competent dancer and so was she. They could hold their own, but when she went left instead of right and he had to guide her, she met his gaze and they laughed. Sharing a joke.

"That could have been me," he murmured for her ears alone when they passed on to their next partners.

They met at the end of the measure and instead of taking her to Poppy or Helena and leaving her, he took her to the supper-room. He found her a glass of wine and some morsels of food. Not that she was hungry, but she ate some anyway, to please him.

"Do you plan to go anywhere else tonight?" he asked her. Sometimes she did, but more often than not she went home to her lonely bed, leaving him to she didn't know what. And increasingly recently, she didn't want to ask.

"No," she said simply. "I thought I'd go to bed."

"Then we'll go home together."

Surprised, she raised her brows but said nothing. She took a sip of wine and stared at him over the rim of the glass. His mouth twitched as he took the glass from her and placed it on the nearest table. "Are you ready?"

She rarely went home with her husband. "Won't they think you provincial?" she said, citing an insult she'd heard muttered behind the fans.

"They already consider me vulgar. I don't care what they think." He paused, and when she set her hand on his arm, drew her closer and added, "But I care for you."

Shock arced through her again. He led her through the main room, pausing to speak to people, and after the second she realized what he was doing. Selecting the people who had avoided her earlier. On her own, she couldn't hope to persuade them to exchange more than a few courteous words. But Max forced them to pay attention.

Sophia received more kindness in that one stroll through a crowded ballroom than she had all month on her own. She tried not to be bitter about that. Even Lady Devereaux smiled when they bade her farewell.

"They love you," she said to him when they'd finally managed to descend the staircase and get to the front door. Guests were still arriving. This was one of the squeezes of the season, and they were leaving. She couldn't feel sorry.

Tomorrow she'd call and leave her card in thanks for the evening's entertainment. She was punctilious in that regard. Never forgot a courtesy.

"They don't love me," he replied. "They tolerate me. I'm a marquess, and it's that they want, not me. They'd have preferred for me to behave myself, not engage so blatantly in business, marry—" He stopped abruptly.

"Marry an earl's daughter?" she suggested softly.

In the carriage, they didn't light the interior lamps. They didn't have far to go, in any case. They sat together in silence, jewels glittering as they breathed. Sophia stared out of the window, watching the carriages coming and going as if it were mid-day and not nearly midnight. Link boys ran from one carriage to another, lighting people's way so they didn't lose their footing. Night-watchmen sat in their boxes, huddled in nondescript clothes to ward off the chill of this spring evening. Sophia had hardly bothered to shrug her cloak around her, safe in the knowledge that she had a fire lit in her bedroom. She'd never known privation, never shared hardship with anyone, and that made her feel uncomfortable sometimes, but what good would it do for her to join them?

Now she wondered if the watchmen had wives who loved them, waiting with comfort, a hot meal, and a warm bed. Her bed was warm all right, but because of the warming pan French's assistant ran under the sheets before Sophia got between them. No other reason.

Her husband's brief moment of chivalry seemed to have passed, because once in the privacy of their carriage, he didn't attempt to speak to her. He'd probably see her home and then go out again. To his mistress, maybe, or to a club or gaming house.

Tears sprang to her eyes. The thawing of their relationship, however small, had led to a melting of her heart. For the last four weeks, she'd desperately tried to harden herself to the life she could expect, of struggle but independence, and now he behaved as if they were together. Properly together. Why? A belated attack of chivalry? And she had nothing, not even respectability. She'd been trying to pluck up the courage to tell him about John's revelations, but she hadn't found the words.

It was too much. Plunged into a life she didn't understand and finding herself at sea, she'd determined to weather the storm. Nobody should get close to her.

Except he had.

A sole tear trickled down her cheek, and Sophia fought to keep the others unshed, stiffening her muscles to fight the impulse. Again. She would overcome this, too, and she'd be proud of herself for doing it.

A pair of masculine hands stole over her shoulders, impelling her to turn around. "Sophia," he said, very softly. "Sophia, don't."

"I'm trying not to," she said, her voice clogged with tears.

With a twist, he turned her into his arms and nothing, nothing had felt as good as when he closed them around her, enclosing her with his warmth.

"Sweetheart, I don't deserve you. I've neglected you dreadfully. I'm so sorry."

Enough to make her dissolve into floods. The tears she'd held back for weeks wouldn't be denied. They cascaded down her face, and she sobbed into his fine velvet coat. Cut velvet, frighteningly fragile, but she couldn't help it now. He held her tight and crooned words she couldn't make out into her hair and against her forehead, rocking her with the motion of the carriage.

Nobody had held her like that. He drew away just far enough to dig into his pocket and produce a serviceable handkerchief. But instead of pressing it into her hand, he mopped up her tears himself until the coach came to a standstill.

"I think we should go indoors," he murmured, "but…wait there. Give me a moment."

He nodded to the footman to open the door and let down the steps of the carriage. Max was closest, so he climbed down and held out his arms.

Beyond pride by now, she went into them, but instead of helping her down he simply picked her up, voluminous skirts and all. She looped her arms around his neck and clung, terrified he'd drop her.

She buried her face in the snowy folds of his stock. He carried her as if she weighed nothing.

"Her ladyship has been taken ill," he said calmly, his voice vibrating against her face.

Yes, that would work. It would explain why they left early and why they came home together. Nobody would gossip about that.

Expecting him to put her down once they were in the house, she braced herself in readiness. But he crossed the hall and took the stairs, her body bouncing with each step. She stayed still, hardly bearing to breathe in case somehow he'd abandon her somewhere along the way but he did not.

Someone murmured "My lord." One of the servants, she didn't know who. Then the familiar aromas of her bedroom filtered through to her senses; her perfume, overlaid with the orange-scented cream she liked to use on her face. A touch of lavender from the sheets. Comforting, pleasant smells that went a little way toward soothing her agitation.

She dared to lift her head only to meet his compassionate gaze. His eyes reflected her and contributed kindness, something she'd not even imagined him capable of. Not that he wasn't always equitable and fair in all his dealings. Just that she'd never associated him with the gentler emotions. She gazed up at him in wonder as he took her to the bed and sat her on the edge. Only then did he release her.

"Better?"

Ah, now he would leave. She cleared her throat. "Yes, thank you." Her voice came out, to her surprise, but it was still hoarse from her bout of crying.

Sadness overwhelmed her and although she'd thought she had no tears left, one trickled from each eye, welling up to obscure her vision and then overflowing. "I want to stop," she said.

"It's been coming a long time," he murmured. "Let it happen." He straightened and faced her maid who stood, hands folded neatly before her. "Her ladyship isn't feeling well. I'll take care of her. You may go."

French barely masked her surprise before she dropped a curtsey and left the room, her skirt swishing.

Sophia smiled through her tears, warmed by his assertion. "You'll take care of me?"

"And so I will. I should have handled this situation weeks ago." Impatiently he shrugged off his gorgeous coat and threw it over a nearby chair. "Let's get this done."

Now he sounded determined, as if dealing with a practical matter like a leaking roof. That made her smile more, for some reason. Probably because the approach was typical of him, to handle problems straight on. Except he hadn't, had he? He'd let her cope on her own for weeks.

"It took someone else to point out my neglect. I'll never forgive myself for that," he said.

He strode to the basin and wrung out a cloth. "Unlike last time, the water is warm."

He snatched up a clean towel, came back, and settled himself on the bed next to her, both of them sitting on the edge. When he slid his arms around her she snuggled close.

The gold thread on his heavily embroidered waistcoat scratched her cheek, but she ignored it and cuddled closer. Her tears still fell, but not with the same vehemence as before. He murmured her name and eased her away from his shoulder so he could clean her face.

"I must look a mess." She wasn't a pretty crier. Tears made her complexion blotchy and her eyes red-rimmed.

He gazed down at her. "You look lovely."

"Only a blind man could say that." She'd allowed French to apply a little rice powder, rouge, and lip stain before the ball, and they must all be smudged.

"I'm not blind. You're lovely."

He made her smile while he worked at clearing up the mess she'd made of herself. After, he patted her face dry.

"You always seem to be cleaning me up," she said, and then wished she hadn't because the last time hadn't gone so well.

He put down the cloth and towel, just dropped them on the floor and reached for her hands. They stared at each other in silence. Sophia bit her lip. She couldn't tell what he was thinking.

"I behaved badly."

Whatever she'd expected him to say it wasn't that. "When?"

"Our wedding night." As always, straightforward. "I shouldn't have gone about it that way."

She didn't know what to think. "I assumed you needed to do it to make the marriage legal."

"No. It didn't matter if we consummated it or not. It was legal." He gripped her hands firmly. "I didn't have to come to you that night. But I wanted to."

"You did?" That thought brightened her mood. "I—I'm not—I didn't think I was attractive to you." No other way of putting it. She'd repulsed him. "Or were you involved with someone else? Are you? I promise, I won't mind—" Although she did. Far more than she should.

"No." He stopped her before she could go into a complete babbling mess. "I think you're lovely. Beautiful, in fact. You're intelligent and poised." He smiled so warmly she caught her breath. "But I didn't want to get too close to you. I couldn't."

"Why not?" She frowned, not understanding. "Is there something wrong with me?"

"No." He hesitated. "Nothing is wrong with you. It was my fault that our wedding night went so badly." Leaning forward, he touched his lips to her forehead. "And then I compounded my mistake. I let you be to find your own way through the morass of society. I thought you were capable of handling it. Fool that I am, I didn't know you were struggling. It took someone else to point it out to me, and that's hard to take. But he was right."

She wet her lips. "Julius."

"Yes. He noticed." With a melancholy smile, he began to undress her. Careful and controlled, he unhooked her bodice, pushed the garment aside, and removed her stomacher. "You had a difficult time tonight. I promise I'll never put you in that position again." He paused. "I'm sorry. I was so bound up with my own concerns, I didn't see yours. That's unforgiveable, so I won't ask your forgiveness. Just let me help you now."

Lynne Connolly

"I forgive you." She said it so softly, but she meant it. "What good does it do to hold on to grudges?"

He glanced down, his fingers busy on her clothing, his gaze catching hers for a brief moment before sliding away. "You're more generous than I deserve. I won't doubt you again."

"You won't?" That sounded so sweet to her, but from a man who questioned every business deal he made in minute detail, it also sounded unbelievable.

"I swear."

When he looked at her with eyes wide, no guile, she believed him.

He eased her gown off her shoulders. It slid down her arms. She stared at him, wondering what he was trying to do. Make love to her? But she was so tired now, and she couldn't be at all attractive.

So gently she hardly felt it, he traced a line with his finger from her shoulder to her inner elbow. She shuddered. Weak and empty after her bout of crying, she felt entirely in his hands, as if he could do anything to her and she wouldn't resist.

With a flash of insight, she wondered if men really wanted that, or if they wanted something else? She studied the light in his eyes and the way his attention followed the movement of his fingers, concentrating on his actions.

He undid the cords at her waist, and then slid off the bed, holding out his arms to her.

When she jumped to join him, her petticoats and hoops slid off her in one cataclysmic move, like earth in a mudslide. All the way down. She stepped out of them. After one long look into her eyes, he gave a small smile and dropped to one knee.

She found the movement attractive, far too much. But that had been her trouble. Over this last month, his appeal had increased. The more he treated her with cool civility, the more she wanted him. She'd even take him as he was before. That contact of their bare bodies had been thrilling, and she didn't know how to cope with it. Or its lack.

After unfastening her garters he slid her silk stockings down her legs so sensuously she flung out a hand for support. And found his head. He had worn a formal wig for tonight's ball, but sometime between the front door and the bedroom he'd lost it. She touched his hair, dark and smooth, the long tail fastened up. "Why do you wear your hair long?"

He tipped back his head, forcing her to move her hand. "Because it's easier this way. Some men prefer their hair shaved, some wear it short, but this way I don't have to bother with wigs most of the time. They itch. I can go bareheaded in the summer, which is infinitely preferable to sweating away under horsehair." He grinned as if sharing a secret.

She grinned back, feeling younger, more carefree.

Gently he lifted one foot and removed her satin shoe and her stocking before placing her bare foot on the floor and repeating the action with the other. She was only wearing her shift now. His hand cupping her foot felt deliciously forbidden, and when he moved slightly, the sensation filled her all the way to the top of her head.

When she shuddered, he rose to his feet in one smooth movement and took her hands.

"Come. Let's get you into bed. You've had a rough evening and you need your rest."

Rest? That wasn't what she was thinking of now. But she was weak and aching, and once he pointed it out, weariness seeped down to her bones. She'd gone one month fighting this way for the rest of her life exhausted her.

But she liked his hand in hers. Wanted to feel more of it.

He drew back the covers of the bed and helped her to climb in. She lay back against the pillows, watching him. To her consternation he covered her up.

Before she could think over what she was saying she risked rejection one more time. "Are you not joining me?"

His eyes widened and darkened, or was that because he'd turned to reach for the candle snuffers? No, because when he looked back at her he appeared the same. A richer expression impressed his features.

"Why would you want that?"

"I don't want to be alone tonight."

If he offered to call French to attend to her she'd kill him. When she felt better.

Thankfully, he did not. Watching her, he began to unfasten the buttons on his waistcoat.

His clothes followed his coat on to the chair in quick succession. Waistcoat, breeches, stockings, shoes, and finally underwear. He tore off his stock and tossed it on the chair, then turned to her, clad only in his shirt.

He could have been wearing a nightshirt, like their first evening, as the folds of his shirt came down to mid-thigh. "I'll stay until you sleep. But you're tired. It drags at you, I can see it, so don't deny it."

If all she could have was his presence, she'd take it. She enjoyed watching him approach the bed, his muscles flexing easily, clearly discernible under the fine linen. Before joining her, he took the snuffers and extinguished the candles in the room, all but the ones set on the bed head.

He crossed to her side of the bed and extinguished those, too, pinching them out without bothering to use the snuffers. Then he walked around, his figure dimly visible, the white linen ghostly in the gloom, and got into bed with her, disdaining the use of the step.

When he lay down next to her and pulled the covers over them both, he turned to face her, his arms open. "Come here."

Gladly, she went to him, felt his arms close around her. "You won't leave?"

"I won't leave."

His warmth surrounded her, his body protected her. For the first time in forever, Sophia felt completely safe. She slept in his arms, drifting deeply into profound, exhausted slumber.

Chapter 11

Max castigated himself for all kinds of fool. Holding this woman in his arms, he let his mind roam free instead of forcing it along its usual rational lines.

What a mess he'd made of his marriage! He could have been doing this and more every night had he treated her with the respect and consideration she deserved. Instead, he'd allowed half-formed rumors and his business to set barriers between them. Any longer, and the barricades would have become insurmountable.

The light of dawn filtered through the bedroom shutters and over the bed. He hadn't bothered to draw the curtains around so the light fell over them. Other than drawing up the sheet so it didn't bother her, he didn't move, but watched his wife as the pale light delineated her features.

She had a fine-drawn face, with softly rounded, full lips and a firm jaw. Heavy eyelids, sweetly flushed cheeks. She revealed an innocence he was loath to disturb. But he would.

On their wedding night, he'd taken her with a cool efficiency and two ambitions. To discover if she was a virgin, which he did before he pierced her body, and to create the possibility of a child.

The act had felt profoundly wrong, or rather, the way he'd done it had. By trying to make the intimate side of marriage easy for her, he'd in fact made it harder. He hadn't known what to do.

He, the incisive, ruthless businessman, had fouled up his own marriage because of indecision. Should he return to her? The two days he'd planned to give her to recover from the wedding night had stretched into a week, and then longer. Easier to let matters slide than to revisit that shocking need that had brought him to his knees when he let himself think of that night and what he wanted from her.

His raw emotions had only grown worse. He wanted her with a longing he fought hard to overcome. Nobody should have that power over him. He couldn't afford to give that kind of control to anyone.

But the more he struggled, the worse it grew. Every time he saw her, he wanted her more, the memory of her sweet body and her trusting eyes haunting him. His body knew, instinct told him more waited for him, and he hadn't trusted it. Had run from it.

Sophia lay breathing softly in his arms, and he felt like the strongest of men, merely because she was here and at her most vulnerable with him.

When John Hayes had returned into her life, jealousy had reared its head, adding to the toxic mix of emotions he tried so hard to tamp down.

Sophia's father had told Max that he'd interrupted an intimate encounter. Although Sophia showed no sign of wanting to resume that, she'd allowed the man near her, seemed friendly with him. Was she thinking of taking her previous suitor as a lover?

Not while Max lived.

She opened her eyes. She gazed at him, and before he could let his clever mind persuade him that she didn't want him, he kissed her.

He made the kiss count. He melded his mouth to hers. Her hand stole out of the covers and around his neck and pulled him closer, so her breasts pressed against his chest. Her nipples hardened, twin pinpoints in the center of all that softness.

When he shifted his head to one side, the better to seal their kiss, she opened her mouth, and he took her invitation to enter. Their tongues twined and caressed.

Moaning, he spread his hand wider where it rested on the small of her back and sent it seeking. Her buttocks were curved, and they filled his hand with a perfection he'd never discovered in anyone before. She just…fit him.

With an effort, he finished the kiss and drew away far enough to gaze into her eyes. Soft brown pretty eyes, if still a little red-rimmed. But that was his fault. "I'm sorry." He couldn't say it enough.

To his surprise she rolled her eyes. "It wasn't all your fault. I pride myself on my courage, but I had none when it came to you. I should have come to you earlier."

He cupped the back of her head with his free hand, threading his fingers through her soft hair. "We could spend the morning castigating each other. Or we could begin our marriage properly. Only if you feel well enough," he added belatedly.

He received a sunny smile in return. "Yes, yes I do. I slept, and I feel better for it."

"Sleep is good for some things." He dropped a kiss on her nose. "Not for others." His concerns dropped away as he gazed at her. "Not for this."

Without warning her first, he flung back the covers, enjoying her feminine squeak of shock. Before she could find her bearings, he unfastened the buttons at his cuffs and whipped his shirt over his head, tossing it aside.

He sat upright, hiding nothing, not least the heavy erection he'd sported for most of the night. Holding her so close, feeling her breasts move against his chest every time she breathed, had had its inevitable effect. He wouldn't wait for her any longer. "It won't be like last time."

Her smile warmed him down to his core.

"Good. I knew it wasn't everything. Otherwise, why would people risk their reputations and their livelihoods for it?"

"Good point." He gazed at her, savoring her response. His nudity gave him strength. He hid nothing, boldly displayed his reaction to her presence. "Do you like what you see? I can cover it up, if you'd like."

Teasing her, he reached for his shirt, but she sat up and put her hand on his arm. She shivered.

"Are you all right? Truly?"

"Truly. It's excitement. I want you to show me everything, Max."

"And then," he purred, "You can show me. I believe once you understand the…fundamentals, you'll teach me a great deal too."

He glanced down at his cock, now primed and straining to get at her. As it had been for the last month. That frustration had only added to his short temper and frantic activity. "Do you want to touch me?"

She was reaching out before he issued the invitation. At her first tentative touch, he groaned, his arousal ratcheting up another impossible notch. He tingled with anticipation, not daring to touch her in return, feeling like an untried boy.

It got worse. Or better, depending on the perspective he took when she dragged off her shift.

"I thought I knew you." He studied her body with avid fascination.

Her breasts were fuller than they appeared when she was dressed, probably because she wore relatively modest clothes. But now he'd seen them, that suited him well, because he wanted to keep them to himself. Hug the secret close, let others guess at their magnificence.

She had large nipples, soft and velvety, but they crinkled as he stared at them. He flicked a glance up at her face before he continued his perusal.

The nest of soft curls at her groin indicated the secrets they ineffectually hid. Her aroma wafted up to him now she'd removed her shift. Delicate and essentially feminine, it teased his nostrils, daring him to move.

He must not frighten her, but he wanted that essence, to know it in every possible way. "Lesson one," he managed to choke out before he eased her on to her back.

She opened her legs, probably expecting what he'd done before, but that would never happen again. Not in that way.

"You don't have to do that. We should learn each other, find out what we want from each other. No holding back."

Instead, he sent her a wicked smile. Her pretty eyes widened when he slowly moved over her and lifted her thighs to drape over his shoulders.

Moving closer, he took a deep breath, surrounding his senses with her, and then he feasted.

She tasted wonderful as he licked her front to opening, gathering her essence, claiming it for his own.

She gasped. "You can't—"

He broke away long enough to say, "I think you'll find that I can," before returning to his self-appointed task. Nobody could stop him now he'd had one taste of her. Not enough. It might never be enough.

When he sucked the little pearl of flesh at the front of her cleft she cried out, pushing his head as if to urge him away. But he held on, licked and caressed her with his tongue, persuading her to let him continue. This was far too good to give up. In any case, if he took her now he'd embarrass himself, probably not last long. He'd gone too long, spent a month ogling his wife, and now he was going to enjoy himself. And bring her with him.

She clutched handfuls of his hair, but not to drag him away, not any more. She cried out, long wordless sighs of sound, as he worked her into a controlled frenzy. He rolled his tongue around the bud, teasing her, and then sucked harder, giving her sharp, concentrated points of sensation to accompany his lavish savoring.

Then he brought his fingers into play and had to fight to keep her on the bed when she jolted up. When he slid a finger inside her wet warmth, her cries increased in volume.

Satisfied she'd forgotten everything except this, he worked her body, lapping her abundant juices. The sound permeated the room as she became wetter and he grew more intense in his efforts to bring her to a peak of delight.

She locked her thighs around his head. He hummed against her flesh, and then introduced a second finger to join the first. Satiny and lush. He blocked the image that came to mind, of his cock buried deeply inside her. It would happen, but not if he tortured himself in that way. Then they'd have to wait.

He couldn't wait. Just another suck, another finger.

The third finger did it. He bent them, scraped her inner walls gently and she screamed. It was like pulling the trigger on a finely tuned pistol, and the result was as explosive.

Her channel convulsed around him and her heels bore into his back, but he didn't stop sucking and caressing until every quiver had stopped. Or paused, because they were about to embark on the next stage of this… He didn't know what to call it. Not seduction, because he was no longer sure who was seducing whom.

When he withdrew, her sigh gave him deep satisfaction. But not enough.

He withdrew his fingers and unwound her legs from his head. She was lax now, like a rag doll. After kissing each inner thigh, bestowing gentle tributes, he drew away and watched her.

Staring at him, her heavy-lidded eyes slumberous with the after-effects of her orgasm, she smiled, making him wonder how he could have held off for so long. And why, for that matter.

"Do you want to learn what happens next?" He needed her permission, to know she wanted this as much as he did.

Her eyes widened and her attention went to his cock. "Yes."

"This is not like last time. You're in control, madam." Scooting to the top of the bed he sat against the pillows, resting against the padded headboard. It was a heavily embroidered and quilted version of his coat of arms. A very suitable decoration for what they were about to do. After all, without this he had no reason to have a coat of arms.

The pointed part at his back told him the bull's horns were making their presence known, but he was more concerned with his fleshly spike. He held out his arms. "Come here."

She blinked. "Over you?"

"Exactly. Come and kiss me. I want you to enjoy your own delectable flavor while you take my cock into your body." He deliberately used the words, explicitly detailing what he wanted her to do to see her reaction.

A smile curled her ruby lips. "Yes, my lord."

Oh lord, that was perfect. As she sat up, her breasts quivered and changed shape, but the nipples still stood proud, jutting at him, daring him to take hold. He would, but he wanted to watch them bounce.

She kneeled up, and then with a sudden decisive move, opened her legs and came over him, straddling him with admirable thoroughness.

"An adventurous woman. My favorite kind."

He held his cock steady for her. Even that practical touch made him twitch. If he didn't get inside her soon, he'd have to think of something else to do to keep her on the boil for the next twenty minutes while he rebuilt his erection. Eager he might be, virile come to that, but he wasn't a god. Or a stone statue, although one part of him damn well felt that way.

She gazed down, bit her bottom lip in concentration, before glancing up at his face. "Will it hurt?"

"I promise you, no." He'd licked her with the idea of opening her up, easing her way, but once he'd tasted her, he'd taken more. Now she was well and truly ready for him.

Her moisture dripped on to the head of his straining cock and he groaned. If she didn't make up her mind soon, he'd have to do it for her.

Far too slowly, she lowered her body on to his. He felt every inch, every fraction of an inch, as she took him deep and then deeper still. Grasping her hips, he helped her, forcing absolute control on himself while she accepted him and accustomed herself to having him inside her. After all, the last time hadn't been pleasant for her.

When her chin went up and she gazed into his eyes, all he saw there was wonder and triumph. A sense of triumph filled him, such as he'd never known before.

He smiled. "You did it. You're in control, sweetheart." That was why he'd chosen this way of making love. He didn't want to take her. He wanted them to take each other. "Now kiss me. Let's see what else we can do."

Her breasts nuzzled his chest as she leaned forward and pressed her lips to his, touching his mouth with her tongue. With a groan he opened, surrendering everything to her. Firming his grip on her waist, he lifted her and then let her ease back down on him, showing her what to do. The next time she moved on her own, only needing him to remain where he was and thrust back into her when she came down again.

Voraciously he sucked on her tongue as they learned each other, finding the rhythm that would bring them both to satisfaction. He shifted her slightly and paid attention to her response as she gasped into his mouth. Better. She liked that. She liked it more when they did it again, and again.

Max drove harder with each stroke, delving deeper. All he had to do was hold her steady as she moved on him. He could use the support behind his back to help push forward and into her. Their kiss continued, never ending as she became bolder, greedier, and he ate at her mouth, thrusting his tongue in harmony with his hard drives below.

She grabbed a handful of his hair, clutched it with a desperation he shared. They'd get there, and this time they'd do it together.

The sound of their bodies slapping against each other echoed around the room. Max opened his eyes and watched her come apart. He held her safe, while for the second time that morning, he made his wife come.

When her channel tightened on his cock, Max was finally done for. He let go, releasing into her. Wild now, he dragged her body down on to his, grinding her against him as he flooded her with his seed.

He heard his own voice as if distanced from it, crying out her name and a succession of breathless gasps. He dragged her into his body, the need to feel her overwhelming every rational thought.

As time passed, he became aware of her breathing heavily. Some sense returned to him. He laid her down tenderly before lying beside her and dragging the covers back over them. He was warm enough, but he didn't want her to take a chill.

Raising her head, he gave her a series of sweet, drugging kisses as they slowly emerged from their post-coital dream-state.

"Now I understand," she said, her voice little louder than a breath.

But Max was so close, he heard her well enough. "Understand what, sweetheart?"

"Why people risk everything for this."

He kissed her. "Yes, they do. I'm in danger of doing it now, because I fear that won't be the last time we do this today."

Her eyes flicked open and then half-closed again as she chuckled and rested against him. "We have to get up sometime."

"Do we? What for? Do you have an appointment you simply can't miss?"

"No, but I thought you would."

He murmured against her temple, enjoying the way he gave her butterfly kisses with every word. "I would cancel an appearance at court in exchange for this. Or a meeting with the head of the biggest shipping company in the world. Anything." Her laugh warmed him. "It's time we had a honeymoon. I should have taken you away somewhere. But then," he added, "I might not have realized what I'd done to you until it was too late."

"Enough," she said. "I've heard enough of that."

He hadn't. He wanted to confess his doubts and his fears about the marriage. Now it mattered more than ever, but for an entirely different reason. But with her happy, he didn't want to spoil the mood.

He smiled wryly. What a coxcomb he was!

Now he had a weapon, a way of fighting back, a way of keeping her. And he would use it.

Chapter 12

The next day they set out for the country. Max's idea, to show her the ancestral home, but also, he explained, a chance to spend time together with nobody to interrupt them.

"In town, your father, Julius, Poppy, my mother and any number of other people distract us. I want some time with you, for us to talk and get to know each other properly."

His country seat was in Buckinghamshire, a day's swift journey or two days of easier travel. They took two. After a stay at an indifferent country inn, they reached Devereaux House mid-afternoon on the second day.

Although she'd expected it, Sophia was still taken aback by the sheer size of the place. They caught a glimpse of it from a distance, swept around a corner of the tree-lined drive, and there it was.

"My goodness," she murmured.

"Yes. And it's just as grand inside. At least it had better be." He gave a wry grin. "I've had workers restoring it for the last two years. They've nearly finished the central block, they said. I need to tell them what to start on next. Perhaps you can help me decide."

He took her hands, and she gladly removed her attention from the house to his face. Today he was smiling, at ease. He seemed much more relaxed here.

"I want you involved," he said. "This will be your home. In future, people will say you are responsible for the creation of this magnificent house, the best in the country."

Leaning forward, he kissed her. He'd done a lot of that over the last two days. Making up for lost time, he said. She wasn't complaining.

"I don't know if I can."

He squeezed her hands. "You have been responsible for investment decisions costing thousands of pounds. You can handle this easily."

His belief in her warmed her heart as much as his kisses. But she had many things to tell him, and some of them might change his mind. In a way, the size of this house was good, since she'd be able to avoid him, and he her if he wished it. She didn't know where to begin, but it had to be with current events rather than past ones.

Except they were bound together.

She turned her attention back to the house. It was huge, of gleaming golden stone, the central block a Palladian masterpiece with ranks of windows on the three main stories. Too many to count. But that wasn't all. Either side of the main block stretched two huge wings, a story lower but in the same style, so the house appeared as nothing so much as a palace. The sun glinted off the myriad windows, delineated fine-hewn stone. One person owned this?

The household of servants has amassed outside to greet her. That seemed worst of all. "We only had four servants living in," she said.

"We have more than that in London," he remarked. "It's needed."

"I can see that."

She didn't hide her wonder from him, and he watched her, his expression inscrutable.

"You like it?"

"Wouldn't that be an insult? Merely to like it, I mean. Isn't it more appropriate to marvel at it, or admire it, or stand in awe of it?"

He gave an easy laugh. "Perhaps. But from you, liking will be enough. It's a lifetime's task."

Easily. But she wouldn't say that now. The house was modern, so probably had the best services, such as kitchen equipment and building standards. So maybe finishing and keeping it beautiful wouldn't take all her time. Although making it truly beautiful would make it worthwhile. A proper legacy.

Max alighted first and helped her out himself. He smiled at her as she descended. "Welcome home, my lady."

Home. Anything less like a home she couldn't imagine, but people did live in comfort in these places. More than comfort if rumor had it right. But luxury wasn't her preference. It intimidated her.

Trying to behave as a lady born to the life, she allowed Max to introduce her to the servants, which he did with aplomb. Luckily, not to every single member of staff, since the grassed area they stood on appeared to be a catch-all for any passing wind. The long range of buildings probably channeled them this way. She had to hold her broad-brimmed hat to keep it in place. But she did have time to gather that many of the servants here were related, and most had served the family for generations.

Also that they didn't approve of her. Although the servants took care to keep their wordless exchanges out of Max's sight, Sophia was quicker and more perceptive. She saw the raised brow one of the upstairs maids exchanged with a footman. They were probably secure in their positions in the household. Perhaps they should take more care.

Not that she was given to drawing a white-gloved hand over the top of pieces of furniture, as some mistresses did. But she'd ensure the house was properly taken care of. As her duty. Anyone who didn't come up to her standards would have to leave, and that included wordless criticisms of her or any other person in the house.

With her hand on Max's arm, she climbed the broad, shallow stairs and entered the house.

The vast hall was high enough to encompass all the main areas and as wide as most London houses. But the painted ceiling drew her attention. People, or beings, flew across the huge area toward a figure at the center.

"My great-grandfather," Max murmured to her. "He was the one who went into exile with King Charles. The king presented him with the marquisate on his restoration. He was a mere earl before that. But not a penniless one."

"How so?"

"Some of the family remained behind in England. Half the family was royalist, half for Parliament. It preserved the estate when many perished." He shrugged. "But ruin comes from many quarters. The Wallaces have lost and rebuilt many fortunes."

"And you built the present one."

His smile was warm. "So I did. The one my father dissipated building this place."

She blinked. "I thought he gambled. That is, I assumed…either that or unwise investments."

"The South Sea bubble did him no favors," Max said. "I learned never to invest everything in one pot from that debacle. But he had money left. The estates were extensive. I sold as many as I could. I had to, to pay the mortgage on this place. My credit wouldn't have lasted long had I not."

"I hadn't realized matters were so dire. I mean, I heard of your family's bad times, but I thought they were relative, not absolute."

Since the danger had gone, she couldn't see the point of keeping the information from the servants who probably knew more than she did in any case. A few remained after the introductions, footmen and a maid.

"Did my maid arrive?" she asked one of them and received assurances that she had.

French and Max's valet had left early that morning so they would arrive sooner than their master and mistress. She had been forced to see to herself at the stop on the road. Not that it had been a hardship. She'd enjoyed the quiet room and the refreshments she'd shared with Max alone. And the kisses. She looked forward to more than that tonight, confident, as she had never been before, that her husband would share her bed. Or she would share his.

A wave of tiredness swept over her at the reminder of bed, but she pushed it aside. She was made of sterner stuff than to collapse after two days' travel. Except she wasn't used to it, as many were. She refused to allow a comfortable journey in a coach furnished with every luxury to vanquish her.

Concerned he might notice her fatigue before she saw this edifice, she turned away and studied the rest of the hall. Paintings, mostly landscapes, hung on the walls, and everywhere but the ceiling was enlivened by decorative plasterwork. The floor was marble, but with very little furniture. She didn't find the place comfortable, but she guessed that was deliberate. "This is a statement rather than a hall," she said.

"It is," he replied, his voice low. If he spoke up it would echo around the walls repeatedly, like in a cathedral. This place was as big as St. Paul's, but a temple for temporal power, not spiritual majesty and just as awe-inspiring.

The staircase was a double—two staircases either side of the space led to a landing above. "Somewhere for the lords to gaze down on the less fortunate," she commented and received a sharp laugh for her pains.

If she had expected the rooms to grow less grand, she was disappointed. The staterooms were enfilade, in a long line along the front of the house, so they got the best views. When the doors to each room were opened, as they were now, she could see right through to the end. They wandered through a huge salon, another smaller salon, a music room, and a state bedroom with a four-poster bed draped in crimson velvet.

She reached for his hand and he took it, his fingers winding securely around hers.

"We don't have to sleep here, do we?"

He chuckled. "Not unless you want to. Nobody has ever slept in this bed. In the old days, it was a mark of favor to receive a guest in a bedchamber. Much as you have your levees today."

She hadn't held many of those. A time when the house was opened to people while she was dressing. She only did that when she was preparing for a ball or something elaborate that would take time. Most of the people who attended wished for her favor in some way, musicians and artists. Someone had even composed an execrable poem to her beauty, in the hope that she'd sponsor the publication of his small volume. Not a chance, although she hadn't told him in those terms. He had excellent taste, however, and had helped her select her fan for the day.

That seemed so far away now. This place was a kingdom on its own. People could live here and escape detection for years.

After the grand chambers where they'd spend time with guests and honored visitors, they passed through to a small antechamber. This contained two pietra dura cabinets of such beauty they took her breath away, the polished marble and semiprecious stones glinting in the daylight streaming through the wide windows. But she didn't want to touch them. They were too beautiful for someone as normal as she.

She'd never felt so inadequate. But this was her house, and Max wanted her to take charge of it.

Dismissing the footman who'd accompanied them, Max strode through more beautiful rooms until he reached a bedchamber, where he closed the door firmly. Another lovely room, but with modern wallpaper in Chinese silk and a canopied bed instead of an old-fashioned four-poster.

"You're not happy," he stated.

She shook her head. "It's just...you said it was grand, but I never imagined anything like this. How could I? It's bigger than St. James's or Kensington."

He pushed her into a chair and knelt before her, taking her hands. "This is our home, and it will be exactly as you wish it to be." He glanced around. "This is your bedroom, should you prefer it."

"Where's yours?"

"Next door," he said promptly. "This is the only suite with adjoining bedrooms, and I thought we might prefer it. But if you want a different room, say so, and we'll make the arrangements. This is our house, Sophia. It belongs to us, not the other way around. My parents were its servants, but that's the last thing I want. It's ours, to do with as we wish." He grimaced. "I used to dream of coming here in the dead of night and burning it down."

She gasped. "But it's so beautiful!"

"It is. But it's a mausoleum. Not a house." Longing entered his gaze. "I wanted a home. I was brought up here. Even the nursery wing is grand.

I never knew a home. Do you know the moment I entered your father's house I felt more comfortable? The furniture was worn but good. The place bore marks from people having lived there. It was a home. I wanted that for our London house, too, and you've done a great deal toward making that happen. But here...I don't think it's possible." He took a deep breath. "I lived here in solitary splendor, no siblings to enliven my days until Poppy came. And all the time building was going on around us. The place still isn't finished. I fear it never will be. Like the bottomless soup pot in fairy tales."

She remembered those stories, and his reference almost made her smile, except he seemed so despairing. Lifting her head, she glanced around the room, taking it in. The blue colors would suit her. They appeared newer than the rest of the furnishings she'd seen so far. "Did you order this room prepared for me?"

His cheekbones gained a red tint and he glanced away. "I wanted you to be comfortable somewhere. But I did it when we were first married. I planned to overawe you. So if you don't like this, please change it."

He did it for her. Even then, he was thinking of her. "I like it." She got to her feet. "Show me the rest of the house, and when we see a servant, we'll order tea for when we're done."

Before she was tired, but now she felt full of renewed energy. He'd just informed her that he needed her, that he wanted her help. That was enough to remind her what she could do. She was a businesswoman, trained to evaluate investment projects. So she'd use her training to this place. Regard it as a business. After all, it was part of the family investments. She would assess the return exactly as she would anything else.

Smiling, he stood too and took her hand, raising it to his lips to bestow a soft kiss on the back. Then, watching her face, he turned it over and grazed her palm with his lips. "Thank you," he said. "I chose the perfect wife, did I not?"

They continued to tour the house, and Sophia did her best to thrust her emotions to the back of her mind and paid far more attention to her analytical brain.

Devereaux Place had treasures, most of them packed in the main block. As they went around, Max told her its history. What Sophia had imagined a modern construction proved to be something else entirely.

"We're coming to the older section. The façade to this part is just that. It covers a much older building."

Indeed, the style and the feel of the house changed from the gorgeous staterooms to the more lived-in library. In fact, the house had three libraries. At least one too many. One was old, another was for show, and another had always been there, originally holding the official papers belonging to the estate that were now safely locked away in the estate office downstairs.

She liked the Jacobean Long Gallery which overtopped the staterooms. It was a long room with window embrasures and a line of family portraits. She noted the family resemblance, the sharp features, and from time to time, the green eyes that were so distinctive a part of her husband's face. Except his sparkled with life and liveliness. When he realized Sophia was taking more of an interest in the house, he regaled her with far more interesting, and scurrilous stories.

Sophia viewed the family rooms, elegant and more modern in design, and the older rooms at the back of the house. That had originally been the front, but Max's father had turned the whole aspect of the building, making the front of the house the back. She began to warm to the place. She liked this part.

The wings mainly contained offices and guest rooms, together with some frivolities like a summer drawing room. "As if this place needs another drawing room!" She turned to him with a laugh.

He shrugged. "You're right. It was built to contain that bureau." He indicated an elaborate desk with a bookcase top. "It was presented to the marquess of the day by King Charles the Second."

She didn't like it. The barley sugar twist legs were only the half of it. "A room for one piece of furniture?" That was when she got her idea. "You worked all your adult life to keep this place," she said. "Why?"

They were alone here, so he could be as frank as he wished. Would he confide in her?

"This house was my father's dream," he said. "It was my mother's dream, too. They were devoted, my parents. Adored each other, even when it became clear there would be no more children after Poppy. There was a problem when Poppy was born, and it rendered my mother barren. At least, that was what she called it in her bitter moments." He paused. "She had many of those after he died."

She had many now, Sophia thought, but didn't say it aloud. "So you wanted to keep it for her?"

"I want her back here. When he died, she left and never came back, except when compelled to. Now she moves from one member of her family to the other. Living with Julius isn't unusual. She lived there before, and then she went to her sister who was ill, and then back to Julius. After my father's death, I had this place closed up and a skeleton staff put in place. It distressed her greatly, and I don't think she's ever forgiven me for doing it."

"I see." Sophia had a word for that. Several, in fact. She'd seen people use objects to lever a deal before, and this was what her mother-in-law was doing. Only in this case, she was using the house as a way of gaining her son's attention and his love.

Sophia didn't give a fig for that. In fact, she gave less. "She has martyred herself for you?"

He shook his head. "It wasn't like that. She never railed against me." He crossed the room, leaned his hands on the sill, and stared out over the home park. "She told me this house was mine now, and I should do as I pleased with it."

"I'll wager she did," Sophia muttered, but kept her voice low. She walked across the room to join him, mustering her courage to say what had to be said. "I do have a suggestion. She's right. This is your house."

She turned her back on the view and leaned back, studying the drawing room. Attractive enough, but not the magnificence of the rooms in the main part of the building. "They spent all the estate money on this house."

"They were determined to make it perfect." He gave a hollow laugh. "Some parts aren't finished. These wings have blank ends, and some rooms have no floors. At the end of the other wing, there's a double story section without floors. There are plans for the development. My next project." He sighed.

"Then don't do it." A suggestion she dearly wished him to adopt, so she had to concentrate, put all her powers of persuasion, such as they were, to work.

Max turned away from the window and straightened, folding his arms across his chest. He was preparing to take his stand. Her heart sank.

"Give me your opinion with no bark on it."

She waved her hand. "This could be a room out of a pattern book. There is nothing distinctive about it, apart from the bureau. I believe your parents had run out of invention or money or enthusiasm by this point. Everything is expected, traditional, as if they'd given the job to someone else and told him to get on with it."

He kept his attention on her face. At least he gave a short nod, so slight she might have missed it had she not been paying attention to his every move. "Go on."

She could tell nothing from his closed-off expression. Now she'd started, she had to plough on. "This part of the house and the other wing are new. There's no history associated with them. And what people need this many rooms? I thought the house my father bought in the country spacious enough, and it had scarcely a tenth of the rooms this place has. It seems wrong, Max. That was why I was uneasy when I saw Devereaux Place first, although I didn't realize it was the reason."

He nodded, but still said nothing. Obviously he understood the value of silence. Already she was getting cold feet, fighting against fidgeting.

But she would not give in. Would not stay silent, because this marriage was meant to last. In these early days, they had a chance to set the terms and conditions, find a path they could walk together. They had so nearly taken separate paths. Only her determination to make the best of what she had and his re-evaluation of her had changed that.

She took a deep breath for courage. "I say move the things worth moving into the main house. Use that bureau to embellish one of the staterooms, for instance. Then demolish the wings."

She bit her lip, waiting for the explosion, but none came. He watched her in silence.

She ploughed on. "This is our children's inheritance. I don't want my son forced to maintain this house when he has no wish to."

"It's under entail," he pointed out.

He sounded reasonable, not a note of anger she could detect, but in Max that was dangerous. He was doing his best to conceal his thoughts, as he did when brokering a big business deal. She could be in danger of watching him walk away again. If he invited her opinion only to spurn her, she would take that as a sign of his lack of interest in her thoughts.

If he discussed the issue, tried to persuade her, that was something else again. She could accept that state of affairs. At least he'd have listened to her.

"Surely the wings aren't part of an ancient inheritance. Aren't you allowed to alter the place the way you wish?"

He gazed at her in silence for a few moments. Then the light returned to his eyes. He turned his head, glanced out of the window again. "I used to play in the tree that stood here once, until my mother caught me and scolded me for it. She told me I had to be more responsible, that the fate of a whole dynasty lay on my shoulders. My father was an only son too. There are no close relatives on his side of the family, none left. All my life, I had to remember who I was and what I represented. When I went into the City, my mother refused to speak to me for a year, until the results of my investments began to come in. Then she relented. Oh, it wasn't *trade*, she said, as if that made a difference. If I could have earned the money working as a stable boy, I would have done so. Anything to regain what my father had thrown away. I was sixteen, Sophia. I never was a feckless youth as my cousins were, never wasted time in gaming houses with expensive mistresses. Because of *this*."

He glanced around the room, disdain in his gaze.

"You say I should throw away everything I worked for, to give my mother the legacy she wanted. I should destroy what she and my father tried so hard to build. That's what you're saying?"

Chapter 13

"It's not your dream, though, is it?"

All the time they'd toured the house she'd watched him as much as her surroundings. Not once had she seen the fanatical spark of ambition light his countenance. He'd shown no pride, only weary acceptance. "I've learned to calculate, to assess, not to put sentiment on belongings. I have my mother's jewelry, poor trinkets compared to some of the pieces I've inherited as the marchioness or those that my father bought me when our fortunes rose. That's all, though. I don't have her handkerchiefs or her clothes because we got rid of those or had them made over. They were just things. They weren't her."

"So what's your business assessment of this place?" Still he regarded her with calm coolness.

She hated it, half-wished she'd never started this, but she had, and she must continue. Couldn't back down unless he gave her a considered opinion. None of that "I forbid it" nonsense he'd used when she'd said she would see John. As if he didn't trust her.

The spark of remembered anger gave Sophia the impetus to go on. "I don't want my son made unhappy by a thing. A possession. So that, for me, is on one side of the ledger. In favor of keeping the status quo, there are few points. Your mother's happiness is an important one."

So was his happiness, and she knew the one she cared about the most. "And the house is undoubtedly beautiful. You might destroy a future treasure.

"On the other side, for the demolition there's the financial aspect. It won't be as much of a burden. Most of the beauty will be retained. The treasures will go to new places. The building materials can be placed into storage for when the main house needs repair or sold. We can get a good sum for accoutrements like paneling, fireplaces, doors, and so on, and any furniture we decide to sell. Floorboards are selling particularly well at the moment, especially good oak ones like these."

She knew that because her father had been forced to replace some of the boards in the back parlor recently after an attack of woodworm. Fortunately the worm hadn't spread very far before they discovered it, but the price of the replacements had shocked them both. Details like those made business far more profitable.

"Are you suggesting we go into the building trade?"

She considered denying the possibility vehemently, but changed her mind. "Why not, if it's profitable? The demolition should pay for itself, if we're careful. Then there will be gardens to plan, or we could put grass over the area and continue the Home Park over it."

"You," he said, taking a step toward her, "are an iconoclast. You see monuments, and you ask yourself why and what purpose. Your practicality overwhelms me."

Sophia lifted her chin. "Better practical than poor."

"Indeed, my mercenary little wife."

He cupped his hands over her shoulders and as always her insides quivered at his touch.

"Come here."

Roughly, he pulled her close and set his lips to hers.

That was the last thing she'd expected. A long discussion, perhaps rejection, especially considering she'd broached a topic he seemed to hold dear. Not this passionate embrace. He spread his big hands over her back, stroked her into submission. Maybe that was the idea. Ah well, at least she'd tried.

After a long, thorough kiss, he drew away, but kept her in his arms. "What I suggest is that we go to bed. Now, with those little Chinese men rioting over your bed curtains. Let them watch. I don't care, but they'd better get used to the sight."

"What?"

"You are perfect for me. You articulated what I've been thinking for a while but dared not do." He kissed her again. "I'd worked all my life to restore this place, and for what? A few sticks of furniture? I like your plan. No, I love it. And it's something we can do together. Let's set our minds to it and get it done. We can get the main part of the work completed in a year."

Dazed, she stared at him. His eyes had regained that passionate expression she loved. He was holding nothing back.

"You mean it? It was only an idea."

"One I'm wholly in accord with. I can afford this house now. I can afford ten of them, but you're right. I don't want to saddle our children with a millstone around their necks. And then it will be 'Oh, it's old, and it's valuable, part of our history. We can't get rid of it even if it is bankrupting us.'" He laughed. "Instead, we'll give them a great house instead of a palace. An exquisite gem instead of a rambling mansion. We'll make it beautiful, you and I, ensure the work is done well. Do you like gardening?"

She shrugged. "Apart from growing a few herbs in pots when I was little, I don't know. I've never tried it. I'm told it's very relaxing." But she needed nothing more than this for relaxation. She melted in his arms. Every time. She laughed up at him, her relief at his acceptance of her idea warming her bones. "I see it more as employing a good landscape artist and working with him to ensure it's done well." She paused. "One thing. I'd like an orangery. I've always wanted one of those, ever since I read it in a newspaper somewhere. I'm not even sure what one is."

"A summer house, lots of glass and filled with orange trees and orchids," he said promptly. "We shall have it done. Sophia's orangery. We'll consult with our gardener to decide where it will be." He hugged her close. "Do you need to see the other wing today?"

Not at all, she thought, but kept it to herself. "No. It will be there tomorrow."

"Although not this time next year," he said, with a joyous laugh. "When we return to London, we'll find someone to oversee the work. I don't want to lay the burden solely on the shoulders of my estate manager, although I'll give him the oversight of the project."

"How will he feel about it?" A man whose job was to care for the estate might not like her plans. Their plans. "And what about your mother?"

He grimaced. "Lansbury won't mind. He's often complained about shoring up the unfinished parts of the house. Since they're all in the wings, he won't need to worry about those any longer. My mother though, that's different. If you don't object to it, we'll go back to London in the near future and tell her before she finds out by other means."

She nodded, her hair catching in the threads of the embroidery on his waistcoat. Forget-me-nots today, on cream. Max never concerned himself much about his wardrobe. He just employed the finest valet he could find. Typical of him to delegate in that way. Concentrating on what he did best and taking time to find the best people possible to do the jobs he couldn't or wouldn't do. Like her. For a man in his situation, she was certainly the practical choice.

When she looked up into his face, that was the last thing in her mind. Her own passion was reflected in his eyes. "Yes," she murmured against his lips. "Let's go to bed."

They accomplished the journey back to the main house much faster than the one out here. "We could keep pavilions," she said.

"No," he replied. "If we're doing it, let's do it properly."

He kept her hand firmly tucked in his, heedless of anyone who might watch and perhaps condemn. She must learn to disregard that impulse. It would lead to a very uncomfortable existence, if she cared what everyone who saw her thought.

Half way along the Long Gallery, he spun her around and dragged her close for another kiss. Deep, hot, and wild, taking away all her concerns. Nothing mattered but this, but him.

Chuckling, he pulled away and grabbed her hand. "If we do much more of that, we won't get to the bedroom. I don't mind. Do you?"

She'd never seen him so open, laughing, and happy, and the sight dazzled her. She laughed back. How could she do anything else? And the thought of him pushing her into one of the window-bays and throwing up her skirts sent a fresh surge of heat to her groin. But she wasn't so desirous that she would initiate the encounter. Their new relationship was too fresh and she too inexperienced to know the etiquette, if it could be called such, in this situation.

"Show me everything," she demanded greedily. "I want to know it all."

He turned back to her, his face alight with laughter. "Everything I know, you will know. But not all at once."

But she had so much time to make up for, so many years of not knowing this. Still laughing, he ran with her, their feet thundering on the wooden floorboards of the Elizabethan gallery. At the end, they turned into another hallway, down a set of stairs, another hallway, and at last the bedroom he'd said was hers.

He slammed the door, spun around to press her against it, and took her in a deep kiss.

A movement and an exclamation of shock startled her into opening her eyes, but Max didn't stop kissing her. This close she saw the stubble on his jaw and the strands of hair that had escaped the neat queue. He touched her lips with his tongue, his request for her to open, and she did, cupping her hand around his head and threading her fingers through his hair. He tasted her, sweeping his tongue into her, licking the roof of her mouth and sending her higher.

While he kissed her, he fumbled at her neckline, dragging away her fichu to expose the upper slopes of her breasts. His touch, so soft, stirred her into action. Moaning, she slid her free hand under his coat, seeking the buttons on his waistcoat. Naked, she wanted him naked, needed to feel his hot hair-roughened skin against her own.

She no longer cared who was in the room. But whoever it was still stood there. The person was against the door. Unless someone was very good as getting through doors silently.

Shock ricocheted through her. The thought of someone in here with them, watching them, sent shivers of arousal through her. Forbidden, wicked, and unexpectedly stimulating.

He must have sensed her change because he drew away. "Sweetheart?" But he smiled. He knew.

She gasped. Nobody understood her like that. She barely understood herself, that impulse that drove her to carry on, no matter who was watching. Her body heated.

She wanted to show other people how much her husband wanted her. How shaming was that?

Someone moved then, a rustle of silk. Max pulled away, standing before her at first, and then he moved aside. A hectic flush heated her cheeks.

French stood in the middle of the room, a gown draped over her arm. "I-I beg your pardon, my lord, my lady."

According to the first law of domestic servants, she'd transgressed. Servants should be silent and invisible. In some households, they were trained to turn their backs when their employers passed by, to give some privacy. Sophia would never dream of requesting that, but in this case she might make an exception.

Her attention went to the gown. "Not that one, French." Why she'd said that she had no idea. Just the first thought that came into her head. Her mind whirling with new knowledge, she wanted time to think, not to expose her new discovery in front of anyone. The gown would do as a distraction.

"Ma'am?"

"It's an unusual color," Max said.

It was. Aquamarine with sprays of white embroidered flowers cascading down to the hem. "It doesn't work well on me. The color is wrong and the pattern too vivid. But I liked the fabric." She gave Max a placatory shrug. "A mistake."

He raised a brow, gave the gown a cursory glance, and reached out his hand to her. "My room, I think."

His room was decorated in warm colors, dark reds with mahogany furniture and landscapes on the walls. Nothing feminine about this chamber. And it looked used, not brand new.

"Has this always been your room?"

"Since I came down from the nursery wing. I resisted the efforts to move into the marquess's quarters. The other end of the corridor from the marchioness's. I didn't want that then, and I want it even less now. But if you want to change, say the word."

"No." She glanced around the room. "The other room is beautiful, and in time I'll like it more. But I love this one." *Because you're in it.* "It's a real room." It had an atmosphere. Someone lived here and imbued it with his presence.

Smiling, he gestured to the bed. "And my bed isn't piled high with clothes." As hers was.

She curved a hand around the back of his neck. "I might have to stay here all night if French doesn't clear my bed. Really, I hate to impose on you—"

With a low chuckle he stopped her mock protests with a kiss. "Where were we? Ah yes." He glanced down and unfastened her bodice. "I felt you tense when you realized someone else was in the room. I knew as soon as we went in." Another hook worked loose. "I assumed she'd leave discreetly, but she had that gown hampering her. I didn't care. I'd have had you anyway." He glanced up at her face. "You enjoyed it, didn't you?"

"What?" Her startled gaze went to his face. He knew. Those eyes—they revealed everything, but when had they started to do that? Before, when she hadn't known him so well, she'd thought him inscrutable. One of his gifts that enabled him to make deals greatly to his advantage. But she saw it now. The heat and the amusement. "I don't know. Just that—"

He had her bodice undone. Gently but with determination, he pushed the silk off her shoulders and sighed. "Such lovely skin you have. I know, my sweet, and I won't ask you to do anything you don't want to do. Perhaps I'll have ancestral portraits brought in here. *They* can watch us."

"I didn't know it was possible."

"All things are possible where the body's concerned. The brain is only one part of it. Your stomach lets you know when it's hungry, so why not the quim?"

She started in shock. She'd never heard it spoken before. She'd only read it, in the more wicked caricatures and commentaries. "That—"

"Let's be frank. We'll try everything and see what we like. Being watched never bothered me, but it's never excited me, either. It seems to excite you." Walking around her, he helped her off with her gown. "Imagine the servants peeking through the jib door. Every room in this house has a hidden servant's door. Did you know that? Perhaps they watch." Her stays began to loosen as he deftly set to unfastening her laces. "I've heard rumors that they do."

"Watch?" Again, that warmth between her legs. Heat and wetness. Recalling what had happened before, that time they'd spent in bed in London, Sophia should have expected it. But the sensitivity seemed more, as if she couldn't bear not to rub her legs together to relieve some of the tenderness gathering there.

He had her stays off and, with a few swift movements, unfastened the drawstrings that held her pocket, petticoats, and hoop in place. He didn't stop there, but bent to undo her garters and roll her stockings down her legs.

"My valet and your maid. Especially French. Would you like them to see you naked?"

As she turned to face him, he got to his feet and smiled down at her, but his cheekbones were tinged with red, always a sign of emotion in him. He was excited, too.

"Only you," she said.

Gently, he removed her last garment, her shift, which, being of fine lawn, concealed very little. But that veil had given her the illusion of concealment. Now she stood before her fully-clothed husband stark naked.

His eyes kindled with heat, and he stripped off his coat and let it fall. He glanced toward the back of the room. The jib door, she guessed.

"There they are," he said. "Should they see me do this?

In one swift move, he dropped to his knees and reached for her. Curving his hands over her bottom, he drew her close and nuzzled into her heat. He took a deep, noisy breath and nudged one thigh with his chin. "Open," he commanded.

She took a step to one side, opening herself to him, and he rewarded her. He feasted. Licking her like the finest sweetmeat, savoring her, he didn't hide his sounds of appreciation. "Mmm," rumbled along her most sensitive tissues, shivers rocking her. He held her close, showing her no mercy as he licked and sucked, breaking away only to say, "You will come. Just think of those servants watching us, seeing what you allow, and what I'm taking. They want it too, but that they cannot have. They can only watch."

His words persuaded her, so convincing she could imagine French standing at the open jib door in her pink Sunday best, watching, side by side with Max's attendant, who had his hand on his shaft.

"Oh!" Sensation jolted through her.

"That's right," he murmured before returning to his task. He delved, and then sucked, curling his tongue around the tender bud. He teased and tugged until finally she cried his name and gripped his shoulders for fear of falling.

Shudders racked her, and if he hadn't stood and held her close so she could lean against him, she'd have fallen. He kept one hand on her cleft, prolonging her orgasm, and another firmly around her waist. She held up her head for his kiss, and he didn't disappoint her. He tasted of her, sharp and feminine.

"Get into bed, my sweet. I'll join you directly. You are so delicious I could eat you all night."

Eat her. Feeling wickedly sensual, she went to the bed. By the heat searing her back, she knew he was watching, so she added a sway to her hips and lingered over climbing on the step. After flinging back the covers, she arranged herself on the crisp linen sheet and leaned on one elbow to watch him.

He stripped for her. Glancing over to the bed, he gave her a wicked grin. "This is for us, Sophia. I don't intend to let you far from that bed for a long time, so prepare yourself to be put under siege."

"That sounds…intriguing."

The hoarse tone of her voice surprised her, but he seemed to enjoy it, as his smile broadened. When he lifted his shirt over his head his muscles flexed, the bulges in his arms and shoulders belying the assumption that a fashionable man should be smooth and elegant. He could be elegant when the need arose, but his body contained fascinating slabs of muscle that betrayed his visits to the boxing saloon and the fencing studio.

In her mind, she dismissed the imaginary servants because nobody should see him like this. This was hers to enjoy.

In the act of stripping off his breeches, he lifted his head and stared at her. "Are you cold?"

She shook her head, a few pins from the wreck of her hairstyle falling to the pillow.

"Then let me see you." He straightened, only his underwear left, his shaft tenting the fabric. A damp spot appeared on the front. "Throw back the covers and open your legs. Show me where to go."

Her heartbeat quickened and she gasped for breath. Dare she? Yes, of course. She wanted to show him, loved to display herself when she saw that light in his eyes, desire kindling passion.

She swept the sheets back, the starched fabric rustling provocatively, and slowly opened her legs. "I'm wet for you," she said, greatly daring.

He rewarded her with a low growl. "I can see that. By the time I'm finished with you, you won't be able to stand. I will take care of you, carry you to the powder room, wash you, and feed you. But here you are mine, and you do my bidding."

"I swore to obey." She didn't mind his autocracy in bed. Welcomed it, because he would give her everything she wanted, introduce her to pleasures she had yet to imagine.

"Then here is where you will do it. This sight is for no man but me. Understand?"

"As long as you swear only I will see you thus from now on." She wanted him to herself. They could play as many games as he liked, but she wouldn't share him. Many men had mistresses, but she couldn't bear to think of him doing that. That thought should have given her pause, but it only made her greedy. "If you want this, come to me."

He inclined his head graciously. "As my lady wishes."

When he stripped off his breeches, she licked her lips. His cock stood finely erect, damp and shiny at the tip, red and hard.

"You want this? You shall have it, madam."

He was at the bedside in two strides and on the bed, but kneeling up. Gripping his shaft, he presented it to her. "Drink your fill," he said, "But not too much. I want you to know my taste."

Would she do that? Her mouth watered. Oh yes, and with delight. She sat, knelt, and then sank back so her bottom rested on her heels. That brought her at the right height. Gazing up into his eyes, which were so dark as to appear almost black, she reached out, cupped his balls. He let out a small sound, a grunt at the back of his throat. So masculine that Sophia smiled.

She licked him and groaned. So tasty. Musky with a hint of something sharp—good white wine, perhaps. Yes, that. Greedy for more, she opened her mouth and took him in.

When she sucked, he gave a cry, and then gave an order. One she dared not disobey lest he took away what was giving her so much pleasure.

"Look at me. I want to see your eyes."

If she opened her legs so she could sink down a little more, she could do that. Suck his cock and watch his face. Openly desirous, he gazed back, watched her serving him. Tasting him. Keeping her hand on his balls, gently massaging, she brought her other hand up to curl it around the part of his shaft she couldn't swallow. Her husband was a big man, and it would take more skill than she possessed to take him in her mouth, although she fervently wished she could.

Would he come in her mouth? Would she like it?

His long groans told her how much he was enjoying her ministrations. But before she could taste him fully, he sat up, grasped her shoulders, and dragged her up to him. Fastening his mouth to her in a fierce taking, he rolled her over so she lay under him and pushed his cock inside.

It dragged at her skin, tugged, and then broke free, rooting deep. She cried into his mouth, and he finished the kiss to stare down at her. His eyes were wild, his hair straggled around his face, making him a savage marauder rather than the civilized businessman that lurked deep inside. Only her knowledge that he existed somewhere inside this man told her she was safe.

And she reveled in it. She'd driven him to the edge, and she wanted to know what life was like on the other side. All her life she'd taken care, ensured her safety but now she wanted to—

"Let go," he ordered her in a wicked whisper.

She obeyed. She could do nothing else. Screaming his name, heedless of anyone who might in reality be lurking nearby, she bucked under him. But his superior strength held her firmly in place while he took what he wanted. Emptied himself into her.

Panting, laughing, he rolled away, but reached for her so she went with him and curled up by his side. Tilting up her chin he kissed her, but although undeniably sensual, this time his kiss was tender. She pressed close to him, savoring his hard, muscular body.

"You're a revelation, sweetheart," he murmured. "A fast learner." He smiled against her mouth when he took another kiss. "Why don't we stay here? Never go back?"

She chuckled. "When the building work begins, you won't want to be within a hundred miles." She lifted herself up on one elbow and frowned.

He touched her forehead, but watched her, didn't interrupt her.

"Shouldn't one of us stay and supervise?"

"You mean you in the country and me in the city?" Now he frowned, too. "No." Flat, unequivocal. "We need to be together, to build on what we've started. This is more than doing our marital duty, or hadn't you guessed that already?"

Swallowing, she nodded. She had, but she'd been half afraid this was his way of enjoying himself while getting her pregnant. Then he'd move on, as so many men did. The promises he'd given her, they could have been in the heat of the moment, or reassurance. Would he want her when she was pregnant? Despite that concern, she warmed when she thought of having his child growing inside her.

His laugh bounced off the walls. "This is better than I could have imagined."

She gazed at him in astonishment. He could laugh, full-bellied and amused, with no hint of sarcasm. Perhaps they should stay in the country, if it meant she saw him like this more often. His lovemaking astonished her, as did his openness in bed.

Only when he drew the sheet down did she realize she'd drawn it over her when she'd moved to raise herself up.

"I want to see you," he said. "It gives me great pleasure."

"I—I'm not used to it."

"I'm delighted to hear it."

Reaching out he traced the outline of her nipple. The tip was still hard and to her embarrassment it hardened more. Tingles spread over her still sated flesh.

"This is what we're supposed to do, sweetheart. We might as well enjoy it."

"Yes."

His hand stilled. "I didn't mean it in that way." His fingers rested lightly on her breast. "I meant that… I'm not very good with words, I'm afraid. Let me show you instead."

And as he took her nipple into his mouth, she reflected that words weren't always necessary.

Chapter 14

"We should get up today."

"Why?" Lazily he reached for her.

She went to him. Over the last three days, they'd rarely left the bedroom, and then only to wash, eat, and chat. Both were insatiable, and once she'd realized how much he loved her taking control from time to time, she got up the courage to do it. They were friends and now lovers. They had built a sound basis for the rest of their married lives.

"Shouldn't we tell Lansbury our decision?"

He rolled on top of her and buried his mouth in her neck. "Even your soap tastes good."

"Can you die of too much lovemaking?" Sometimes she thought so. How could she have ever been afraid of this?

"We can try." He smiled down at her, totally open.

She smiled back, like an idiot. He'd pampered her, fed her, and made love to her until she'd lost count of the number of times. The only times she'd been dressed were when she'd donned her robe to visit the powder room. Or to go into their private drawing room to take an informal meal.

She still hadn't finished her tour of the house, but she was in no hurry to do so. Besides, since he'd embraced her plan so enthusiastically, it wouldn't be there for much longer.

"We should make lists. You know, the rooms and what they need."

He propped himself up, which only served to bring his cock nearer to her cleft. Already she was dampening for him, her body readying itself for his possession.

"We'll ask the steward to inventory the wings first. He probably has one ready. Then we can decide what we want and which building materials we can salvage and sell. With the London building boom, we could bring some items to town to sell."

"Another business?"

He kissed her. "Everything is business." He rotated his groin, driving his cock closer, but not there yet. "Almost everything."

"Even then, we're trying to make a child for the marquisate. An heir," she pointed out.

"Don't you want a child?"

More than anything, she discovered. She couldn't explain it properly, but she tried. "I want to bear a child to you. I want your baby." She swallowed, knowing she was taking yet another step into the trust of intimacy. He held so many of her secrets now. Just not the one John had vouchsafed to her. She'd have to tell him soon, but not when they were like this. So close.

She'd been giving herself those kinds of excuses for the past three days. If she didn't tell him before they got back to London, he'd see the information as a betrayal. And it would be, of a sort, because she'd be sending him into battle unarmed. He had to know, even if it meant she wouldn't have this anymore.

At the thought, alarm sent a bolt of sharp awareness through her, and she swallowed.

He noticed, of course. "What is it?"

Her heart ached. "May I tell you later? There is something… But not here, not like this."

His eyes turned grave and his mouth flattened. "I don't like secrets. I'd prefer there were no secrets between us."

"There won't be." Giving a tiny moan, she arched her body toward him. "Later. I'll tell you later." What had he turned her into? In three days, he'd shown her so much she wasn't the same person as she had been when she'd arrived here. Her rationality had turned to mush, together with her resolution.

"How can I resist?" he murmured, coming down to her. He licked her breast until her nipple tingled, and then turned his attention to the other. "You taste of salt and soap and perfume…and me."

"It doesn't sound very pleasant," she said, but she gasped when he took her nipple into his mouth and sucked. He'd learned what she loved along with her, and he used his knowledge to the greatest extent possible to bring her the greatest pleasure. He was very good at that. She gave a grateful moan when he rolled his tongue around the very tip of her breast, where her senses gathered. She'd beg him for more, but he was already giving it to her.

Gently he parted her folds and slid two fingers into her wet crease. He brushed her clitoris as if by accident, watching her face avidly. "Open to me."

"I'm open." To prove it, she squirmed against his hand. Her flesh softened.

"I can feel that. Open your eyes. Don't close them. Watch me. I want to see your every reaction. I want you to see mine."

Thrills coursed through her, sending her heart pounding. Completely open? Slowly, he pushed a finger inside her. He'd found a spot inside her that sent her *in alt*, and he touched it now, so gently she thought she'd explode.

"I can see you," he said. "All of you. You love this. When I do this—" He touched her inside again, just stroked it and she flinched, tightened around his finger and then whimpered. "Oh yes," he murmured. "Just like that. But don't close your eyes. Your eyes are so expressive. I can see everything you're thinking."

"Or I let you believe that," she murmured as her senses settled enough for her to think again. When he sent shots of sensation through her, her mind stopped working. All her thoughts coalesced in that part of her he was pleasuring. He'd told her the more scurrilous names too, some of which she didn't know. She delighted in repeating them to him and listening to his chuckle.

He kissed down her body, making humming sounds, the vibrations purring against her skin. "You have the most exquisite navel." His breath skimmed over her stomach. "Perfection should be celebrated."

He kissed a tiny ring around the indentation and paused to dip his tongue before travelling further down. He nuzzled into the bush of hair at the apex of her legs. Flicked out his tongue to touch her with the tip of his tongue, gone before she'd registered his presence. Opening her legs, she invited him in. He took it, sucking her bud hard, in fierce contrast to his tenderness of a moment before.

Lifting her hands, she grabbed a handful of his hair, holding on as he tasted her, his skill enhanced by the way he'd learned her body over the last few days.

When she heard the sounds he didn't bother to hide, they impelled her higher. Instead of moving, she held on. If she shifted, she'd dislodge him, and right now she'd do anything not to have that happen.

He sucked and pushed a second finger inside her, and she thought she might just die. Then she looked down at him and found him watching. "No, I won't close my eyes." He didn't have to ask. In any case he had his mouth full. His lapping and sucking made every part of her body sensitive, not just where he was concentrating his attention.

In one, decisive move, he surged up and flipped her over. "Up," he said. "On your knees."

"You can't look at me like that."

He laughed. "Nothing but the truth now. I don't need to watch your eyes to know that. I can feel it. Now do as you're told, wench."

That made her laugh too, but when he tapped her backside as she gingerly rose up for him, her mirth died. Three days ago, she was a relative innocent. She'd let him lead her to places she had no idea existed, and she wasn't sure she could live without experiencing them with this man. He was making himself indispensable to her.

He nudged her with his erect cock, and she moaned when she felt his first steady entry. Unspectacular, but then it didn't need fireworks for her to sigh in eager anticipation. This was her favorite part. Or maybe that was when he entered deep, or maybe when he kissed her, or—it was all perfect.

How had she lived without this?

Pushing deeply inside her, he stilled. "Tell me if I hurt you. You look wonderful like this. Your bottom is rounded, peachy, inviting me to take and take again. I can't stop where you're concerned."

Shreds of courtesy remained, even while she felt his excited entry. He drew nearly out of her in one smooth move and then slid back in again, his move seemingly never-ending. Yes, deep and deeper still, until he nudged her inner walls aside, making a place for himself there.

His place. Totally his.

The next time after he withdrew, he slammed back in, the impact jolting her forward, but he was ready for it. He gripped her waist, dragging her against him to stop her forward momentum.

"Brace yourself, sweetheart. Here we go."

No mercy now, and none wanted. Deep, hard thrusts, pushing against her with every stroke, taking her. Owning her. She would give anything to have him do this.

"Don't stop," she said between gasps. Her arms trembled, threatening to let her down so she locked her elbows to keep herself steady for him.

Sophia was a fast learner, and she put her expertise to use now. If she rocked against him as he drove into her, she could create that smacking sound as their bodies collided and open her body to him as much as possible. As much as she dared.

He roared her name, growled it, ordered her to give everything up to him. "I'll take care of you," he said. "Forget everything but me, everything but this," punctuating his words with harder thrusts until she howled with ecstasy.

But she didn't come. Instead, he brought her to a plateau of awareness, of a place where his every touch thrilled her, and all she knew was him. All she wanted to know.

At last he curled one arm around her, dragging her closer, and touched her clitoris, pinched it in time to his thrusts. And the currents of sensation turned into a river. Crying his name, she jerked, and her passage tightened around him in involuntary spasms as she lost her breath to her orgasm.

Dimly, his voice rose, and he gave one shout before he jetted his seed deep inside, deeper than he'd been before.

With breathless laughter, he leaned over her, lifted her up so she could rest against him. Then kissed her shoulder and her neck before easing her down on to the sheets and gently withdrawing, as tender now as he'd been fierce a moment before.

"Rest, sweetheart. I'll order some food and hot water."

He lifted away from her, leaving her momentarily bereft, before she slid into deep slumber. Before she went completely under, he murmured, "Dream of me."

She'd certainly do that.

* * * *

He woke her with a gentle kiss and a touch on her shoulder. Smiling, she looked up at his relaxed face, and he smiled back.

"They've brought us breakfast in the next room," he said, referring to the private drawing room attached to the suite. Her boudoir.

She sat up, not bothering to draw the sheet around her. It was a bright spring day, and her husband had seen everything she had to offer. Besides, she wanted to see that glow in his eyes. He didn't disappoint her. The golden glow returned when he perused her naked body.

He cupped her breast, testing its weight. "You shouldn't tempt me," he said. "You need sustenance. Besides I wanted to tell you something. Lansbury is back from his travels. It seems someone sent for him when we arrived, but he was on the Nottinghamshire estate and it's taken him this long to get back." His mouth firmed. "As if we were transgressing on his property. I'm keen to start the work as soon as we can, so I'd like to interview him. But it was your idea, so would you prefer to be present?"

Out of all the husbands she could have chosen, this was the one for her. He wanted her to be with him? Some men would have taken the suggestion she made as their own and taken all the credit for it as well as the responsibility. John would have. Even in the highest throes of her madness for him, she knew that.

The thought of John sent a chill racing through her, and she suppressed a shiver. She would tell him, and if they were dressed, her task would be easier. Naked, she was completely open with him, as he'd encouraged. She couldn't bear it if he took her news badly while they were in that state that had brought such pleasure to them both. He might spurn her. Better done when they were armored, albeit with every day clothes.

"I'd like to, if you don't mind."

"I'll tell him we'll see him in an hour." He glanced at her and the corner of his mouth kicked up. "Two. I know women prefer to take their time dressing. Would you like a bath? I can order one for after breakfast."

A bath would take far too long and would disrupt the house while it heated the water. But she didn't care. "I'd love a bath."

"I'll give the orders. Now come and have your breakfast before it gets cold."

Before she could leave the bed, he dragged her close and kissed her again. "Don't think I won't have you back here as soon as I can. Or yours, it makes no difference. Or the library, or maybe we should try the state bed downstairs."

Her laugh rang around the room. "And then we can receive all the honored guests there, remembering what we did."

He snorted. "I don't think the bed even has sheets on it, but it could be interesting. Imagine the maids walking in on us. There is usually someone there, dusting or cleaning or suchlike. They'd just have to work around us, wouldn't they?" His smile broke out again. "I rather like the idea of that."

Taking a deep breath, he drew away and climbed down from the bed. He picked her robe off the floor and offered it to her. "But you have to come here to claim it."

His wicked grin told her what he wanted her to do. He was daring her. Although she'd become much less shy with him over the last few days, she still balked at the idea of walking around naked. Her modest upbringing went deep. But she put on a sultry smile, recalled the last experience they'd shared in this room, and flung the sheets aside with a flourish. Glancing up at him, she found the footstool and climbed down. Then she sauntered toward him. His eyes darkened, and she presented her back so he could help her into her robe. When he did so, he tightened his arms around her waist and kissed her shoulder and, when she turned her head, her mouth.

"You're deeply tempting," he murmured against her lips. "We should tell Lansbury to wait."

"No we should not. Let him make a start with the inventory, and then we can come back to bed."

He smiled. "So practical. That gives us extra impetus. The sooner we're done, the sooner we can come back here."

Only when she left the room with him did she realize that not one twinge of fear had accompanied her actions in the last three days. Finally, Max had achieved what she'd tried so hard to do—to dissipate the fear that John had engendered in her. No longer did she flinch when a man touched her intimately, not even in an automatic reaction.

John's attack had frightened her more than she cared to admit. She'd had to force herself forward, force herself to accept the hand of the man she wanted, to lie down for him, and to take him into her body. In fact, she couldn't wait until they'd finished with the steward and could get back to their own devices.

After a full breakfast that Sophia felt she deserved, she went to her room where French waited for her with a suitable day gown. Green, a pretty pea-green, not at all like the emerald of her husband's eyes. She felt strange, dressing for the first time in days, even in something this simple. French didn't comment, but her thin lips pursed.

When Sophia went through to the drawing room to meet her husband, his appearance almost undid her. Although dressed in country clothes, he appeared more like a man she had met in the city than the man she had spent the last three days with. What a difference clothes made to a person.

However, when she took his hand, he felt the same. She smiled at him and received his warm smile in return. He took her to the small office on the ground floor of the building.

There, Lansbury the steward waited for them. He was dressed in neat, practical clothing. A pair of gold framed spectacles adorned his face, behind which a pair of blue eyes sparkled. Sophia held her judgment in reserve. She was far too suspicious, from her Dealings in the city.

The man bowed low. "It gives me great pleasure to welcome you to this house, my lady," he said, with all the unctuousness a marchioness could wish for.

Sophia certainly didn't appreciate that, but perhaps the last marchioness preferred it. He would have to work out how to deal with her. However he might have done his research. The news of her marriage was public knowledge after all and not difficult to research, even on the road.

"It's a pleasure to meet you too, Lansbury."

He glanced to Max, who indicated the rent table. The piece of furniture dominated the room, a large round table with small drawers set around it. She bent to study one of the labels pasted there. "A to D," it said.

"Tenants," Max explained. "When they come to pay the rent on quarter day, their records are kept in these drawers."

"How many tenants do you have?"

"We," he corrected gently and glanced at Lansbury.

"At the last count, my lady, two hundred and sixty three on this estate."

"A good number." It seemed a reasonable number for the main property. Not just farmers, but perhaps villagers, too.

"A trifle low, if anything," Max said. "But we have other concerns."

He touched her elbow, and she forced herself not to sink back into his arms. This touching was exquisite torment in the early days of their relationship when they needed to learn each other. They'd risen too soon, but they had their duties, the reason for their marriage. She could never ignore those.

They all took a seat at the table, Max and Sophia remaining close.

She watched Lansbury closely when Max explained their plans. At the first mention of the word "demolition," the poor wretch closed his eyes and shuddered. Interesting that he didn't try to hide his reaction from the man who had jurisdiction over him.

Max had informed her that Lansbury had inherited this position from his father, who'd held it before him. That happened not infrequently, and perhaps he was as dynastically minded as Max's family. Even in her natural home, the City of London, families hoarded rights and privileges jealously to pass down to their descendants. So why not a land steward, an important position in any great family? He would have his own assistants and discuss possibilities with his master, instead of simply taking orders.

Lansbury's mouth twitched as if he were in pain at a couple of points, and half way through, he opened his eyes and fixed Max with a hard stare. The twinkle had gone.

When Max finished, Lansbury paused, and then said, in a perfectly modulated voice, "Do you think that's wise, my lord?"

"Yes." Typical of Max to answer the question and no more.

"Who gave you this idea, pray?"

By the way he carefully avoided looking at her, Sophia knew what he was thinking. And he'd be right. The notion had come from her.

Lynne Connolly

Max glanced at her, smiling fondly. "My wife merely began the idea. It is what I want, what I've always wanted." He lost the smile when he returned his attention to his steward. "See to it, please. I want an inventory drawn up as quickly as possible, and the plans pushed forward by the end of next month. By then, we'll have a schedule for the work. By the end of the year, the project should be well underway." He gave Lansbury a hard stare. "No procrastination. If anyone demonstrates that, get rid of him and find someone who will do the work." His intentions were perfectly clear. If Lansbury didn't want to do it, he would find someone who would.

Lansbury's prominent Adam's apple moved in his throat as he swallowed. "Yes, my lord. I cannot help thinking that we should let the notion mature for a while." Then he glanced at Sophia, but only briefly. He flicked his attention back to Max as if she meant nothing at all. "You have plenty of concerns."

Sophia considered his suggestion and read what he was saying underneath the words. "I'm sure we'll cope."

"I was thinking we could use Denton while the work here progresses," Max said, naming another of his estates. "Or just stay in London."

So he'd thought of it, too. If she fell pregnant, it wouldn't be wise for her to be around a large demolition project. He had a house picked out for her. But if she agreed to that, she might well be left out of future plans.

"Is Denton nearby?"

"Tolerably," Max said. "It's not a large or showy place, but it's comfortable and ample."

That sounded like a house she'd like, but Sophia knew where her duties lay. She had to be a marchioness, not a country lady. Which meant this house. Without the wings, it would still be much larger than anything else she'd known.

But she'd fight that battle when it arrived.

"Have the inventory ready by the end of next week," Max said calmly.

When Lansbury gasped and began to protest, Max interrupted him. "There is such an inventory. It merely needs bringing up to date. Checking. Ensure everything is listed in room order and in order of contents, please."

"My lord, you have lived in London for a long time. You have rarely visited this place. It would help if you allowed yourself some time to accustom yourself to the plan."

Max leaned an elbow on the table and smiled beatifically. Sophia had seen him do that, when he'd just struck a deal that he wanted. She wouldn't trust that expression if she were Lansbury.

"One of the reasons I live in London is because I can't afford this house. Or I couldn't when I started to recover the money my father frittered on this place. I have no intention of passing this burden on to my own children, so now is the time to do it. When Sophia suggested it, I realized it was exactly what I wanted. So do not try to make me accept the house as it is."

"My lord, I drew up plans for the completion of the unfinished rooms in the east wing."

"Very diligent of you, Lansbury. File them away. We won't need them now."

Sophia would have felt sorry for the steward, but for the fulminating glance he threw Max's way when he thought his master wasn't looking. She guessed what Lansbury planned. He would contact the dowager, and then war would be declared. She could foresee unpleasant times ahead, but as long as she and Max remained determined, then they would see it through.

Sunshine streamed through the window onto the rent table, illuminating the conversation between the men. So polite, with so many tense undertones.

With no more to be said, Max courteously helped Sophia to her feet, and they left the office to the man who would reluctantly supervise the project.

"Perhaps you should employ someone solely to oversee the work," she said.

Max snorted. "And antagonize him further? I think not. He must do it or resign. There is no shortage of good land stewards. If the work doesn't suit him, he can find another place. Which he will do without much difficulty, as he has a good record."

Heedless of who might see them, he spun her toward him and kissed her. "With you, I can see this through. When you said it, I realized it was exactly what I wanted. And I won't allow you to shoulder the blame, either. It is our idea and our project. Part way through, we'll mention that we'll need the grounds re-done and let him look around for a good designer. Perhaps restore the park to the way it was, or instigate something new."

"Won't that be expensive?"

He kissed her again. "But less than the building. More to my taste, too. I'd prefer to look out of my window and see acres of green lawns and flower gardens. Perhaps a fountain or two."

His heated smile melted her.

"But for now, I think we've done all we can. What would you like to do? By the way, that gown…very becoming."

He wouldn't have noticed it a short time ago. Now she could return his smile with interest and move closer, teasing him with glimpses of her cleavage. "We never finished that tour."

"So we didn't." He grimaced, and then brightened. "If we do that, we could work up an appetite for all kinds of things. What do you think?"

"And the bride visits?" She added an innocent smile. "Your neighbors will expect a dinner, won't they? Once they hear you're in residence, they'll want to visit us."

"How will I bear it?" His voice softened, grew more intimate. "I will sit next to you and whisper naughty things in your ear while they think I'm asking you if you want more tea. How much will you bear of that before you make your excuses?"

The thought heated her blood. The nature of the wickedness appealed to her far beyond anything she thought possible, especially with him.

He moved away and offered the support of his arm. "Are you ready for your tour, my lady?"

Now wishing she'd never mentioned it, but also anticipating the tour with more than an expectation of seeing more rooms, she laid her hand on his arm. They went upstairs.

The butler met them in the main hall. "My lord, you have a visitor."

Max exchanged a smiling glance with Sophia. "Bride visits?"

"No, my lord, although several people have called since you arrived. I gave them the information that your lordship was unavailable." He coughed behind his hand. "This visitor has arrived from London, or so he tells me, and he is most insistent that he sees you. Lord Winterton, my lord. He has been here but an hour."

This time Max's glance showed alarm. "Julius? He wouldn't have disturbed us unless he considered it necessary. What on earth could it be?"

"Was it just his lordship Lord Winterton wanted to see?"

Max clamped his arm to his side, trapping her hand. "Whoever he asked for, he's getting both of us. I wonder why he didn't send a message?"

The news worried her, but it might be nothing. "He could have business in the area."

Max's arm relaxed. "You could have the right of it. He does have a small property not far distant. Let's find out."

The butler had left Julius to wait in the Blue Parlor and sent to the kitchens for refreshments. So when they entered the room, a maid carrying a tray of small delicacies accompanied them.

Max pulled her back, spun her into his arms, and delivered a quick but passionate kiss. "Since I will have to wait, I need sustenance until I can get you back into bed."

They made their way into the room when Julius waited for them.

Julius wore the kind of country coat that only a London tailor could make in a rich dark brown that enhanced his fair good looks. Elegant as always, he regarded them unsmilingly. Then he got to his feet and bowed. "It's good to see you looking so well," he said.

His attention went from one to the other of them. Sophia didn't know what he saw, but he would see her a whole lot more relaxed than she had been a few days before. Whoever would have thought she would have been relaxed in a palace?

Max's eyes narrowed, but he said nothing until the maid had arranged the refreshments to her satisfaction and left the room. Sophia busied herself pouring the tea while the two men exchanged small talk about conditions on the road, politics, and anything else that didn't concern them personally. Tension increased. By the excess of cordiality exchanged, Sophia knew that Julius did not plan to discuss anything trivial.

She took her seat and her part in the conversation. "Did you find yourself in the area, or is there a purpose to this visit?" she said. "Not that you're not always welcome here you understand. Just that you're worrying me."

For the first time, a smile spread over Julius's features, slow and appreciative. "I do like that. A woman who isn't afraid of speaking her mind."

"You must know many such women." She wasn't the only woman in London with a forthright temperament. "I have no patience with dancing around a subject when it's an important one."

"You are percipient, ma'am."

They were seated too far apart to touch, but Max's glance was a visual caress, and she smiled back.

"You're a woman of decided character. I always thought so, although I didn't know everything about you. I still don't."

When they turned their attention back to Julius, his eyebrows were raised.

"Interesting, I do wish you well. But the news I have may have implications none of us want to deal with." He paused. "Are we at any risk of being overheard?"

Max shook his head. "The maid who served us is one of the family who has been with us the Devereaux for generations. If word gets out, she knows, as do the others, that I will dismiss every one of them."

"Fair enough. And I will also take steps if what I say here is heard anywhere else."

But what was so important that it merited this level of discretion? Sophia took a quick breath and lowered her gaze. *Not that, please not that.*

And why the hell hadn't she told Max before now? Sophia braced herself ready for when the sky fell on her head.

"This news isn't easy. I verified it before I came and the proof is available should you require it," Julius said. "I brought copies with me. I made the copies myself and I have the originals locked up at home."

"Did you stumble on this…evidence?" she asked, unable to wait until her fate was upon her. She needed the answer now.

He gave her a hard glance, his eyes chips of pure sapphire, and about as expressive. "No. I went looking. I need to protect my friends and my family. Why? Do you know what I'm about to say?"

She shook her head. What if he were to tell something else? But perhaps she could claim some restoration by relating some of the news herself. Was it too late? Panic rose to choke her. "It's something my father said," she said, blurting out the information before she could out-guess herself. "I didn't know what to think, or what to say. I wanted to research it, but I didn't have time."

Julius leaned back and crossed his legs, resting his cheek on one outstretched finger, his elbow on the arm rest of the elegant, brocaded chair. "Go on."

Yes, it was that. Sophia longed to reach for Max but she dared not. Afraid to even look at him. "I met…someone in the park, who gave me some news."

"Whom?" Julius rapped out.

"Julius—" Max said in a warning tone.

"I beg your pardon, ma'am. Whom did you meet in the park?" Julius made it sound like a tryst when it was nothing of the kind.

"John Hayes," she said quickly. "I couldn't stop him approaching me. I was…that is, my father considered him as a candidate for my hand before I married M-Max." Oh now she was stammering, something she hadn't done since childhood. But then, few things had meant so much to her. She ploughed on. "I didn't believe what he told me. Why should I? But it sent me to my father. I wanted him to say that John was lying, that he had tried to create trouble between Max and me." Ironic, since at the time they had enough trouble of their own. But now, John had succeeded, although not in the way he intended.

"You met your old lover in the park?" Max said, voice low and controlled.

Sophia shivered. She hadn't heard that tone since the day before they'd left London. She'd never wanted to hear it again. Not directed at her, anyway.

"He came to see me," she said. "That is, I never arranged to meet him."

"John Hayes," Julius said, either not noticing, or more probably, choosing to disregard the ice in the air, "is working as a political secretary to the Duke of Northwich."

Shock sent a stiffening chill to her bones. Everything froze. "The Duke of Northwich?"

She dared to look at her husband. His expression rivalled Julius's for sheer impartiality and coolness. She could be sitting between two icebergs, either of which could crush her. The duke?

"John never told me who he was working for, but he introduced me to Lord Alconbury, Northwich's son. Max knows about that meeting."

"You didn't think to ask him?" Julius said. "Your lover?"

"He was never my lover!" Stung by the accusation, she turned on Max. "You know that!"

"Only because your father stopped it," Max snapped back. "But I interrupt. Pray continue."

Julius shot him a hard glance, but Max ignored it. All his attention rested on her. That wasn't fair, either, but she couldn't bear to relate what had really happened between John and her. Not with these hard, powerful men listening. Her humiliation. It was bad enough that her father knew, but now, now she couldn't bear it.

All the horror and the distress she'd thought she'd buried deep inside came back up, sending bile to burn her throat. "John was never my lover," she said. "I can only repeat that." She'd tell Max later, if he gave her the chance. Surely he would. "He told me something I found it hard to believe." She swallowed. Would it sound any more real if she said it aloud? "That my father is not my father."

Max frowned. "What are you talking about?"

"My father, James Russell, didn't father me. Didn't—"

"I understand," Max interrupted. "You needn't go on. Why would he tell you that?"

She closed her eyes, gathering strength, then opened them again. "Because it's true. When I visited my father...Russell, he told me the truth. They put the date of the marriage back a year to make the dates match."

"Did he know?" Julius said.

"Yes, he did. He was paid to marry her. But their marriage, I always thought it was a good one, and he said so." She swallowed back the heaviness that filled her now. How much so if she had been forced to tell them what really happened with John? And why would they believe her? She'd met John twice and shown no sign of rejecting him. How would Max see that? That she was planning to recommence their affair? That would be sheer betrayal, especially since she hadn't fallen pregnant yet. An unspoken rule in society was that a woman didn't stray until she'd borne her husband a legitimate heir. Not that everyone always obeyed that stricture, but most did.

She swallowed and finished her story. "My father said he always considered me his daughter. He didn't know who my mother's lover was or why they chose my father to marry her."

"Because he was out of the circles we move in," Max said promptly. "It's obvious."

"More than that," Julius said. "They had enough wealth to care that she didn't get closer to her lover. Enough to ensure her future life was comfortable. Was your father good to her?"

"I think he loved her. I *know* he did. He was distraught when she died. He doesn't show emotion, doesn't trust easily, but he trusted her as he trusts me." She needed something, some assurance, because she felt Max's withdrawal like a physical thing. He was no longer with her.

She'd known he was cold, but now she knew more. In the last few days, he'd given her something that was infinitely precious to him, and now he'd withdrawn it. She might never see it again. Never feel his caress or bathe in the tenderness of his presence. Her future stretched before her in a bleak, unbroken, featureless path. If he withdrew his passion, she couldn't bear it. Didn't want to think about it.

She was terrified that she'd lost Max. Rather than that, she'd risk everything, even humiliation, if she had to. "I didn't like John. I didn't want him anywhere near me. He's not my lover. He never was. He courted me, persuaded my father to trust him, but then he went too far. He tried to rape me."

Chapter 15

Max heard her words in cold fury. Hearing that she'd met her lover once more, that she'd talked to him, and then that she'd kept such a secret from him... How could he trust her ever again? Or even love her? He'd almost persuaded himself. Even now, anger simmered through him because he couldn't keep his mind straight around her, couldn't think of her as he did everyone else—with the distance that came of liking, not loving. The news about her parentage meant less to him than this.

She had betrayed him by not relating the meeting in the park. That struck him to the heart. Accordingly, he took the action he always had and withdrew behind the shields that had taken him a long time to construct. He was a fool to let them down, even for her. Instead of a partner, he had—what? A breeding machine?

No, he couldn't bear to think of her like that. And now she wanted him to believe the act with Hayes hadn't been with her permission? That if her father hadn't interrupted them, she'd now be married to John Hayes instead of him? Except her father had seen him, Max, as a better prospect.

Russell loved Sophia. He would want the best for her. A marquess and a wealthy one, moreover one he knew would take care of his beloved daughter.

Except she wasn't his daughter, was she?

Sophia rose to her feet in a swish of silk and hurried to the window, where she stared out at the grounds. She gripped the sill as if she'd never let go.

Max turned to Julius, trying to get his whirling thoughts in order. "So this Hayes, who works for Northwich, dropped poison in her ear? For what reason?"

Julius glanced at him, and then at Sophia. He got to his feet. "You have other matters to resolve. Don't worry. I won't be going anywhere tonight. I'll retire to whatever room is available and rest for an hour or two before dinner. Call me if you need me. There is more news, the matter of the proof I told you about, but nothing is more important than this." He turned at the door. "Nothing. Listen to her."

He left, closing the door quietly behind him.

What could he do? He should leave. This woman had kept important things from him. "How long have you known about your father?" Had she been fooling him all along? He kept his voice steady, his tones cool. He couldn't think properly. Perhaps more facts would help him.

"Just before we left London. That night you…consoled me."

He knew from the choked tone of her voice that she was weeping. Still he didn't go to her. "It was because of that?"

"Partly. It was a shock. I knew I had to tell you, but what difference would it make? What would it do to our marriage? We were barely on speaking terms, and I didn't know how to talk to you. This is new to me, the society, the life, and in my innocence I thought it would be easy. My father is wealthy, my mother was a member of the nobility. How hard could it be? Impossible." She stopped abruptly and her shoulders shook.

He could stand it no more. "Ah, God, don't cry!" Crossing the room Max seized her and turned her into his arms. He didn't care. Didn't want to know. He had her now, and for his own peace of mind he was keeping her. So he might not love her as deeply as he'd considered, wouldn't give her his entire trust. She had committed the sin of omission, as bad as lying. While he could understand her motives, she'd crippled him, sent him into battle with half the map missing. But did she understand that?

Sophia clung to his waistcoat, sobbing into it, her tears no longer silent. "I—I thought we had found each other. I'm so happy with you. I wasn't afraid!"

He remembered her flinching from him on their wedding night, the movement that had driven him away, that had made him so reluctant to take her properly. In the end, doing his duty had been all he could do in the face of that silent rejection. "I thought you didn't want me. That you wanted your lover, the man your father interrupted you with."

She shook her head. Tears still flowed down her face, and he groped in his pocket for his handkerchief.

"I didn't want him. John said he…he'd make sure of me. That he'd ruin me for other men." She paused and sucked in a breath. "I thought he meant my virginity, but he meant to make me pregnant, or at least create the possibility of my being in that state."

"And knowing what had happened to your mother, your father took the same path. Forced someone else to marry her." His voice hardened.

"Ask him what he saw. John Hayes wanted to snare a wealthy wife and control of my father's business."

Max intended to, but not for the reasons Sophia supposed. To his shock he found himself saying, "I believe you."

Did he? Yes he did. That made sense. Hayes had his own way to make in the world, and marrying the master's daughter was usually a sure way to success.

Julius had said to trust his instincts. Max chose to do that now. The woman he'd spent the last few days with wasn't one who would lie to him about her affair with another man. She wouldn't have met a man in secret. The park was hardly a secret place, in any case. No, what she said made sense.

He did believe her, truly. He recalled her behavior on their wedding night. That was more than virginal nervousness. It was fear. Actual fear, as if she knew and didn't want what was to happen. Had she expected him to take her roughly, hurt her, even?

While he held her, he carried her to the large sofa and sat down with her sprawled across his lap. She clutched his waistcoat and sobbed her heart out.

The heat of anger rose slowly inside him, Max made two resolutions. One, John Hayes would pay for what he'd done to Sophia. Two, he'd uncover the secret of her birth.

If she was a Dankworth, what did that mean? That they forced her into his arms in the hope that she'd betray him and the rest of the Emperors? Maybe. In that case, he'd win the war.

He couldn't tell his wife until he investigated further. If Russell didn't know who had fathered her, she would not, either. She was so distressed he wouldn't upset her further with speculation until he knew more.

The Jacobites were dangerous, perhaps more at this delicate stage of international affairs than they had been when overtly attempting to win back the Crown. They could tip the balance so slightly, yet have profound effects. And Max had no doubt that their agents would work towards bringing down the Hanoverian dynasty that currently ruled the country. Whatever the cost. To call someone Jacobite was to call him schemer. The Dankworths were prime examples of the breed.

No, his heartache set against all that potential danger was a small thing. Except it loomed large for him. At last he'd thought he had found someone to share his life with, and now—

Sophia shifted in his arms, moving close to him, and his cock stirred. Her tears had subsided to the occasional sniff, and while he was sure his waistcoat was soaked, he wasn't about to move to find out. He held her tightly and waited, occasionally touching his lips to her forehead or her temple to assure her he was there and she was safe.

She said nothing, and after five minutes he knew why. A soft snore told him that she'd cried herself to sleep.

Lifting her, he crossed the room to the door, and after a bit of juggling with the doorknob, got it open. A footman waited outside at a discreet distance. Max jerked his head upstairs and the footman preceded them. After hesitating at the door to her room, he decided to continue using his own.

She barely stirred when he slid off her hooped petticoat and her shoes so she could lie down better. He'd call her maid to help her with the rest, to sit with her until she woke. He needed to have words with his cousin, see that proof Julius talked about.

He gazed at his wife's tear-stained face and for a moment allowed himself to picture what he could have with her. He would much rather lie down with her and hold her until she awoke. Yesterday he'd have told Julius to go to the devil and done just that, but today... She'd kept important information from him. He needed to know why before he could let her in any further. That one fact niggled at him. When they'd come here, she'd known Russell hadn't fathered her. She'd kept the information from him. Why?

He left her to sleep.

Julius was in the chamber he usually used when he visited, in the main part of the house. A grand guest room, commensurate with his status as the son and heir of a duke. And a beloved relative. Max tapped and went in on his "Come!"

Julius was sitting in front of the dressing table idly filing his nails. He'd dispensed with his coat and wore instead a magnificent dressing gown in blue and gold brocade. He'd dropped his wig on the stand his valet had placed ready and sported his natural hair, golden blond, cropped short, clinging sleekly to his well-formed skull. When Max entered, he quietly put down the file and turned his chair to face him.

"How is she?" he asked.

"Asleep," Max said briefly.

"Is it true about Hayes?"

Instead of punching his cousin, Max forced himself to contain his violent response. "I have no doubt that it was. What her father thought was a seduction...wasn't. He arrived in time to prevent the bastard completing the act, but not in time to prevent the man from terrifying and hurting her."

"Thus it took you weeks to instigate normal relations," Julius said. "Impressive speed, considering the circumstances. Would you like me to kill him, or will you do it?"

"He's all mine," Max said between his teeth. "I want more. I will make him pay. He'll suffer for a long time."

"Good. But I might kill him anyway," Julius said. "How many women will he serve the same way?"

Max hadn't considered that. "Perhaps I'll castrate him." He would get enormous satisfaction from doing so. Except he might find he had a glorious castrato voice. The castrati were the toast of society. If Max cut out his tongue as well, the man wouldn't have the chance. Nor would he be able to spread any more lies.

Something he had in common with Julius was his cold temper. He could think through it better than when red-hot rage took him, and for that reason it was much more dangerous. He felt scalding fury for Hayes. He wanted to see the man's guts on the end of his sword. Not the fancy small sword he used in town, either.

Julius shrugged. "We shall see. But for now, we need to leave him alone, let him think he's free."

"Agreed," Max said shortly. Because more was at stake than his happiness, loath though he was to admit it. "What do you think he's up to?"

Julius picked up the nail buffer and passed it over his forefinger. "Something unpleasant. He's working as a political secretary for Kirkburton, or at least that's what he's being paid for. Probably a dirty dog. Paid for carrying messages, instigating conspiracies, anything to disrupt the regular order of things. By the way, I was on my way north, which is why I'm here."

"Visiting a remote estate?"

"Chasing Tony." Julius drove the buffer over the surface of his nails with a savagery rarely seen in that activity. "He's gone off on a harebrained scheme of his own. He has some idea that he's unearthed a nest of spies."

"Where?"

"Lancashire, where else?" Another grimace. "Tony is rushing into something he doesn't understand. He's not an idiot, merely impulsive."

"Of course." Max felt some anxiety for his cousin, but after all, Tony had been in the army. He could take care of himself. "So do you plan to continue?"

"I want to know your plans, if you have any. Northwich is up to something. I don't know what, but after a few years of relative peace, suddenly he's moving. I don't know what or how, and that worries me."

"What about your father?" Max asked. The all-powerful Duke of Kirkburton had previously taken a serious interest in the Jacobite peer.

"He has other matters to deal with." Julius took a deep breath and expelled it in a heavy sigh. "This is to go no further, Max. My father isn't well. We're not sure what it is yet, but he tires far too easily. The slightest exertion exhausts him. I don't like it. My mother is harassing me to allow Helena to go home, to be her support at this time, but I will not allow it. Helena wouldn't help our father. He has people to care for him. She still wants Helena to dance attendance on her. Helena doesn't wish for it, although now she feels guilty about it. It allows my mother to apply more pressure. So I can't spare much time on Tony. You should know I'm eternally grateful to your mother and Poppy in staying on, but my mother may prevail on her yet to leave and let Helena go home. I will fight that every inch of the way. I've discovered a few distant relatives who could serve beautifully as a companion to Helena, though I'm still interviewing professional candidates. I will find someone." He grinned. "Perhaps in Lancashire."

Max shrugged. "My mother doesn't like your mother. She'll help with Helena just to disoblige her."

"Good to know." Julius didn't look surprised. He probably knew already. "It doesn't make me any less grateful."

"We'll head to London tomorrow. I'll keep an eye on affairs for you. If necessary, Helena can come and stay with us." Max knew as well as Julius did that once the duchess got Helena back in her house, he would have to enlist an army to get her back. Not because Helena didn't want to go, but the duchess, whose diminutive size and frail appearance concealed a powerfully determined personality, would not let her leave again.

"Thank you. I hope it won't come to that. In that case, you'll have to move Caroline too, and her nursery and all her nursemaids."

Max didn't bother to point out that Julius was spoiling his daughter mercilessly. Julius already knew. Instead he turned to matters closer to his heart at the moment. "Is there anything I need to do once I return to London?"

"Once you've taken care of your wife, you mean?" Julius dropped the buffer carelessly, but somehow it landed exactly parallel to the nail file. "Do that first. If a problem arises with Helena that you can't easily solve, I'll take care of it when I return. Sophia must be the priority." Gracefully he rose and crossed the room to the table set by the window, which had a worn leather pouch on it. Out of it, he drew a sheaf of papers. "There is a mystery around your wife, and I believe I've hit upon the truth, or at least some of it." He turned, holding the papers. "I have the originals locked up at home, but I made copies for you."

Max raised his brows. "That important?"

"Possibly. And when I say original, some of them are merely records of records. Well, then."

Max got to his feet and went to where Julius stood. They bent over the table.

"This is a copy of the record of your wife's parents' marriage. They married in Italy, at the Embassy in Rome. They let it be known that they married a year before the actual date, for obvious reasons. I don't know who else was present, but probably the bride's parents."

"Lady Mary Howard," Max said. "One of those Howards?"

"Distantly. She isn't a Norfolk Howard specifically. Her family was a minor branch and lived in Lancashire." He gave Max a telling glance, one brow arched. "Strange how that county keeps appearing. Her father was the Earl of Morningside. Although he was an earl, the family had fallen on hard times. They sent Lady Mary to London to find a wealthy husband, under the aegis of the Duchess of Northwich."

Max swore.

"Indeed. Lady Mary became pregnant. There is no doubt that Russell isn't the father of her child. He wasn't there when the baby was conceived. I have an idea who was. I enquired as to who was in Rome at the time Sophia was conceived." He paused. "A few names cropped up, but I narrowed it down to one. I think her father is the Duke of Northwich. That would explain his extreme interest in her. And sending a spy into Russell's household."

Max closed his eyes and let rip with as many foul curses as he could think of.

Julius turned over the paper as if Max had said nothing untoward. "I like your wife. I believe her when she says she was nearly raped by John Hayes, who we know is working for the duke, probably was working for him all along. Either he wanted to make sure of her for herself, and she is a considerable heiress, or he wanted to push her into your hands. Your alliance with Russell was well known."

"Is Russell working for Northwich?" Max couldn't believe he could be taken in so extensively. He'd trusted Russell. If his father-in-law was a charlatan, Max might as well give up now with obviously flawed

Lynne Connolly

judgment. So much of his business depended on personal relations with someone and a degree of mutual trust. If he doubted his judgment, he might as well throw in his hand.

"No," Julius said. "I'm sure that he was not. Otherwise he would not have ejected Hayes from his household. Maybe Northwich wants him. I think Northwich wants to expand his interests in shipping. After the Forty-five, much of his property was confiscated, but he was never convicted of any direct involvement with the Stuarts. He's regained most of what he lost, or rather, his son has, and he's moving again. A shipping empire in control of a Jacobite? Imagine what they could do with that. His son has extensive interests, but so far he hasn't moved to help his father. I am watching."

Max sighed. "Alconbury. Yes, I've come across him in the City. We politely ignore each other." But not for much longer, if he approached Sophia again.

Julius nodded. "Fair enough. You should perhaps warn Russell. He may not have been aware that his wife had close connections with the Northwiches. That wasn't how he found her, after all. He married a pregnant woman for a considerable sum of money, ostensibly given by his father-in-law, the Earl of Morningside. He wasn't to know that Morningside didn't provide the sum."

He put the papers down. "These confirm what I've discovered so far. I'll leave them with you. So what does that mean to you?"

Max had been assessing the information. Swiftly, he shuffled through the papers. "Either the duke is sending a cuckoo into our midst in the form of his daughter, or he intends to claim her and ask her to work for him. I won't allow Sophia to become a pawn in this game. That goes for you too, Julius. She is nobody's pawn."

Although his heart ached, he tried to think clearly. "She didn't realize until recently that Russell wasn't her father. And Hayes tried to rape her." Rage surged up once more, and he took a moment to regain control of his emotions. "Her father told me he'd interrupted Hayes seducing his daughter and he realized how vulnerable her position as his heiress made her. The inducements he offered me..." He shrugged. "Everything I've ever wanted. I can restore this house, I can support a wife, and I'm a force to be reckoned with in the City. I can't trust her. No," he corrected himself hastily. "I *do* trust her. But she visits her father, and his house is compromised, is it not? Russell is a clever man. What if he's in league with the Dankworths? What if he let Hayes into his house voluntarily and then saw me as a richer prize for his beloved daughter? He knew Sophia wasn't his get, knew it all along."

"Then he offered his daughter as part of the bargain," Julius said tersely. "Yes, I see. You can't deny Sophia her visits to her father, and she trusts him implicitly, does she not?"

"I believe so."

"You can't tell her," Julius said. "None of this. It could affect the safety of the country, if what I suspect is coming to pass. Northwich's ambitions in the shipping industry concern me greatly. It could affect the nation's security. So you can't tell her, not until we know more. Can you do that?"

He'd have to return to keeping secrets from her, in case she let slip too much to her father. What a wretched situation, to keep confidences from his own wife! "I won't keep the secret of her parentage from her. I'm sorry, Julius, but she deserves to know."

Julius stared at him. "And what will she do? Rush around to confront her father? Warn him that we know?"

Max shook his head. "That's her affair. If she does, we'll just have to live with it. However, I won't let her too close to my most sensitive papers, the ones that don't concern her father." Max frowned. He could, but it would be hard.

"I can't change your mind, can I?"

Max shook his head.

"I'll continue with my research," Julius said. "I have a strong feeling that I haven't reached the bottom of this puzzle. There's something left, something I haven't seen or been allowed to see." He glanced at the clock over the mantelpiece. "When are you serving dinner? Or should we have private meals?"

"No."

Only one niggling seed of doubt remained, and Max hated himself for it. She hadn't told him about the meeting with Hayes in the park and what she'd learned there.

Was his lovely wife a Trojan horse? Unwittingly carrying secrets to her father? He refused to believe the alternative, that she was complicit in some scheme to trap him into working with the Dankworths, and thus, the Stuarts. No, he trusted her, but he didn't entirely trust the man she called Father.

Odd that the man had no idea that Northwich could be involved, or that he hadn't made enquiries. Unless a deeper secret existed, one he hadn't discovered yet. What he knew was bad enough.

Discovering the secret she'd kept from him about her parentage when she'd had ample opportunity to reveal it sent a thorn under his skin. It would irritate him until he could remove it. One way or the other.

Chapter 16

Sophia didn't approach the subject that lay between her and her husband until they were nearly in London. After a disturbed night's sleep in the same mediocre inn they'd used on the way there, she sat in the coach framing her question. Until she realized she'd never get it exactly right. So she came out with it. "Who was my father?"

He turned his head sharply to stare at her, eyes wide and very, very green. "What?"

"You didn't stay with me when Julius was at the house. That meant you talked with him, and he had news that you didn't tell me. I know it could be other things, but I don't believe so. It was about my father, wasn't it?"

True, Julius could have discussed all manner of things, but during this journey she'd caught Max looking at her and then away when she met his gaze. And staring at her speculatively. He knew. All her instincts told her. "Who is he?" she insisted.

He kept her gaze this time and took a deep breath. "Julius discovered evidence that points to the result. It doesn't prove it beyond doubt. We don't have proof, only speculation."

She waved her hand dismissively. "Don't prevaricate."

Despite the gravity of the situation, he smiled, but shook his head. "You shouldn't be able to do that. Make me smile, I mean. Especially when I have to tell you. I'd hoped to avoid this, but how could I hope to keep this from you?"

"You can't. I'd badger my father until he told me."

Julius answered her swiftly. "He knew your mother had a child when he married her, but not who the father was. Likely if he asked, either they didn't tell him or they lied."

Fear clutched her heart. "Why would they do that?"

"Because they wanted to keep the true parentage secret." He bowed his head, before lifting it and meeting her gaze.

The outskirts of London came into view, houses straggling along the road now they'd crossed the Heath. They didn't have too long before they got back to their town house. He might want it that way, because then he wouldn't have to share a coach with a hysterical female. Not that she would. She had shed all her tears when she'd relived the experience with John. Washed the experience clean away. Now she felt nothing but anger that someone had used her, had thought so little of her that he would think she was his for the taking.

John Hayes meant nothing to her any more. Only this man, folding his hands together tightly, preparing to tell her an unpalatable truth, meant anything to her.

"Whoever fathered you, that doesn't make Thomas Russell any less your true parent."

"I know that." She did. Her father had brought her up to believe in truth and honesty in business dealings. He'd told her to hold her head up and believe in herself. Except for that one last betrayal when he'd thought John had ruined her. Even then, he'd done what he considered best, removed her from John's influence and found a husband quickly. Yes, the man who'd reared her was her father. But the other could claim her. "So who was my father?"

Max met her gaze. She wouldn't be deterred.

"Do you wish me to make enquiries of my own?"

"No." Again the hasty answer. He took her hand, turning his back on the window to face her. "We believe your father might be the Duke of Northwich."

She gasped and clapped her free hand over her mouth, as if to trap the knowledge in there. Her husband continued to steadily deliver the news. "The evidence is pointing that way. We don't have absolute proof, but we're hunting for it." His clasp on her hand tightened. "Sophia, I didn't want to tell you until we had more evidence."

"So the Duke of Northwich paid for my mother to marry my father? And he was my father?"

"Yes. That's what we've discovered. There could have been a scandal because your mother was very young. Seventeen."

She nodded, wordless for the moment.

She was a duke's daughter? An illegitimate one to be sure, and an unacknowledged one, but the change in her station dizzied her. All very well for religious men to preach that all men were the same under God, but reality was different. "Who else knows?"

He frowned. "Julius and me. And presumably Northwich."

And perhaps her father, too.

"Before we married, in law you were Sophia Russell." He withdrew his hand.

She frowned, not understanding his retreat. Didn't he want to touch her? He certainly hadn't had that problem at Devereaux House. She longed to return. Trouble lay ahead, not behind them.

"Now you're my wife. Never Northwich's daughter."

"Do I resemble him?" Curiosity led her to ask. She'd never met him, although she had met his son. Her brother? Did Alconbury know he was her half-brother? She had so many questions. Her father had told her he didn't know who had begotten her. Was he telling the truth?

"Not really."

"What does Northwich look like?"

"Like Alconbury, but older."

He seemed determined to answer her questions, but no more. If she dropped the subject then so would he.

"Doesn't it mean anything to you?"

He gave a careless shrug. "It doesn't affect who you are, does it?" He fixed her with that intense gaze.

"I suppose not. But—" Strangely she wasn't upset, not at all. Merely curious and shocked.

Perhaps because his comment was true. It didn't affect who she was. Since learning Thomas Russell hadn't fathered her, she'd come to terms with a lot of things. Mostly that he had cared for her despite knowing that. Her mother had never hinted, not from word or deed, that she'd ever had a lover or a scandalous past. Or even that she knew the Dankworth family.

But it affected Max. "Your family—the Emperors—they're the enemies of the Dankworths, aren't they?"

His mouth tightened, and little lines appeared at the corners. "You could say that. They seem determined to antagonize us. They're Jacobites, and they dislike us because we're loyal to the Crown."

"It's more than that," she said as they lurched over a pothole in the street. But she was so used to them she hardly noticed it. "It's bad blood."

"It's always more than that, Sophia. It's never simple. Personal dislike, little acts of spite over the years, everything adds to the central argument. They're Jacobites; we're not."

That sounded so rational she could almost believe it. "There's more."

"Perhaps. Does it matter?"

"I suppose not." The last thing she wanted to do was upset him, because when that happened, he went silent. She'd had that painful reality thrust on her in the early days of their marriage. He refused to engage, wouldn't discuss anything he didn't want to, throwing up a barrier she couldn't surmount. So she dropped that part of the discussion. "I'm just… surprised."

"Since your maternal grandparents weren't very wealthy when your mother married your father, we suspect the money that paid for the marriage came from the duke," he told her.

Yes, that made sense. She hadn't reached as far as that in her reasoning. More than how it affected her. "Is it over then? Do we let the matter rest?"

"Until we hear from him."

Shock reverberated through her. "Do you think we will?"

"Yes, I do. The duke has planned this. Although I think that he wanted Hayes to have you. Not me."

"But he knew of your business dealings with my father."

He shrugged. "I hadn't expected you to realize that part. I shouldn't underestimate your intelligence, should I?"

She shook her head. "No. So my—Northwich could have wanted me to marry you and ordered John to…do what he did, because then he has me here. With you."

So absorbed in the situation was she that she hadn't realized they were so close to their house until the carriage came to a halt. She'd missed all the outposts, all the places she usually marked when she was in the city she knew so well. Everything, all her concentration on what was happening inside the coach.

* * * *

Three days later, Sophia knew for sure that her husband had removed the intimacy they'd shared at Devereaux House. Oh, he was more friendly, and he came to her bed at night. But he never stayed. She didn't wake in the morning to see him smiling sleepily at her, and she missed it. Very much indeed, so much that her loneliness was almost unbearable. Before Max, she hadn't realized how alone she was. She'd called it independence, had prided herself on her free spirit, but really she'd been alone. Without the one person she'd needed, wanted to call her own. Then she'd found him and lost him. All because she hadn't told him the truth about her parentage. As he'd said in the coach, what did it matter who had fathered her?

Except that it did. She was a daughter of the hated Dankworths, and presumably Max found that hard to bear. Although she wanted to ask him, reticence filled her, because she feared his rejection. Now, after what they'd done, what they'd been to each other, if he turned his back on her she would fall apart. He said he did not care who fathered her, but he must, because he was definitely more distant. When she asked him, he pleaded pressure of work. But it was more than that.

She'd started arranging her levees, the time when she appeared in her bedroom and people visited her there. She discovered she disliked them. She preferred to spend her mornings more productively, not listening to people who wanted her patronage, not because of herself, but because she was the Marchioness of Devereaux.

She went through her days, letting routine slot into her life, but as if it were happening to someone else. A sense of distance separated her from those around her, as if she were the exalted being some insisted on treated her. She was not; she knew that, but she couldn't get them to see, nor would they believe her if she told them. The Marchioness of Devereaux was somebody else. Not Sophia Russell of the City of London.

Then came the day they broke the news about Devereaux House to her mother-in-law. Max, who had pleaded outstanding business to absent himself too often since their return, asked her if she wanted to be present when he told his mother.

"Since I had the original idea," she said, "I should take at least part of the blame," and received the sweetest smile she could remember from him since their return to London.

They visited his mother at Julius's house, where she was still in residence with Poppy. The dowager had made herself at home, although, as she explained to them, not encroachingly so.

"I will probably go to Kirkburton House when I can. Julius is interviewing suitable companions, and it can't be long before he finds one for Helena. But the duke needs me. Or rather, the duchess does." The slight curl of her lip told Sophia exactly what her mother-in-law thought of that. "Unfortunately, I can't leave my brother in his current state to her tender mercies. He deserves better. A little kindness and consideration will go a long way toward his recovery."

Sophia's relationship with her mother-in-law had thawed since the early days of her marriage. At least the duchess didn't repudiate her, treat her as a pariah or someone to be tolerated.

After their return to London, Max squired her to balls and routs, took her driving in the park, displaying them as a couple for all to see. If anyone had suspected their previous coldness was anything but the marriage settling down, he dispelled the notion now. As a result, people started to talk to her. Really talk, as if they liked her. Not that she fooled herself about that, but she was on her way to being accepted.

On the way to Julius's house today, Max had told Sophia how ill the Duke of Kirkburton was. Although mildly hurt that her husband hadn't told her before, Sophia understood that the duke didn't want his condition bruited abroad. He was only remaining in London because his special physician refused to leave the city. Besides, taking a prominent medical man to his private house would encourage the kind of attention the duke appeared to want to avoid. "I was unhappy to hear that he is not well."

"He will recover," her ladyship said firmly. "He always has. It will be no different this time. Winterton isn't ready to assume the mantle of the dukedom. It wouldn't suit him."

Sophia wondered about that. Already, Julius took much of the responsibility of the dukedom. But he'd done it by stealth, taking none of the credit, claiming to be a fashionable fribble who cared for nothing more than the design of his waistcoats. Sophia and anyone who bothered to look further could soon tell that wasn't true. But people rarely looked beneath the surface, in her experience.

"I took Sophia to Devereaux House," Max informed his mother.

"I know."

Sophia exchanged a glance with Helena who raised one brow very slightly in the kind of droll look guaranteed to make Sophia laugh. Helena had seen the house, then, and had similar thoughts to Sophia. But had she considered the drastic action Sophia had? She was about to find out.

Her ladyship turned a dazzling smile on her daughter-in-law. "Did you like the house?"

"Yes," she said, because she had. "It's very elegant." At least she'd enjoyed the memories she'd made there. Most of them. Even breaking down in that horrible way when she'd used the word she'd been avoiding for months. Because Max had been there for her, had taken care of her. That went a long way to reconciling her to what had happened. And he hadn't rejected her—not exactly.

She exchanged a glance with Max now. Let him break the news. His mother would probably assume it was all Sophia's fault anyway.

"We took some time to survey the newer parts," Max said carefully. "Unfortunately, the wings aren't built as well as the main house, and they're already showing signs of damage. The roof leaks in part, for instance, and some of the rooms aren't completed. It will cost a lot of money to repair." He paused.

Here was where his mother would tell him that he had more money than Midas, and he could repair it.

She didn't. "Then demolish those parts," she said. Her eyes met her son's.

Sophia had positioned herself so she could see both participants, far enough along the sofa she shared with Max that she could see him. His mother sat opposite without turning her head too much and drawing attention to herself. Her father had used her as an observer for years that way. Many businessmen disregarded her, until they learned better.

So now Sophia saw Max's eyes widen, and his mother's slight, satisfied smile. *Please let him have the sense to accept her suggestion as if it were hers alone,* she thought.

"But that house is your life's work, Mama."

The dowager's smile faded to nothing, and she shook her head and swallowed, her eyes glistening. "It was your father's life's work, my son, not mine. That house killed him. He became obsessed with it, his every waking moment devoted to it." Tears glistened at the inner corners of her eyes. One spilled over.

With a small murmur, Poppy moved closer, proffering a handkerchief, but her mother ignored it although she gave her daughter a slight smile.

"I will say this. I have kept silent too long. When you restored the fortunes of the marquisate, Max, I became so afraid you'd continue. But how did I tell you? You appeared to love the house."

"I do," he said. "But the original part, the part I grew up in. I grew to hate it later because of all the noise and disruption."

The dowager sighed. "The more he built, the more he became obsessed with building more. It was like an illness." She glanced at Poppy and then back at her son. "After his death, I couldn't bear to live there. I turned my back on it and stayed with my family instead. Poppy, I'm sorry. I should have—"

Poppy covered her mother's hands which were neatly folded over her fan in her lap. "No, Mama. It would have been worse, would it not, if you'd brought me up there? And Max couldn't have worked from the country house. Could not have achieved half of what he did." She paused and favored Sophia with a glance.

Sophia met her eyes, secrets exchanged between women.

"I thought the house was cursed," the dowager concluded. "I never wanted to see it again because it took my husband away from me. But how could I say that to you? It's your inheritance."

Max closed his eyes and took a deep breath. When he opened them again, the green depths were bright. "You would come back if I—we—did this?"

"Yes. For a while, although I enjoy visiting my relatives. I like being useful." Now she gave Sophia a steady look. "I will come when I'm needed." When there were children.

"Mama, I'm so pleased. When we toured the house…I didn't know what to do."

Only Sophia knew what that slight hesitation meant and she sighed in relief. He had the sense not to tell her their plans.

"I hadn't realized how much some parts were deteriorating."

"As money grew tighter, he economized." She sighed. "But he didn't stop. I begged him to, but he did not. You will do this?"

Max exchanged a glance with Sophia and reached out his hand. Gratefully, she put her own in it. He squeezed it, and his eyes sent her an apology that she felt no need of, but gratitude sent a warm glow through her anyway. "We ordered the inventory brought up to date. We'll move from there."

"You could sell some of the materials."

Just as they'd discussed, but Max received the suggestion with thanks. "We may need your help, Mama. I can't be there all the time, because I still have my investments to oversee."

"You'd like me there?"

"Only if it doesn't upset you."

She scoffed. "I want to see it."

At last Sophia understood the woman. She'd remained with Julius because she felt needed, and it kept her away from her home. The home she detested. Every new stone would have reminded her of her husband, every one a contributor to his early death.

Sophia left Julius's house much relieved, and from the new spring in his step, Max felt the same way.

In the carriage he drew her into his arms and gave her a smacking kiss. "I feel so much better. I feared my mother would never talk to us again."

"You did well."

He shrugged. "I wanted to give you the credit."

"I'm sure the notion would have occurred to you eventually."

That dry remark earned her another kiss. "But you said it. We could have gone through the rest of our lives fighting to restore what was badly done in the first place, both of us dancing around the subject. Never do that. Promise me."

"Never do what?"

"If you feel something, say so. If you want something, say so."

How could she do that when what she wanted most of all in the world was his love? He didn't trust her still. He didn't confide in her, and he kept his bookroom, where he kept all his important papers, locked. Against the servants, she was supposed to think, but she knew better. So did he expect her to ask for that? She fell silent, not knowing what to say. Then recalled his words. "You must ask, too."

"Oh, I will." Heedless of the crowds surging outside, he kissed her properly, licking into her mouth with leisurely thoroughness.

That wasn't what she'd meant, but it would do for now.

Chapter 17

Sitting at his favorite table at Lloyd's Coffee House, perusing his list of meetings and conclusions, Max lifted his head to order another coffee. He'd stay here for another hour, listen to the gossip, and let the place wash over him. If he missed anything about London, this was it. This place had given him so much, and he'd entered it as a welcome haven, away from the malicious rumors about his father and ruin.

A flash of bright color outside the window attracted his attention, and he glanced up to see something he knew. Someone. A gown, aquamarine with white flowers embroidered over it. Pretty, but Sophia didn't like it. She'd asked her maid to get rid of it. He wasn't in time to see the face of the woman passing by. But she wore a familiar broad straw bergère hat and a short cloak covered the top part of her body.

Sophia. On her own?

He started to his feet and, after throwing a few coins to the woman at the cash desk, heedless of the amount, strode out of the coffee house. What was she doing in the City on her own? She knew the place, few better, so what more reason for her to have at least a maid? Or was French somewhere close? He saw no one, much less a footman in his livery. She should have those two at least. Her father had warned her of the dangers of being an heiress. The dangers of people lying in wait to abduct her. That had been one of his main reasons for arranging his daughter's marriage to Max. That she would be out of danger.

Not like this she would not. His anger rising, he pushed past a few urchins lurking around the coffee house. He covered his purse with his hand and carried on, but the short delay had been enough to let her get ahead of him.

Just as well she was wearing that gown. Anxiety for her safety warred with anger that she would do such a foolish thing.

He turned a corner and saw her ahead of him. She scurried down the street, not looking to right or left. Speculation filled his mind as he tried to race after her down the crowded street. The traders, beggars, and citizens seemed to be conspiring to prevent him catching up with her. Shouting wouldn't do any good, as sound filled the air, noise he usually took for granted but now grated in his ears. People jostled him but he ignored the pleas for "Jest a penny, sir," and "Chair, guv'nor?" and hurried along. He followed her through a pedestrian-only alley. More thronged the area, forcing him to slow his pace, and then he realized where she must be headed.

Covent Garden, away from the City and toward the West End. Fear overcame his anger. She could be waylaid, maybe robbed. He needed to catch up with her.

Another street, and then they emerged into the wide open space of the Covent Garden piazza. She was half way across the space, walking quickly on one side of the shacks that opened at night to spill out notorious madams and whores. Luckily, this being noonday, they were closed and shuttered. On the other side of her, cabbage-leaves and rotten fruit marked the site of the fruit market, but that had closed now, all but a few stragglers. All this was familiar to him, marked as he passed. But his attention remained on the figure in the bright blue gown now closing on a house at the far corner of the Square.

Max came to a sudden halt. Someone slammed into home from behind, apologized, and moved around him. Max hardly noticed. All his attention was riveted on the two figures. Two now. Sophia had reached her objective, it seemed, and was now busy lavishing John Hayes with kisses.

He held her tightly and returned what he received.

No. His head spun. How so? He lost all reason for a moment, and pure red rage flooded his soul, heating his blood to boiling point.

After all this, all he'd done, all he'd been through, to find this at the end?

Red fury filled him to the brim. He, who'd previously prided himself on his cool temperament. He would kill her. No, he'd send her into the country. She could stay there and rot, for all he cared.

* * * *

Sophia arrived home in plenty of time to dress for dinner. A letter lay on the salver on the demilune table in the hall. Without waiting for anyone to present her with it, she snatched it up. Hand delivered, and the seal on the back was plain. Interesting. Her father generally used his company seal, proud of the address he had every right to send a missive to, but perhaps he was in a hurry. Or one of his assistants addressed the letter for him, because she didn't recognize the handwriting on the outside. Breaking the seal, she went into the back parlor, waving away the footman's offer of tea. "I'll have it upstairs," she said absently.

The back parlor looked out over the garden. Light flooded in and apart from the distant sound of carriages in the street at the front of the house she could almost imagine herself in the country again. Standing in front of them, Sophia broke the seal and unfolded the letter, scanning it quickly. She'd have to answer it tomorrow or she wouldn't have time to change for dinner.

Then she read it again.

She was right in that the letter was from her father. But not the father she knew. The other one, the Duke of Northwich.

My dear,

I hate to introduce myself in this way, but I see no alternative. My son said he met you at a ball. You were introduced to him by my secretary, John Hayes. Alconbury informs me that you have left the haven of the City and entered into matrimony with the Marquess of Devereaux.

This news disturbs me, especially since I have news for you that you may consider distressing. You have probably heard information over the last few days which is, to say the least, flawed. There is more, much more, and I need to tell you without delay. But personally.

Believe me, I mean you nothing but good. I can hint at some of the reasons for my distress. In my youth I was profligate, I admit that now. I had affairs with many women, but, my child, not with your mother. However, I know one who did.

The late Marquess of Devereaux, the father of the man you married, had a habit of following me, and sometimes he would take what I did not. I fear that has been the case here. Believe me, Lady Devereaux, I do not vouchsafe this information with any pleasure. I have incontrovertible proof of what I say, but I will not trust any messenger or third party with this.

I will say no more in this missive. If you wish to discuss this matter further, I will send a carriage for you. Believe me, I will be discreet. If you visit the Royal Exchange and take the south exit, the carriage will be waiting for you. Bring one maid, nobody else. The driver will ask you if you are Mrs. Smith. If you do not come, I will endeavor to make contact with you another way.

Believe me, I remain your servant in this matter,
James Northwich.

The flourish seemed almost insolent.

Unseeing, Sophia groped for a chair. She read the letter, and read it again.

What on earth could she do? If this were true… No, surely not. She could already be pregnant with a child born of incest. It didn't bear thinking about. Pressing a hand to her stomach, she forced away the nausea threatening to overwhelm her. Memories of what she and Max had done came vividly to her mind, and her belly roiled.

She couldn't tell him. Who could she tell? Julius was out of town. If she told Max, he'd move heaven and earth to discover the truth, probably storm around to Northwich's house and try to throttle the truth out of him. Any excuse to confront the man who'd made his family's life a misery.

Northwich said he had incontrovertible proof. She needed that proof. Maybe she should confront him herself.

Relief swept through her. She could confide in one person. Must, because she could think of nobody else.

The sound of voices in the hall brought her back to herself, and she screwed up the letter and thrust it into her bosom as she left the room. She had just enough time to change before dinner, barely enough.

She hurried upstairs and into her dressing room, where French had laid out the aquamarine. They were attending the theater later. She couldn't quite remember what the play was. Not that she'd be going now, and certainly not in this gown.

She raised her voice. "French!"

Her maid came scurrying in. "I expected you would arrive in the bedroom, my lady. I beg your pardon."

"Did you put this out for me to wear?" She fingered the aquamarine. It really was pretty, but she disliked it more now. She couldn't think why she'd bought it. Too garish, too bold for her taste.

French touched the gown. "I thought you might like to try it on and see if your first opinion was the right one. It is exquisitely fashioned. You would perhaps try it out before you disposed of it."

If she weren't already agitated and distressed she might have taken French's suggestion. As it was, she needed a scapegoat and an object would be better than a person. "Remove it. I don't like it. I don't care what you do with it." Something caught her attention on the hem of the gown and she bent to examine it, eager to discover a flaw she could use. She hated to be thought of as capricious, even by her maid. "Is this mud? How on earth did this gown get mud on the hem?"

French frowned and joined Sophia in examining the gown. "It's that dratted Daisy," she said, naming her assistant. "I'm sorry ma'am, but she's proving most unsatisfactory. Careless, and now I think she's dishonest. I knew she was borrowing garments without permission. Probably to impress her beau farther along the street. I'll see her turned off for this. See if I don't."

"No. Set her to work as a housemaid," Sophia said. They were short a housemaid after one had been discovered to be in an interesting condition via one of the footmen. Sophia had turned off the footman and sent the maid to a foundling home to have her baby there. But that left her short-staffed, and while the footman had been quickly replaced, they were still down one housemaid.

Telling that she could think of that at a time like this. "I'll see to the details myself, but I won't be going out tonight. I'm not feeling well."

"Oh, ma'am, do you need anything?"

French had been with Sophia for most of her life, coming to her when Sophia was thirteen, so she'd seen her mistress in several states before now. French had seen to Sophia's personal needs without fuss and with efficiency. She would have to go tomorrow.

When she thought of the meeting, her stomach churned. She turned to the chamber pot. French held her steady while she brought back what she'd eaten that day. She gasped and clutched the edge of the chair on which the chamber pot rested.

"I'll put you to bed straightaway, ma'am."

Her eyes streaming, her throat sore, Sophia gratefully took the handkerchief French handed to her. "Let my husband know, if you please. I believe it was the patties I had earlier today. I thought they were a little suspect. Oysters are difficult."

"My mother said you shouldn't have oysters when there wasn't an R in the month," French said. "But it's only just turned May. Unfortunate, my lady. I'll see if the cook can find you something to settle your stomach. What should I tell his lordship?"

"Just that I'm not well and I won't be going out. Tell him it's nothing to worry about, I just ate something that disagreed with me."

"Yes, my lady. And I'll see to the other matter, while I'm about it, but I still think you should turn Daisy off. Dishonesty is dishonesty, and she'll be making off with the silver next."

Sophia waved French away. "She's just a feckless girl who doesn't think properly, but she's a hard worker. Tell Foster to keep a close eye on her for a while. We'll see how she does." She couldn't care less about

Daisy, if she had taken clothes without asking. "You can send to the agency for another assistant in the morning."

French sniffed. "A trustworthy one this time."

Tenderly, she handed Sophia a glass of water to rinse her mouth with, and then her tooth-powder, so she could clean her teeth while the maid unlaced her. Sophia found herself tucked up in bed in no time, with the promise of a nice cup of tea and a bowl of broth. She accepted the tea, but refused the broth with a shudder. "Perhaps in a while," she said.

She should have expected Max to come upstairs to see her. But when he entered the room, she had to fight not to shout at him to leave immediately. Her stomach, which had settled, stirred anew, and her throat tightened so she could scarcely breathe. She'd seen this man naked, she'd made love with him. And he could be her brother. Even the slightest possibility made her feel sick and set her limbs to trembling.

Max flicked out the skirts of his coat and sat on the bed, lifting his hand to place it gently on her forehead. "My poor Sophia! What do you think is wrong?"

"Oyster patties," she said with a grimace. She'd enjoyed them, one of her favorites, but she had to blame something. "I'm feeling a bit better already." A blatant lie. His presence made her worse. Because God help her, she still wanted him. Images of their time together flashed through her mind, making her clitoris swell and throb in shameful desire. She could not feel like this toward her own brother, surely?

He regarded her, an edge of coldness in his eyes. "There was a matter I wished to discuss with you. But it will wait." He smiled, dispelling the chill. "Would you like me to stay with you?"

She tried not to shake her head too vigorously. "I'd like to sleep now."

He nodded. "Probably best. You must let me help you."

Gently, he lifted her and helped her to lie down. Sophia repressed her shudders, not knowing if they were desire or distaste, knowing they should be the latter, afraid they were not.

She was a vile person to want him so much. If it were true. If it was not, Northwich wanted to see her about something else. But she had to have that proof in her hands. Needed to know the truth. If it was, it would cause a scandal the like of which London hadn't seen for years. They'd tear her to pieces. And bring Max and the Emperors down with it.

So why didn't Northwich use the information to do just that? Perhaps he meant to. She didn't know.

* * * *

Sophia was relieved to discover that, after a brief visit to her chamber in the morning, Max had appointments for the rest of the day.

"I hate leaving you like this, but send a footman to me if you feel any worse."

"No need." Sophia had ordered a meal, more for self-defense than anything else, because she still felt ill. She made a show of buttering a slice of toast and biting into it with relish. "I feel so much better," she assured him once she'd devoured the mouthful. "It must have been the patties, because there's nothing wrong with me now. I shall visit my father," she added as an afterthought, "so I'll be in good hands."

When Max leaned over the bed to kiss her, she turned her head so his lips skimmed her cheek.

He grunted, kissed her forehead and straightened. "I still feel I shouldn't leave you."

She waved her hand. "Go, go. I promise I'll contact you if I feel worse. But it was just bad food. Don't fuss, Max."

He left the room smiling, which was more than she did an hour later. With French in tow, she climbed in the sedan chair she'd ordered and let them take her to her father's house.

She'd thought of wearing the aquamarine, just by way of spite. She didn't want any of her favorite clothes tainted by what she was about to do, and she could discard that gown without a qualm. But in the end, she chose an unremarkable green with a modest hoop, almost reverting to her days as a daughter of the City. In those days, she'd worn more modest and less flamboyant garments. She also chose an enveloping brown cloak with a hood, in case she saw someone she knew, and a hat with a very wide brim. Wide so that the chair-men moaned when they saw it, for fear she wouldn't get inside. She managed.

Her father was at home. He'd set out on his rounds of his office and the coffeehouses shortly. Today was a Mercer's Guild meeting day, so she'd purposely set out early to catch him before he left.

He greeted her, as he always did, with a smile, and she surprised him with a hug, desiring that they not be disturbed. Once they were sitting in the privacy of his office, she handed him the letter.

"I hate to bring you further distress, Papa, but you need to read this."

He scanned the letter quickly, then read it again, paying more detail to it.

"Do you think it's true, Papa?"

He glanced up at her and down at the letter. "Your mother was a good woman," he said. "While we were married, I never had cause to doubt her. If she transgressed before our marriage, I believe her when she said it was only once. But she wouldn't tell me who. Or in what circumstances, for that matter. Her father paid her portion. I presumed the money was his, since he was an earl. It appears it was not." He put the letter down. "I take it you plan to attend this meeting?"

She nodded.

"Do you think he will tell the truth?"

She shrugged. "I don't know. But I have to hear it, don't I?"

"Why not tell your husband?"

Heat rose to her face. "We—that is, I—"

Her father sighed. "The feud with the Dankworths." She nodded again, pleased he understood without too much detail. The thought of her and Max together imposed on her mind, as it had intermittently through the night, and she pushed it away. If she never got to do that again, she'd curl up and die. But she couldn't if, by some outside chance, what Northwich was saying was true.

"I still think you should tell him," her father said now. "This is a grave matter."

"But if I tell him, he might not want me anymore, even if it's not true!" she wailed. Even to her own ears she sounded more like a lovesick girl than a grown woman. But she couldn't help it. Suspecting what she did, she still wanted him, but she doubted he'd want her. He was deliberately and carefully putting ground between them. When he came to her bed, he didn't stay the night, and already she missed him. Sinful but undeniable.

"Daughter, if this is true, you have to tell him," her father said now. "I already deceived him by not telling him of your birth. That was wrong, and I will never cease to castigate myself for not putting him in control of the full facts."

"Do you think I don't know that?" Her voice lowered to a snarl. "Have I married my own brother? Do we need to make the knowledge public?"

"I don't believe it's true. But I do understand that you need to know. I will accompany you if you wish."

She shook her head. She couldn't bear the thought of anyone else in the room if what the duke had told her in the letter was true. In any case, if her father was seen entering the house of a known Jacobite sympathizer, he'd be immediately suspect in the City.

She couldn't bear anyone else being hurt by this affair. "No, Papa. I can go alone. He won't hurt me. After all, he's done what he can so far to ensure my safety." Sending a spy to watch over her could have two meanings, and one of them might be that he wanted to protect her. John had acted on his own that day. She was sure of it.

That also indicated that the duke was lying about the Devereaux connection. But she had to know for sure.

After ten minutes' further wrangling, he finally accepted her decision. "Take French and Horton with you." Horton had, like French, been with the Russells for years, and acted as footman, but not liveried, as the ones she used now were. He'd be more discreet. And Horton was huge. His early prize-fighting career had made an already large frame even larger.

The fact that she'd have a strong man with her heartened Sophia. So she bowed her head meekly. "Yes, Papa, to both. If the duke has undeniable evidence, I will have it off him."

"I doubt that," her father said. Steepling his fingers, he flexed them, a habit of his while thinking. "He won't give you such proof easily, though he may allow you to take a copy. In any case, the proof is likely to be in parish registers and witness statements. He may have obtained signed legal documents."

"Lies that he can use to tear us apart. If he wants to use this information to threaten me, he will be mistaken. "If it turned out to be true, she'd tell Max everything and retire, live in the country, or even leave these shores altogether.

Her father regarded her for a moment, his eyes far-seeing. Sophia knew better than to interrupt him.

"I think he may have used this as a ruse," he said. "If you're his daughter, he may realize that you won't see him at his request, but would take your husband with you. But if you think that your marriage is in peril, and that your husband would be damaged by the knowledge, Northwich might expect you not to tell him."

He touched the letter. "I will keep this. It's your proof. I'll lock this up in my safe."

He glanced at her and she nodded her permission. If she took the letter with her, the duke could well purloin it, and then what proof did she have of her suspicions?

"If need be, I'll vouch for you with your husband. But you had better tell him you went today. One way or the other, you must."

Her heart ached, but he told the truth. "I will. I swear. One way or the other, I'll tell him."

"The duke won't hurt you." Her father placed his hands flat on the desk, the pressure turning his fingertips white.

She almost smiled when she spotted the smudge of ink in its accustomed place at the side of his left hand, where he rested it as he wrote.

"If I even suspected that, I wouldn't allow you to go. But it's not his way. He wants you for something. Either that, or he wishes to meet the girl he fathered. Although he has never expressed such a wish before. Any time this past twenty-five years he could have asked. He could have created great trouble between Mary and me, but he did not. He could have asked after Mary's death, but he did not. No, he wants something from you, and it will be something to do with your marriage."

"He wants me to spy on my husband," she said flatly. But despite that knowledge, she felt better. Infinitely better. She could talk to Max, and he need never know the horrible suspicions that had clouded her mind this last day.

Last night he'd shown her the first true tenderness since Julius had broken the news about her parentage. But she'd sent him away.

But the possibility existed that her father was wrong and the duke did have proof that she was the daughter of Devereaux. "What if he only recently obtained the proof?" She worked hard to keep her hands folded neatly in her lap over her fan instead of wringing them or biting her nails, her habit as a child when distressed.

"That is a possibility," the man she would always call her father said. "He would want you to create disturbance in that case. Scandal that would break Devereaux. Or he might want to threaten you with exposure, use the information to get you to do something for him."

Spy. In that case, she would refuse.

Having beaten out the arguments with her father until they could think of no other possibilities, Sophia consented to take a dish of tea while her father ordered her a chair to take her to the Royal Exchange.

Her heart in her mouth, Sophia set forth, with her two attendants close behind.

At the Exchange, she dismissed the chairmen and went toward the nearest set of stairs that led up to the gallery where the shops were situated. The large cobbled area that formed the central part of the building was where men often met to discuss business, somewhat like the old Roman forum, which she'd been told was on the same site. That was one reason she liked shopping here. It was close to where she used to live, and she liked thinking of the continuity of purpose. People using this place for the same ends for generation after generation.

Not that she intended to do much shopping today. For appearance's sake, she went into a shop and bought a fan. If anyone saw her there, she could show it to them as her reason for being here. It wasn't a particularly distinguished or pretty one, merely acceptable. She just pointed at it and said, "That one," waiting only long enough for it to be packaged and handed to French, who took it without comment. They proceeded along the gallery, their feet clacking on the wooden boards under their feet, and down the stairs at the end.

Outside, a carriage waited. It was obviously a private one, since it was well-kept with a pair of horses much too fine for hacks harnessed to it. The two attendants were much too superior for the hire vehicles that thronged London. She waited. The footman approached her and bowed. "If you would step inside, Mrs. Smith."

She would. So did the footman and French. The man would have turned away the servants and held out his arm to block them, but immediately Sophia stepped out of the carriage. "I go with them or not at all." They might not be too much protection, but they were all she had. Like her father, she considered the possibility that the duke would try to harm her extremely unlikely. He stood to gain nothing from that. The footman relented, and they climbed in.

"Stay in the hall when we arrive, please. If there is any trouble, French, you run for help, and Horton, get me out of the place."

"Still not sure about this, miss," Horton mumbled.

A man of few words but possessed of much muscle. Sophia was glad to have him with her.

"It's very important, Horton. It's not as if this is the first time I've run an errand like this for my father." That was how they'd presented it to Horton—as one of the clandestine messages she'd sometimes passed along. Most concerned cargoes and sometimes illegal cargo her father didn't want to be associated with. An anonymous word dropped in the right quarters usually ensured the vessel concerned was investigated without delay. Part of the work of a City merchant, but not one that was bruited abroad. But she wasn't wearing a mask today, as some ladies did as a matter of course against the dust and dirt of the city. She'd considered it, but concluded that a masked lady entering the house of a prominent peer might evoke more gossip, not less. She contented herself with pulling her hat over her forehead and keeping her head lowered. She fastened the cloak and draped it over her gown so that only a glimpse of dull green would greet any curious onlooker.

Her stomach fluttered with nerves, but that only added to her determination to see this through. With her father on her side, she'd cope with whatever happened next. And his reassurance, that the message was a ruse to get her there, eased her mind rather than making matters worse.

The carriage jolted its way through the uneven streets of the City and smoothed out on the broader, newer roads in the West End. Sophia didn't look out of the window but sat in a corner of the vehicle, keeping her head down. She didn't want to be seen in case Northwich had tricked her and exposed his crest on the other side of the carriage. It appeared unmarked, but she didn't want to take any chances. Risking the short journey from carriage to door and back again was bad enough.

The Northwich house was in a side-street off Berkeley Square. They'd once owned a grand mansion in Piccadilly, close to the one still owned by the Duke of Kirkburton, Julius's father. That had long gone, dissipated in the fortune the Dankworth family had given to the Cause.

Now the duke had reassembled much of his money, and they had re-established themselves in society. Some even thought they were romantic, with their long allegiance to the Stuarts. Sophia wasn't one of them.

The carriage came to a halt, but Sophia didn't move until the door at the top of the shallow steps opened. They were expected. She climbed down quickly and hurried up the steps, doing her best not to appear furtive, disappearing inside.

The hall was a typical one for these houses, with a black-and-white tiled floor and a lantern swinging overhead, its glass panes glittering in the spring sunshine. The stairs curved up to a single landing, not as large as her own house, but elegant. Family portraits lined the stairs, generations of Dankworths looking down their noses at whomever dared to intrude. Without removing her outerwear, Sophia prepared to wait.

But she didn't have to. A footman in dazzling blue-and- red livery bowed. "If you would follow me, ma'am. The duke awaits." He showed no sign of surprise or even interest in her presence.

She removed her hat, cloak, and gloves and handed them to French. She didn't want anyone else to touch them.

How many women did he usher in to the duke? While Sophia hadn't heard that Northwich had a particularly bad reputation, she assumed he found feminine comfort somewhere, since he was a widower. The house smelled of lavender and mint, unpleasantly pleasant. She liked it, and she didn't want to. She didn't want to like anything about this house.

The footman opened both parts of a double door leading to a well-appointed salon. The furniture was modern in style, French and gilded, and the upholstery a pleasing shade of apple green. Very fashionable with a Continental air. Just what she'd expect of a wealthy Jacobite. Except she wasn't used to thinking of the breed as wealthy.

A man unfolded himself from one of the chairs by the window. Unlike the airy feel of the room, he was dressed in dark, rich colors. Dark red cloth for a coat and a slightly lighter red for the waistcoat, but when he moved, a sprinkling of brilliants sparkled and then stilled. As he did, standing before her, drinking her in.

"I'm very glad you decided to come." His voice was low, hardly stirring the air, but it throbbed with emotion. "I'm glad you don't powder."

She lifted her hand to her hair, dressed simply but left its natural dark brown. Such an odd thing to say. "Why the personal remarks?"

"Because this meeting is about personal appearance, in part. Please, do sit."

Inclining her head, she allowed him to seat her in one of the apple-green chairs. "Before you ask, I don't want refreshments," she said, forcibly reminded of Persephone's sojourn in Hades. Persephone had eaten a few pomegranate seeds and been forced to stay in Hades for that number of months every year. She didn't want anything clinging to her when she left this place. She didn't care how rude she sounded; she wanted this meeting over and done. Every minute here tore at her nerves.

"Very well." Flipping back the tails of his coat, the duke took a seat opposite her.

By his side stood a small table containing a leather portfolio. Closed as yet but she had no doubt it contained interesting information. Equally certain was that the papers wouldn't be leaving this house with her, if they were the originals.

The Duke of Northwich was tall, lean, and graceful, but he had a sharp staccato way of moving that unnerved her. He did it now, leaning forward and studying her face.

She'd had enough. "I'm not my husband's sister, am I?"

"An interesting way of putting it. Why do you say that?" He smiled, easy and superior. Her hand itched to slap his smug expression away.

"Because it was the only way you could get me here without my telling Devereaux."

His smile broadened. "Clever, too. Your family inheritance."

"So tell me your business. I can't spend too much time here."

"Of course not. I hope you'll forgive my receiving you alone, but I'm about to impart information that must go no further, for the time being. I want your promise."

She wasn't that foolish. Keeping a secret from her husband was a sure way of driving a wedge between them. "You don't have it. Tell me, and I'll decide what to say and who to say it to. Otherwise I leave here now."

Gazing at her, meeting her eyes, he said nothing. The silence tactic, but he'd chosen the wrong person to attempt to intimidate that way. She sat up straight and met his gaze, gave it a full minute, and then said, "Your decision. Insist on that promise, and I'll leave now."

He sighed. "Very well. It's imperative that I tell you, and I must trust that your discretion matches your intelligence. And your common sense. I will tell you what you need to know, and I have the proof here, should you wish to see it."

"Of course."

A grin cracked his face briefly. "No copies. And the papers do not leave this house."

She marked the way he said that. He must have a safe on the premises, then. "Agreed."

"First, what do you know?"

He wanted her to go first. Not surprising. She'd do the same thing. But she wasn't playing that game. She'd tell him no more than he already knew. "That the identity of the man who fathered me is a mystery. That my father is not my father. Except that he is." Her turn to smile. "How's that for a conundrum?"

The smile she received in return held no warmth. His light blue eyes showed nothing. "Indeed. As you say, the man who fathered you is different to the man you call father. So who do you think he is?"

She took a chance. "I know he's not the Marquess of Devereaux."

"How do you know that?"

She paused, thinking over her answer, not afraid of breaking the flow of the conversation. He would not trick her into revealing anything she didn't want to. "It was too obvious a ploy."

Tilting his head to one side, he said, "My ruse didn't even merit a sleepless night? How disappointing. Then why are you here? Alone."

"I've brought two people I trust with me."

He flicked his fingers into the air in a dismissive gesture. "Servants. You can never trust them. They're a necessary evil."

But the expression in his eyes changed. Triumph or amusement. She wished she knew him better so she could tell what it was.

"You're curious. Well may you be so. The secret I have to impart is not trivial, nor is it one you can dismiss." He paused. "Are you sure you won't have tea?"

"Positive." She made a fuss of drawing her watch out of her pocket and flipping open the lid. The delicately enameled dial told her nothing she didn't already know. Her internal clock was working fine. "You have ten minutes. I told you I wouldn't stay long."

"Very well." He sighed. "A shame. You're as blunt as my son. I despair of Alconbury. I truly do. The man has no subtlety."

"Good for him." She doubted that. The Alconbury she'd met had clever eyes. He was probably capable of taking his father on at any game the older man chose. She nodded to him, an invitation to continue. He must realize she meant what she said. She wouldn't stay here much longer, and if he challenged her threat, she'd make good on it.

He reached for the portfolio.

Chapter 18

Max nodded to his cousin, Lord Malton, as he entered the main room at White's, prepared to spend at least an hour with a bottle of wine and a newspaper. "Marcus Aurelius, how are you?"

Marcus shuddered, as Max had known he would. But he got his own back.

"Tolerably well, Maximilian, tolerably. Thank your lucky stars you only have a sister to care for is all I can say. How is the divine Poppea?"

Max held up a hand in surrender. "Poppy is well. She's staying with my mother at Julius's at present, although Julius is out of town still. But better than sending Helena to the tender mercies of her mother."

"And you married, did you not? A girl from the City?" Marcus raised a thin, dark brow, showing all the superciliousness of the blue-blooded aristocrat.

"She is, and proud of it." He met his cousin's gaze steadily. "As am I."

Even more now, when he realized his error in imagining for one moment that she'd have met John Hayes clandestinely. Once his unreasoning anger had subsided, the truth had struck him between the eyes. He hadn't needed to see the face of the woman to know she wasn't his wife. But he'd stayed, to discover her identity. The vision had infuriated him all over again, but for completely different reasons.

He would make a few discreet enquiries and discover why his wife's maid would dream of betraying her mistress.

"My error."

Max accepted his cousin's apology. Marcus sometimes took his status too seriously.

"Ahem." A waiter stood at his elbow, not with the wine and newspaper, but a note.

Max glanced at him and scanned the note. "You must excuse me, Marcus. My father-in-law awaits me downstairs."

"Not a member?"

"No point. He has nothing to gain from it."

Max set off downstairs to meet Russell. He stood in the main foyer, wringing his hands. One glance was enough to tell Max this wasn't about business.

"What is it?"

"I have news." He swallowed, obviously finding it difficult to tell him.

A sense of urgency seized Max. Something was wrong. "Out with it, man. Just say it."

"John Hayes was found dead this morning. Footpads, they're saying."

"But you don't think so." Neither did he, after recent developments.

"Not for a minute. I'm afraid, although I regret his death, he was not an admirable character."

"To say the least." Try as he might he couldn't feel sorry. "I appreciate your promptness in telling me."

"Who do you think it was?"

Max's mouth turned. "There is no 'think.' It was Northwich. Who else? Perhaps Hayes threatened to expose him." After the meeting in Covent Garden, the duke would be anxious to cover his traces, to leave no link behind. Hayes knew too many secrets, Max guessed. To that end, he'd sent men to find Hayes and bring him for Max to question. He'd had enough of tiptoeing around the problem.

Once he'd ascertained the identity of the spy in his household—obvious when he put his mind to it—he decided to take action of his own.

"You took Sophia home before you heard this? I know she was planning to visit you."

Russell's hesitation sent a cold dart of warning through Max.

"What? Where is she?"

Russell swallowed. "Sophia has gone to the house of her—of the Duke of Northwich."

Alarm raced through Max. He took his father-in-law to a quiet corner where they could speak privately. "Tell me. Now and fast."

Swiftly, Russell told Max what had happened. "She had French and our footman, Horton, with her."

Max closed his eyes briefly and groaned. "Leave it with me. I'll deal with it. When did she leave you?"

"She was to meet the carriage at the Exchange. It would drop her back there when they were done and she'd get a chair home."

Fighting to stop himself grinding his teeth, Max growled instead. "You thought he'd do that? The man's a traitor and now a murderer."

"I didn't promise Sophia not to tell you, you understand, but she assumed it."

"Sophia can assume all she likes. Leave the matter with me." Max strode to the booth where the porter sat and snapped a few orders before handing over a gleaming guinea and grabbing his sword and hat.

Russell joined him at the door. "What will you do?"

"The only thing I can do," he said, and left the building.

Northwich's house was barely half a mile away. He'd walk. By the time he reached his destination he'd have his temper under control. Probably. If the man had hurt Sophia, then he'd kill him for sure.

After a moment's indulgence, allowing himself a brief vision of running his sword through the blackguard's heart, he set his mind to what lay ahead and what he would do. He knew, but with the thoroughness that had made him a wealthy man, he wanted to make absolutely sure. Although at a pinch he could just give in to his daydream and leave a bloody corpse behind him. Depending on what he found when he got there. The messenger he'd sent to his house would take care of the rest.

He rapped on the door of the Northwich house impatiently and, when he entered, tossed his hat at the footman. "I've come for my wife." Glancing around the well-appointed hall, he spotted French sitting on a hard chair, a cloak draped across her lap and a hat resting in it. A man stood by her side, not in livery, but if he wasn't mistaken, that was Horton. His only ally in this place. "Wait here," he snapped and, ignoring the protests of the liveried attendant, headed for the stairs. Another stood at the base, blocking his way. He placed his hand on his sword and stared at the man. The coward moved aside. Pity.

A door upstairs was flung open and someone roared down, "What is the meaning of this commotion?"

Good, he wouldn't have to open every door until he found her. "Merely my lateness has caused your servants some distress," he said, taking the stairs at his leisure. Seemingly so, but his feet ate up the stairs until he stood before his nemesis. One of them, at any rate. He sketched a bow. "Good afternoon, Your Grace."

"All the better for seeing you, my lord."

Said in such chilling tones that if looks could kill, Max would have dropped dead on the spot. Fortunately, he was immune. He heard her voice from inside the room.

"Max?" Sophia sounded bewildered, frightened almost. What had the bastard done to her? Casting the duke a black look, Max strode past him and into the room.

Dressed as un-flamboyantly as he'd ever seen her, Sophia sat in a chair set at an angle to the window, just enough to allow the afternoon sun to dazzle her. Just as well the sunshine of an hour or two ago had, with the volatility of spring, been overcast by threatening rain clouds.

He gave her a sunny smile as if nothing were amiss, forcing every bit of his dissimulation to the fore. Northwich must not know what Max had discovered, or that he was alarmed. As hard as business negotiations could be, this was ten times harder, because the result was so close to his heart. "Good afternoon, my dear. I thought I'd better come to find you, since it looks like rain. I don't want you catching your death of cold."

He found a chair and without ceremony dragged it to where she sat. With a little maneuvering, he got her chair moved a fraction. That would make her more comfortable. He set his own close to it. But at the kind of angle that meant he could see both her and his antagonist.

Northwich closed the door gently—far too gently—and came over to his chair. He took his seat and reached for a worn leather portfolio that sat on a table by his side. "We were about to get to business, but I wasn't expecting to have to present this to two people." He put the portfolio on his lap and folded his hands over the top. "I'm not sure I should vouchsafe this to anyone else."

Max gave him a heavy-lidded, lazy stare. His very best. "She would tell me anyway. We have no secrets from each other. Do we?" He glanced at Sophia.

Her tongue emerged to flick against her lips. As if he were an automaton, his mind went straight to his groin, that tiny gesture reminding him of the last time they'd been together. And the one before that. But they had some way to go before they could find their way there again.

Sitting here next to her, Max vowed he'd get there or die trying. She would get out of this intact and alive. So would he.

"No, we share everything," Sophia said in a breathy voice.

Her steady tones were completely gone, and he felt her disturbance as his own. He longed to hold her on his lap and rock her, as much to comfort himself as her.

"Tell him," she said.

"I could show him," Northwich purred. "On condition none of these papers leave my possession."

Typical of the man to create a drama of the affair. What was he up to now? He had some spurious documents that told another lie? "Tell us. I'll look through the evidence and I'm sure my wife will want to see them, too."

"It is her business," Northwich said smoothly, "But if she doesn't object, whatever it is, who am I to argue?"

"Indeed." Max gave away nothing. Waited the bastard out.

With a heavy long-suffering sigh, Northwich unfastened the portfolio and removed several documents. They were of differing sizes, and some of the papers were curling and torn at the edges. Originals, then, or made to look that way.

"I'd appreciate copies of the relevant documents," Max said.

"Then you will have to live with disappointment. I have copies, but they reside elsewhere. You will not find them; they aren't in any obvious place. However, you are welcome to peruse these." He handed one over.

A distraction. Max glanced at the top one. It bore an impressive seal, one he had to support with his other hand because otherwise it might tear the paper. The writing was archaic, spindly, and the ink faded to brown. Hard to hold, hard to read. He laid the thing on his lap. "For now, tell us in plain English." Enough delaying tactics.

The duke turned his head and addressed Sophia directly, blocking Max out of his conversation. Max settled back to listen. "My dear, recent events might have led you to believe that you're my daughter. My previous ruse discounted, that seems the obvious conclusion, does it not?"

Previous ruse? The one he used to get her here on her own without telling him. The one that had made her so ill yesterday. Her excuse of bad food hadn't convinced him, but she obviously needed her rest so he'd let the matter be, intending to talk to her today.

Sophia nodded. Max watched like a hawk.

Northwich continued. "I need to take you back in time. You obviously know of my royalist preferences. Although I do not indulge in treasonable activity, I will always remember the time I spent abroad in the company of my father. We left with the last true King, and we returned when it became obvious that conquest counted for more than right."

Max stifled a yawn, only half-feigned.

Northwich ignored him. "You have to understand that we were living in Italy, hand to mouth, and times were difficult. All of us took our pleasures where we found them, much as King Charles the Second did when he was in exile. And like King Charles, not all our liaisons were sanctioned by the Church. King James the Third was difficult to live with. He has a melancholy that makes him despair, and after a time his wife left him." He shrugged, a what-can-you-do expression. "A man has his needs. A new family appeared at his court. One was a beautiful girl, and I had the pleasure of making her acquaintance. I introduced her to the King, and

Lynne Connolly

that is where, I believe, the erroneous conclusion was made that you are my daughter. You are not. You're the daughter of James Francis Edward Stuart."

Silently he handed her the papers. Just as silently, she took them.

Max watched. Wanted to reach for her, but forced his whirling senses into order.

The Old Pretender's wife had left him in '26 or '27, moving to live in a convent. Sophia was born in '29. What was her mother's family doing at that time? As if he'd asked aloud, Northwich spoke again.

"The woman you considered your mother was a convenience. A good name and loyal to King James. They agreed to help. So Lady Mary Howard brought you to England and claimed you as her daughter."

Sophia wasn't even the daughter of Lady Mary? What on earth was happening here? "Who was her mother?"

"A lady called Maria Rubiero. She was a long-term companion of the King, and she may have caused the rift between the King and Queen. In order to expedite a reconciliation, it was decided that her daughter should be spirited away." He inclined his head in a gracious gesture. "I did so."

Sophia sat far too still in her chair, her expression betraying nothing.

"So you decided you'd act?" Max was far from believing him. The story made sense. More than if she was Northwich's daughter. Because many men had illegitimate children, and they didn't go to such lengths to hide them away. That aspect had puzzled him.

But the daughter of a would-be king who'd asked his loyal courtier to do this for him? Oh yes, Northwich would do that. Such a strong lever would enable him to retain a strong presence in the court of the Pretender without any obvious attendance.

Leaning forward, Northwich placed a hand on hers, where it lay on her knee. Max wanted to knock it away, to hurl the papers across the room and drag her out of this place.

He did not. Instead, he sat completely, utterly still and set his brain to work.

She even had the look of a Stuart, with her full cherry-red lips and heavy-lidded dark eyes. Her rich brown hair also spoke of her heritage. High cheekbones, an air of arrogance that all the Stuarts had, whether they deserved it or not. She moved like a princess, or maybe that was his partiality speaking.

But if she were—oh, God, that meant strife. And more. He couldn't think of that now. Nothing was more important than she. *His wife*. After everything else, that was what she was.

A carriage drove by outside, and then another. One stopped.

Finally, when he was sure he'd regained control of his body and his voice, Max spoke. "It means nothing. A spent movement led by a drunk and a feeble melancholic. It has nothing to do with us. Besides, if any of this was proved, she'd be illegitimate."

Northwich spared him a glance. "Royalty is different. They have the power to legitimize who they may. Illegitimate children have ruled the country before now." He turned back to Sophia, ignoring Max. "My dear, I know this is a shock. It would be an honor to call you my daughter. Believe me, had I been the one, I would not have acted as I did. I would have found a way to claim you." His voice was soft and caressing. "I did what I could to honor the child of a man I owed my loyalty to. You are precious, a rare commodity."

Max bided his time. Sophia was his.

The duke knelt before her. *Oh, God.* He bowed his head. "You can be a queen, Sophia. I can make you a queen, or a queen in waiting. You are free of the taint that has damaged the royal family in the past few years. You are untried. The usurper George is old, his grandson young and under the influence of a man many people dislike. Call yourself Stuart, proclaim your identity. I have all the proof you need. This time we will succeed."

She gazed at Northwich, her expression inscrutable. Max couldn't tell what she was thinking, but he prayed to God she wouldn't take the bait.

But he was right. She was British, brought up here, not like the Italian brothers who had been the main hope for the Jacobites. With another Stuart, an attractive one, Northwich could make more trouble and make more room for himself. The Hanovers, who'd never really liked Britain, might give in. Not that they had before, but the King was old and frail, his mind wandering on occasion. What better time to stage a coup d'état?

"Did Hayes know?" he asked suddenly.

"He discovered it," the duke replied with a curl of his lip.

Thus, Hayes had died. That was the real reason. Not the unpardonable thing he'd done to Sophia.

Enough. Closing his mind to everything else, Max concentrated on his wife. The battle was fought here, now, and without swords. A duel, hand-to-hand, for the heart and soul of the one woman who meant so much to them both, for entirely different reasons. He had to claim her. If she refused to come with him, she'd become his enemy too. That would kill him.

                     Lynne Connolly

He got to his feet in one graceful movement that cost him much more than he let them see. "Come, my dear. We'll hardly have time to dress for dinner, and after all, we have to get our priorities right."

Sharply, she turned her head and met his cool gaze. He worked at keeping the fury from his eyes, from his countenance. He lowered his lids and gave her his best aristocratic disdain.

Heedless of the papers strewn in her lap or the duke's hand gently resting over hers, Sophia got to her feet. Let the documents fall to the floor as if they meant nothing. "I'm ready," she said, as steadily as he. She glanced at Northwich and spoke one word. "No."

Max held out his arm, and elegantly she laid her hand on it. He'd never been more proud of her. Her hand trembled slightly and then she controlled it. Pressed a little harder into the cloth that covered his arm. He braced his muscle for her, to allow her to all the support she needed.

He led her to the door. Then turned, as if struck by a sudden thought.

"By the way, Northwich, I'm keeping your spy."

Sophia stiffened, but said nothing.

In the hall he helped her into her cloak and hat himself, leaving French sitting on the hard chair. At the last moment, he gave the maid a cool nod, an order to follow them. He would have left her, but he couldn't in all conscience leave her to this man's un-tender care. He led the way outside.

As he'd half-expected, Northwich's carriage, with liveried servants, stood outside, four black horses shuffling and stamping. No doubt waiting to take her home. No discreet return for her.

Behind it stood his own town carriage, the one they used when they wanted to be noticed, with the four matched grays and the crests proudly painted on each door. And the footmen in livery. She turned, her face a picture of wonder.

"Get in, sweetheart," he said gently.

He handed her up himself and followed, after ordering Horton to see French safely to his house. The vehicle jolted into action. "Why the carriage?" was her first question.

Resisting the temptation to haul her into his lap, he explained. "Because Northwich planned to send you home in *his* carriage, with *his* liveried footmen. He wanted to show us estranged, and that he had you." He took her hand and kissed it. "A princess."

She gave a shaky laugh. "I'm not a princess."

"You could have been. He was right. You could have started the trouble all over again." As relief crept through his system, allowing him to focus on more than one issue, he wondered how many more bastards the Old

Pretender had sired. His wife had cited adultery when she left him. And Northwich had the right of it—where a man couldn't inherit a title if he was illegitimate, a king could. He'd be legitimized by Act of Parliament. Or she. Dangerous to even think that way.

He'd have to speak to Julius and the rest of the family. But not today. Not now. He had much more important things to do now.

She scoffed. "What would I do?"

"I suspect, whatever Northwich told you to do. He'd stand for you as Bute stands for Prince George." The reputed lover of the Princess of Wales, Lord Bute, a Scottish Tory, had an unreasonable influence on the princess's son, the heir to the throne. Northwich no doubt saw himself in much the same way.

She was shaken, but still Sophia, still his. In his heart, he triumphed. He'd won, although he didn't fool himself, they still had trouble to come. If he held her, he'd never let her go, and he wanted observers to see them entering the house undisturbed by their recent trial.

The carriage arrived outside their house, and despite Sophia's plainness of dress and subdued demeanor, Max helped her alight like the princess she was, and into the house. He didn't stop there, but took her straight upstairs to the bedroom. His room. No, not any more. Their room.

Chapter 19

"Shouldn't I go to mine? Aren't we going to the theater tonight? Won't it look strange if we aren't there?"

Max concentrated on removing her hat and cloak, and then tenderly helped her off with her gloves. Sophia let him minister to her, treat her with care.

What shocked her the most was how steady the news left her. "Do you think it's true? That I'm a king's daughter?" Really true? She didn't yet understand how it could be. And had her mother's family left the country and returned without anyone being any the wiser?

Gently he pushed her down on a sofa by the window and took the place next to her. "First we talk. Clear everything up, get it out of the way. Where shall we start?"

One thing puzzled her. "What did you mean about French? What has she done? She's been with me since I was a child."

His eyes turned grave, the golden sparkles dimming. "I didn't want to tell you this, but I have to. French has been spying on you."

She gasped in shock. "Why would she do that?"

He lifted her hand and kissed it. "I made some enquiries. She came to you when you were thirteen, straight from Northwich. I don't know if he set her there to ensure your safety as well as to report your doings. You are, or were, very precious to him."

"Only in the sense that he could use me."

"I don't know." He touched her chin, stroked a gentle finger down her throat. "Or perhaps he did care. He's not a monster. He's a man with misguided principles." He paused and his mouth set in a hard line. "But I might be revising that opinion. Sweetheart, I know the man did something to you I find hard to forgive, but still I hate to tell you. John Hayes is dead."

Shock hit her hard. "Dead? How?"

"Footpads, it's said."

She snorted in a most unladylike way. "Footpads?" She didn't believe that for a minute. "You mean a footpad called Northwich?"

"Yes. When I heard that, I knew the game was much more serious than we'd supposed. It went far beyond a feud between two families. That Northwich, a clever man, would risk murdering a known associate, that he'd take that risk, meant you could be in danger too. But I fear Northwich will never be brought to justice for Hayes's demise. I would have left French with him, were it not for that. With your permission, I'll send her to one of my minor estates to work as a maid. I can ensure her safety there, but I don't think Northwich wishes her dead, or she'd have gone with Hayes last night. Hayes knew too much about his master's dealings, and Northwich knew I was planning to take him and question him. He had to go."

She couldn't bring herself to care about the man who had used her so badly. Not even hatred. She just didn't care. Sadness suffused her. She should be feeling so much more, and if she'd known this earlier, she would have.

Now her husband stretched his arm behind her, his posture protective. "Yesterday French tried to separate us. Together with John Hayes. I was in Lloyd's, in my usual place, when I saw a woman in your aquamarine gown pass by the window. That's a very distinctive gown unlike any other. So I followed, but I wasn't fast enough to catch up with you— her. She hurried across Covent Garden Piazza and met with a man. John Hayes, to be precise. They kissed. In the street no less, and then went inside a house there. Most of the houses in Covent Garden are devoted to one thing—the pursuit of pleasure. I was supposed to believe you were meeting Hayes for an illicit tryst. Then come home and rail at you, perhaps send you away. You'd be on your own, looking for friends." He gazed at her, waiting for her.

"But I didn't—"

"I know, sweetheart, I know. I never doubted you. I knew it wasn't you as soon as French met Hayes."

"Why?"

"Because of what happened in the country. What you told me there and your reaction. You'd never meet that man voluntarily. My first thought was that you were being threatened in some way. Then I realized it wasn't you, and I knew who it was."

"French," she said dully.

"As you say. French. There is a resemblance in height and coloring, and across the distance of a square as busy and as large as Covent Garden, she could pass for you. I'm right?"

She frowned. Yes, she'd sometimes asked French to attend her dress fittings when she had no time for them. Ladies found it useful to have a maid who resembled her in height, build and coloring. "Yes. But it's only a passing resemblance."

"When she was in your gown with your favorite hat, it was more than that. She had her hair done the way you prefer, too. I saw her mainly from the back."

She gave him a wondering stare. "You noticed all that?"

"I notice everything about you." He grazed her cheek with his knuckle. "I knew that wasn't you. I knew you wouldn't meet John Hayes on your own, much less take him as a lover. That was when I realized French was in league with them, and it was she who'd taken your clothes and met Hayes. Because I'd sworn I'd never doubt you again. And I did not. But you were ill, and I couldn't speak to you about it." He gave her a soft smile. "It was nothing to do with oyster patties, was it?"

She shook her head. "It was the vile lies Northwich said to get me to come to his house alone. And he was trying to isolate me, wasn't he? I did that all by myself."

"He failed. You were never alone."

Her mind started working once again. Once she'd gained Northwich's assurance that she hadn't married her half-brother, her brain had clicked back into action, making her wonder what on earth she was doing at his house. She'd been in the process of excusing herself when Max had arrived. "No, I don't think so. John did it because he wanted to. Perhaps the duke had decided he'd grown too close to me and was in danger of winning me over. The duke wouldn't want that for me, would he?"

"No." Of course not.

"A princess should marry a prince. Perhaps Northwich's own son. John Hayes introduced me to Alconbury. Was he also planning for his marriage to a princess, illegitimate perhaps, but also possibly the start of a dynasty?"

He said nothing for a moment. She knew that expression. When he was working out a complicated deal or weaving something into his plans, he looked like that.

"You're right. Hayes wouldn't feature in Northwich's plans for you and his attempt at winning you wouldn't have met with his approval. A creature, a tool, wouldn't be allowed so much power." He smiled. "We spoiled his plans, did we not? With the able help of your father. I don't think he suspected the half of this."

"You thought—"

He took her hands gently in his. "I drove myself mad with speculation, but in the end, one thing remained. One thing is true through all of this. You're mine, Sophia. Your parentage is immaterial now, because you're my wife. A Wallace."

That statement affected deeper than anything else since they'd left Northwich's house. Tears threatened to fall, but she forced them down. He was right. "Yes. I am the daughter of Thomas Russell and his wife Lady Mary, and now I'm the wife of Maximilian Wallace, Marquess of Devereaux."

She'd found where she belonged. She was home.

Max took her hand. "I want to touch you properly, Sophia. Show you how I feel about you and how sorry I am that I doubted you for a single moment."

"But you said that yesterday—"

He interrupted her. "That was when I knew. I didn't doubt you, not for a minute."

He glanced down at her and shook his head. "Too many clothes," he said as if that were the most important thing in the world. He stood and held his hand out to help her up. Her heart beating double-time, she got to her feet.

He pulled out the pins that secured her fichu to her gown. He tossed them on his dressing table, before drawing the piece of gauzy linen away and dropping it on the floor.

"What are you doing?"

"Undressing you." He paused to remove his own coat, letting it fall disregarded to land in a heavy *thump* on the floor.

"Why? I'm fine, Max. I don't need to rest."

"You may not. I need this. I need to touch you, to claim you."

"Oh." That answer took her aback somewhat.

"Not surprised at discovering you're a princess, but surprised I want to take you to bed?" His mouth quirked in a half-smile.

"A little surprised, but this news… I'll let it sink in. Even if it's true, it doesn't alter the person I am. Not to me, nor to the rest of the world. I'm still the daughter of a Cit, and I'm still married to you."

He paused and gazed at her face. "Exactly. And you're still the loveliest woman in London."

"I was never that."

"You are to me."

The way he looked at her, eyes sparkling, she believed him. Her body heated when he gazed at her, desire naked in his eyes.

"And you're right about that, too. It doesn't alter who you are. The woman I love."

What Northwich's news had failed to evoke, Max managed now. Her mind reeled, and she'd have fallen if he weren't holding her steady. "You can't."

"I've found it surprisingly easy," he said, his smile returning. "It happened all on its own. Of course I love you, Sophia. I could give you myriad reasons, but in the end it means nothing next to the way I feel when you're by, the man you make me. I'm a better man for knowing you."

While she was still stunned immobile by his words, he went to work on her hair, removing the frivolous scrap of lace fashionable women called a cap and tossing it away. It floated to the carpet, and he tossed the pins on his dressing table.

"The first time I saw you, really saw you, I thought you brought light to the room."

While he spoke, he was busy about her, divesting her of gown, petticoats, and unhooking her stays. He dumped pins and bows on the dressing table as he worked as efficiently, if not as neatly, as any lady's maid. She'd worn the type of stays that fastened down the front today, an old pair from when she used to dress herself most days.

Someone must have stuffed her head with flock. "You love me?" she repeated stupidly.

He smiled. "Of course I do. Yes, Sophia, my wife, my true sweetheart, I love you."

He asked nothing of her, but lifted her and laid her on the bed, as he had that other time, stripped quickly, and joined her, snuggling close.

She shivered.

"Cold?" he asked.

She shook her head.

Only then did he kiss her. Small sipping kisses at first, slowly lengthening, so they became luscious. Then he gave her his tongue, licking deep into her mouth and persuading her to do the same to him in return. They played, danced, kissed until she found difficulty remembering what life was like without it, without him in her and her in him.

His cock pressed hard into her stomach, dampness marking her where he had released some of the nectar of his body. She wanted it, ached to feel him inside her, but she wanted something else first. To learn him. To show him without words what he meant to her. And what he'd just told her meant. Her heart, her mind filling with warm wonder, she slowly drew away from him, smiling. She swept her hands over his chest, glorying in the hard-packed muscle and the tiny nail heads of his nipples, hard against her palms.

"I do love you, Max," she said, her heart in her throat, because she'd never said that to anyone else, not even her father. "I couldn't imagine living without you."

"Nor I you."

Tenderly, he cherished her, making her feel like the most precious porcelain figure, the most delicate silk. He stroked her body, cupped her breasts so the nipples stood proud. He bathed each tip with his tongue and sucked gently, first one, and then the other, until she cried for him for more. He obeyed her, licking a line around the rosy tip before drawing it into the heat of his mouth. Curling his tongue underneath, he pulled, sending arrows of sensation straight to her heart.

Crying his name, she curved her hand around his head and dug her fingers into his hair. He released her nipple and paid attention to the other, murmuring "So sweet," against her skin. He dropped countless kisses around her breasts. Then he kissed a trail up to her throat where he played and lingered around her pulse points, turning her into a totally sensual being.

He gazed into her face. "You are essential to me, Sophia. My wife, my love—everything."

Smiling, she drew him close and kissed him. His words, his caresses all said the same thing. He loved her truly. "I don't know how long I've loved you either. When I saw you at my father's house, when you came on business, it was as if you brought your own atmosphere with you. You seemed separate. I always knew when you were in the house, because I could feel it. Is that love?"

"I don't think so, but it might be a start." He touched his lips to hers. "For me, it's not being able to imagine my life without you in it."

So simple. She nodded. "It is that. After a while, I couldn't bear the thought of you moving on. It was only business, I thought. You didn't notice me."

"Every time." He murmured the words against her lips. "I always noticed you. But how could I say anything? Foolishly, I thought of other people's expectations, not what I needed. And it is need, Sophia. I was so afraid today that I'd lose you. If you'd gone with Northwich, I couldn't go with you. But I didn't want to alter your decision. It had to be yours."

"It was. It still doesn't seem real. But I don't care. It doesn't alter what I am, does it?"

"It makes you more precious to some people. I swear I'll protect you with the last breath I take, but for your own sweet self, for no other reason."

"Oh, don't say that!"

She touched her finger to his lips and he sucked it in, caressed it with his tongue.

"Don't think about it. Or even believe it. We're here, and I'm going nowhere. Not without you. You really thought I could do that? Become a political pawn?"

He released her finger slowly, his green eyes bright. "I don't know. Honestly, I don't know what I'd do. It's tempting, the chance to wield power. But even if I wanted it for beneficial ends, it would be distorted."

"I'll just have to try to influence people as a marchioness instead of a princess," she said, smiling. "I'll deny everything else."

"Rumors will still spread."

"Damn them," she said, cinching him close.

His laugh vibrated through her body. "Damn them all," he said. "We should stay here. Forever, if need be."

"Why not?"

Once more he took her mouth in a long, leisurely kiss, thrusting his tongue deep into her mouth and letting her explore him. They indulged in some play, kissing and stroking. But when she wriggled her breasts against his hard chest to bring herself a little ease, he laughed, and for the first time, his voice held no shadows.

He was happy, and she was making him that way. That knowledge gave her a huge amount of satisfaction, warming her all the way through.

As he did when he moved lower, toying with her navel and the skin inside her hips, making her flinch and cry out.

"Take it," he said, his voice rough. "Take everything, and then I'll give you more."

Shuddering, she sifted her hands through his hair, seeking out the hard male strength beneath the silky locks.

He gave a throaty chuckle and moved farther down her body. "Dark hair, and that luscious pink center. You are so beautiful, my love."

She'd never considered that part of her beautiful, but since she thought his cock not just arousing but a perfect design of power and tenderness, she could understand.

He sipped at her, gentle at first, and he ran his tongue over his lips, gathering her taste. "Delicious too," he said.

Then, with a growl, he broke. Diving in, he sucked her clitoris hard, making her cry out, her body jerking up into the heat of his mouth. He opened wider, sucked more lavishly, licking and sucking, driving her impossibly hard impossibly fast.

Shoving his hands under her rear, he drew her up, held her steady while he ate at her. He was a man starved, ravenously devouring her and sending her higher with every suck, every lick.

Opening his mouth wide, he sucked, and to her shock she realized he had all of her in the compass of his jaws. Pleasuring every part of her, his hands holding her up so he could reach the heart of her.

Fluttering shocks radiated up her spine, to the top of her head and out, encompassing the ends of her fingers and the tips of her toes. He owned all of her, and she gave herself gladly, completely.

"I'm yours," she gasped as he drove her to a fiery peak. One that drove thoughts of anything except him from her mind. It washed her clean, left her limp and stunned.

As he lifted away from her, cool air swept over her, leaving her refreshed, born anew. She gazed into his beloved face, so open now, no secrets between them.

"Ready, my love?"

"Yes."

She knew what he meant. To make love without stint or hindrance. For the first time they'd be making love openly, both acknowledging what the other meant to them. Everything.

Although she wanted to explore him too, smooth her hands down his body, take his cock in hand and taste it, lavish her attention on it as he'd just done to her, she held fast. For now they needed to join their bodies and their hearts. Needed it.

"Max, I love you."

"I love you too, Sophia. My heart."

Taking his cock in one hand, he guided it to her, and slowly, so that she felt every tiny invasion, he thrust inside her.

Sophia let out her breath in a long sigh. "I want you here all the time."

"Impossible. But you know I'm there in spirit. In the middle of a ball, at the theater or even at court I'm here, inside you. Where I belong."

Lynne Connolly

She cupped his cheek. "It feels like that?"

"It does. I was created for this, Sophia, my love."

His movement appeared an organic development of their joining, a sway and dance only they shared. He took her mouth in a deep kiss, and she responded eagerly. Tasting her most intimate juices on his lips sent her higher. The dance grew more frenzied but it was all a part of what they were and what they meant to each other.

Everything, always.

He lifted up, never taking his attention from her face, and pressed her palms against his chest, made free with his body. And when she looked down, she saw where they joined, his cock pistoning in and out of her slick depths. Every movement brought her new and higher sensations, the touch to her interior channel shocking now, delivering more with every stroke. Bracing herself against the mattress, she came up to meet him, completing her part of the dance. His eyes grew brighter, wilder, and again he laughed in simple joy.

"That's it, love. Give yourself to me. Nothing else matters."

It didn't. She came with a completeness that enveloped her in heat, swept through her with a new understanding of what ownership meant. He owned her because she allowed it, and in return she had him. "I'm yours, always," she told him at the height of her passion, before words left her completely.

"And I belong to you." His cock jerked inside her and he came in short, hard spurts that rocked him. His muscles tensed, each in high relief, unconsciously displaying his superb physique as he came.

He half closed his eyes, sweat gleamed on his forehead and over his body, and she wanted to claim it for herself. Take all of him and absorb it.

His breath shortened into gasps and then he collapsed on to her. Still, in the throes of passion, he had a care for her.

With a growl, he circled her with his arms and rolled so she was nestled against him. "I can't let you go."

"I don't want you to." She pressed a kiss against his chest, the sparse hairs nudging her lips. "I won't let you go, either."

A thought that had nagged at her since their marriage jolted her mind again. Fully relaxed, no block between her mind and her mouth she said, "Will you always feel this way? Can this last?"

He stopped her questions by the simple expedient of pulling her down for a kiss. "Yes. There is nobody in the world like you, sweetheart. No others that I love. None as clever, or as graceful. Let yourself be beautiful, sweetheart, and others will see it, too. We won't always see eye to eye, I know that, but never concern yourself with that. I won't stray, I swear it now."

"Even if I never let you into my bed again?"

"In case you'd forgotten"—amusement coloring his voice—"this is *my* bed. Soon to be our bed, I hope and pray. You'll have to use your room sometimes, for your levees and suchlike, but here is where you come at the end of every night. Or I'll come and join you. I never want to wake up alone again."

Now she smiled. She went back into his arms and laid her head on his shoulder. "I can hardly believe it."

"Which part?"

"That you love me."

He cracked a laugh. "So after a day when you learn you're a princess, that's the concern that affects you the most? That I love you? Believe me, that part was easy."

"I'm not a princess."

"But you are of royal blood. And you're mine."

Growling, he kissed her and they lost each other in their kiss.

Smiling, he touched her chin as their lips separated. "Do we go out tonight?"

"We should. Let people see us."

"We should." But neither made an effort to move.

"Let's go back to the country to tomorrow."

She smiled at him, completely and deeply his. "Yes, let's."

Meet the Author

Lynne Connolly lives in England with her family and her mews, Jack the cat. She comes to the USA every year to visit her publishers and readers. She was born in Leicester, England and was brought up in a haunted house. She is part Romany, and in her spare time she loves reading the Tarot as her grandmother taught her, and making and filling dollhouses.

Turn the page for a special excerpt of Lynne Connolly's

Rogue In Red Velvet

If Connie loses her standing in society, she risks losing everything...

except Alex.

When country widow Constance Rattigan finds herself in a notorious London brothel instead of at the altar, only one person can save her from the auction block. Alex Vernon walked away from Connie once before, when he discovered her engagement. Now that her fiancé has betrayed her, Lord Ripley doesn't intend to leave her again. But Connie has other ideas... She won't marry him until her name is cleared.

Alex decides to make Connie's wishes come true, but it's not that easy, even with the help of his powerful relatives known as the Emperors of London.

On sale now!

Chapter 1

March, 1754

The library door crashed open, shattering Connie's peace and admitting the last man she wanted to be alone with. Pretending unperturbed tranquility, Connie put her pen in the standish. She clasped her hands on top of the book she'd been working on to still the trembling his presence caused.

Wide-eyed, chest heaving, the normally elegant, cool Lord Ripley, slammed the door and put his back to it.

She met his blank, dark stare and cursed her fluttering pulse. Whatever had put him in this state, it couldn't be trivial.

He blinked, straightened and assumed the town bronze most of his sort used like a cloak, covering whatever he felt beneath. He gave the perfectly tied strip of linen at his neck a twitch, arranged his sleeve ruffles, then straightened his wig. As poise and elegance returned, he transformed from a hunted fugitive to a gentleman and pushed away from the door. He strolled to the old, scarred table at which she sat. "Here you are."

What a ridiculous statement. "I believe I am." She read a line in the journal before her, more to look away than because she needed to, and took a steadying breath before she met his eyes once more. "May I help you, Lord Ripley?"

"I merely wondered why you lock yourself away here every day, Mrs. Rattigan. And I came to see if I may assist you in any way."

"I'm perfectly fine, sir. I doubt you could help me, or have any interest in doing so." She'd avoided him for three days and wanted none of his games. She didn't care why he'd shot in here, only she wished he'd shoot out again, just as fast.

"Is it something too difficult for my paltry brain? Are you a bluestocking, ma'am, that you labor here day after day without joining the revelry?" In full control, his society manners polished as ever, he walked to her side of the table and loomed over her.

Her heart beat faster and her breath quickened. She worked to hide his effect on her and castigated herself for a fool. He wasn't interested in her in that way, much less when she had her hair scraped back in a knot, wore no cosmetics at all and had donned her old clothes in preparation for the dusty work. She was just an excuse, an escape from something. Or someone. She was no empty-headed miss. She was a respectable widow, but it didn't stop her becoming tongue-tied. "I—I—"

"You find yourself bored by our antics. You'd rather study Plautus, or is it Marcus Aurelius?" Chuckling, he leaned over her shoulder, flipped the book closed. With one long finger, he traced the name on the cover. "Saucy stories perhaps?"

The door opened and admitted Miss Louisa Stobart, one of the young ladies invited here to meet Lord Ripley. Connie's godfather had confided to her that he might choose a bride from among them.

Now she understood why he'd shot into this room like a pursued fox. Miss Stobart had been the most assiduous of Lord Ripley's pursuers, indefatigable in her chase. He'd been escaping her.

For a change, Connie was in charge. How delicious.

Lord Ripley straightened and gave Connie such a look of pleading that she almost laughed. "Help me," he mouthed, before assuming his easy smile and facing his tormentor.

She would have preferred that he said that in different circumstances, but what she dreamed at night remained between her and her pillow. This would do. A little gentle revenge was called for. She slid the book over to his lordship and pointed at random. "Here is a word I cannot read, sir. Do you see?"

"No, ma'am." Bending over her shoulder, he peered then looked at her.

Far too close, his breath heated her cheek and her heart quickened. This close, he'd see her reaction for sure. Inwardly, she groaned. She hadn't bargained on him doing that. She should have shoved the book away from her.

His eyes widened slightly. He turned his attention to the book. "I think it says wormwood. An old spell book?"

She laughed. "An inventory, sir. As you well know."

His shoulders relaxed under his country-coat. In an ordinary man that slight movement might remain unnoticed, but Connie had spent the last few days watching him surreptitiously. He was the most handsome man she'd ever seen and while she could tell herself that she was merely observing, it did no good. For the first time in her life, she longed to be younger, wealthier and socially higher ranking. Then she could compete. Instead, she'd dressed in a practical country gown that would survive hedgerows and house dust, and hidden away here. "Yes, of course. Wormwood."

Thank goodness he straightened.

Miss Stobart stood on the other side of the table, her delicately draped pink silk gown mocking Connie's sturdy dark green garment. Miss Stobart's was a fashionable ideal of a gown to be worn in the country, sprinkled with exquisitely embroidered spring flowers. Miss Stobart's gaze skimmed over Connie and to his lordship. Her ruby lips pursed in a winsome pout. "Sir, I had hoped we could take a turn in the gardens. I quite thought you had promised me at breakfast."

"I had no idea." He glanced down at Connie. It was her cue to say something.

"I'm so sorry to interrupt your"—*Courtship? Pursuit?* —"walk. Of course you must go."

Miss Stobart drummed her foot against the wood floor, maddening in the quiet library. "Indeed sir, I quite thought you'd forgotten me, so I came to find you." Her voice was sweet; her foot was not.

"I beg your pardon, but I had promised today to Connie for some time now." He gave her an easy smile.

Connie stared at him in astonishment. He'd used her first name. She wasn't aware he even knew it. When he put his hand on her shoulder, she nearly leaped up. His skin wasn't in contact with hers, due to her modest gown and fichu, but it might as well have been. She felt it like a shock of recognition. Of what she didn't want to consider.

"Connie and I are old friends." The familiarity of her first name implied he was much friendlier with her than anyone had imagined. "When she mentioned her task, I immediately volunteered to help. Her—er—errand is something I am particularly interested in."

Not to mention, he didn't have the faintest idea what she was doing. She'd never discussed her project in company and nobody had expressed an interest except for her godfather, whose commission this was.

He was casting her as his rescuer when he hadn't asked her first.

"It is a special project I've been meaning to undertake for some time." Should she lie, draw out the moment? She wasn't used to being the center of attention.

Miss Stobart fixed her cold, blue eyes on Connie, probably for the first time since she'd arrived.

Connie gave the young woman her sweetest smile. "My visit here provided the perfect opportunity."

"A bluestocking?" That was the second time in ten minutes she'd been accused of that. Did everyone in society who opened a book get accused of that?

Miss Stobart's lips curved in a superior smile. She clearly considered herself the victor in this encounter. After all, who would not? Connie was below the notice of a young lady of marriageable age and considerable fortune.

"Not exactly." She glanced at the book.

Leaning over her once more, Lord Ripley flipped the volume over, revealing the faded label on the front. "It's an inventory of the house from the sixteenth century. Family history is important."

Damn, she couldn't torment him anymore. He'd guessed right. "Lord Downholland has particularly wished to gather all the documents pertaining to the house in one place. I merely offered to assist him."

"And I offered to assist Connie," he said smoothly, back in control. "I'm sorry, Miss Stobart, but her claims had precedence."

Wonderful. He was fast making an enemy on her behalf. Miss Stobart would resent her intensely if she came between the chase and ensnarement of her quarry. "I'm only doing this until my fiancé arrives."

Miss Stobart relaxed, nodded regally. "I see. But Lord Ripley has other commitments."

"I'll be down directly, ma'am." He walked to the door and held it open. "If you would not mind waiting for a few moments, I would greatly appreciate the time."

Miss Stobart swept through and he closed the door behind her.

Breathing deeply, he slumped against it. He met Connie's gaze and smiled. "Thank you."

So that was what she was good for. A distraction. "I'm not prepared to act as your chaperone, sir."

Laughing, he waved a hand in one of the most elegant movements she'd ever seen. "I would be eternally grateful to you if you did so." He sauntered toward her. "I never thought I'd be in need of one, to be truthful."

Connie resisted the temptation to move away. She was not afraid of this man, or intimidated by him, even though he had just gone from being the object of her fantasies to a real live human being. His panic, his silent appeal for help had transformed him in her eyes. Although, sadly, his appeal remained.

Seizing her hand, he dropped a kiss on the back, and immediately restored it to her. "I can't thank you enough, ma'am." He grinned wickedly. "Connie."

"I wasn't even aware you knew my first name."

"I do."

How did he know her name when she wasn't even aware that he'd noticed her? Had he made a point of learning it?

"Connie, I truly appreciate your help. Is there anything I can do for you in return?"

"You can answer this. Why is it so important to avoid Miss Stobart?" She dared to turn around and look at his face, bracing herself for the visual contact, as she always did when she looked at him. "You raced in here as if the hounds of hell were after you. Surely you have enough address to avoid her?"

He perched on the table by her side. Too close.

Anger was taking the place of curiosity. She no longer cared about the social gulf between them, or her dowdy appearance, or anything else other than the consideration that he had treated her badly. "Sir, I'm a widow, from the country, but I'm not prepared to be treated as if I don't exist."

His eyes darkened as he gazed steadily at her. "I owe you an apology. I am truly sorry if I implied anything of the kind. I meant it. I owe you a favor. Anything."

The devil take him. What she could do with was an extra pair of hands, and someone who knew how to read the spidery old writing she was fighting every day. She folded her arms. "Very well, since you ask. I want an assistant in this task. I agreed to help my godfather gather the books he'll need to compile a family history. It's proving more difficult than I imagined. Some of the books are heavy and stored in virtually inaccessible places."

His broad shoulders eased. "I would be honored to help."

"Even if it meant getting a speck of dirt on your clothes?"

"Even then." His lips curved in a disconcertingly attractive smile.

Meeting his eyes became more difficult and she fought the urge to fidget. She'd have to change her chair, it was becoming most uncomfortable. "I'm working at this task most of the day. Until my fiancé arrives."

"Dankworth, yes." He snapped the name as if Jasper had done something to annoy him. "I should wish you happy, I suppose."

"Content will do. Thank you."

He quirked a brow. That irritating smile returned. "Contentment only? You don't wish for wedded bliss?"

"Not in the least. A rational partnership is my dearest wish." It was the truth. Love had done nothing for her. She wished for a comfortable marriage that would improve the lot of both parties, nothing else. She'd decided that years ago, and now her ambition was within her grasp, she'd do nothing to change it. "The marriage will suit my godparents, who have been kind to me and have no child of their own to inherit their estate."

"They know about Dankworth, then?"

Did he? Eyeing her pen, she wished she could take it up again and lose herself in the old inventories. She didn't want her decision questioned in this way. What good would it do? "They know he can be foolish on occasion. Marriage will settle him and ensure heirs for the estate." She tired of this game. This man was only baiting her. "I understand you're here seeking a bride, sir. You won't find one in this room."

"Will I not?" He leaned forward, pressing home his advantage. His citrus and spice scent was altogether too seductive. His low voice hinted at unforgiveable sins. "You're not formally betrothed yet, ma'am."

"I will be very soon." She wasn't very good at flirting, never had been. She scraped back her chair, got to her feet, and made a business of shaking out the skirts of her drab green gown. "You cannot show the guests such discourtesy. They are here for you, at least a good many are."

He grinned wryly. "It would be more discourteous to run away screaming. If I don't have this escape, I might very well do that." He stood, took a few paces toward the door, and turned back, the skirts of his country coat swinging around thighs that filled out his breeches creditably. "I see I must confide my predicament and throw myself on your mercy. Miss Stobart is determined to trap me into a connection I have no desire to acquire."

Miss Stobart had either ignored Connie or treated her with barely concealed contempt since her arrival. Connie had heard rumors as well as witnessed Miss Stobart's relentless pursuit of his lordship.

He sighed and scrutinized the silver buckle on his shiny black shoe. "I suspect my father put her and her mother in the way of finding me here. The old man wants me married and as soon as possible. The truth is, I was caught in a compromising position with Miss Stobart at a ball and I decided to leave London for a while until the affair blew over." He lifted his hand as if to run it through his hair, but he was wearing a fashionable wig.

From the color of his brows, she'd say his hair was dark underneath and she had an irrational but powerful desire to see it for herself. To touch it, in a way entirely forbidden to her. Annoying that this unwanted desire wouldn't leave her. His confession didn't endear him to her. *Compromising position* could mean anything from a private conversation to full-blown seduction.

"The incident happened at a ball," he continued. "Miss Stobart said she'd torn her gown and asked me to help her pin it. So there I was kneeling at her feet in an anteroom when her aunt dramatically flung open the door. She'd been clever enough to bring witnesses."

That wasn't so bad. "Didn't you explain your task?"

"They chose not to believe me. Miss Stobart swore it was a declaration of marriage. It was not, but my absence from town was advisable. She chased me here." He closed his eyes, and when he opened them they were filled with surprising bleakness. "I must sound like the veriest coxcomb, imagining every woman in the house after my hand."

"No indeed, sir. You are from one of the foremost families in the land, accepted everywhere, and in possession of a large fortune. Why should you not think that?." Since he was being so honest, why should she not do the same?

He arched a brow. "If I said I wanted to be desired for myself, I'd sound foolish. But it's true. Connie, I have few friends, people I can be honest with. It would be a privilege if you allow that between us."

Friends? Damn, but she still wanted more. Not that she could have it, and Connie had become used to not having what she wanted. Friends would do. "Very well."

"And I'll devote a portion of every day to helping you."

"Thank you, sir." Exquisite agony to have this man so close, but she'd bear it. Worse that she was liking him more.

"Alex."

She blinked. "I beg your pardon?"

"I want the privilege of calling you Connie. In return, you must call me Alex, especially in private. You do me a great favor, helping me to avoid the ladies, particularly Miss Stobart. She's done everything she can to compromise me."

"What about me? Won't I be compromised?"

"You're a respectable widow, soon to be formally betrothed. You told me so yourself."

He had her there. "And in any case, I'm of an age where I cannot be expected to be on the hunt. Isn't that right?"

"I wouldn't say that." He raked her with his eyes, once, twice, from head to toes.

Every part of her body tingled. How could she bear this? "I'm eight and twenty, sir. I'm far too old to consider husband hunting seriously, even if my arrangement with Jasper didn't exist." He might as well hear the truth. "If it weren't that my godparents had chosen me, I'd be well on the shelf."

"They might consider you decrepit. I certainly don't. But you have my word, Connie, I'll behave. Just don't leave me to their mercies." When he moved back, she caught the scent of citrus and masculinity. He was too real, with her in this room, a man rather than a symbol of power and influence.

"Why don't you just leave?"

He shook his head. "I promised my father I wouldn't. He's an old curmudgeon, but he's the only father I have. In a week, I will be kicking the dust of this admittedly charming house off my heels. I just need help until then."

So he could help the old widow woman sort out the dusty books. The situation appealed to her underused sense of humor. If she could bear his presence, and since he'd dropped his society mask she found him much more agreeable, then she could watch the play unfold and smile. As a widow she was allowed more leeway than others, and even if rumors came her way, she was safe. Jasper would arrive any day now and then her quietude would be at an end. She would be an engaged woman. "Very well, but not for long. Until you leave."

"Thank you, Connie. You do me a great service and I won't forget it."

She might as well make use of him. "Be warned, Lord Ripley, I intend to work you hard collecting volumes from the dustiest rooms in the house."

"Alex."

He must look at all women that way and the gullible thought he did it just for them. More fools they. Connie wouldn't join them.

* * * *

Alex left the library smiling. If Connie Rattigan thought her plain gowns and quiet demeanor had prevented him looking at her with more than usual interest, she was much mistaken.

Her determination to avoid the house party had intrigued him at first. Then he wondered how she could think of becoming betrothed to anyone belonging to the Dankworth family. Of course he was biased, since his mother's family were constantly at odds with the Dankworths, but Jasper, in his opinion, was a typical example of the breed. He didn't deserve her. Glad to find her betrothed absent from the party, he'd looked at Connie and liked what he saw. The more he looked, the more he liked.

Discovering her lair had become an obsession that had lightened the otherwise dull visit. He'd traversed several corridors more plainly decorated and much narrower than the more gracious ones in the main part of the house. But he'd failed in his quest.

So it was ironic that he'd found her by accident. He had been escaping the wiles of Miss Stobart. Running away. He'd wandered into the older part of the house, to explore a little. Like many country houses, this one had been added to over the years. Lower ceilings and narrower corridors than in the modern part of the house attested to its age. He'd ducked into an old library, lined with shelves of books that looked read instead of just for show.

When he turned a corner and discovered the lady facing him full-square, his smile vanished. If he wanted to get past her, he'd either have to retreat or beg her pardon and squeeze past. The narrow corridors that a moment ago had seemed quaint now took on a more sinister aspect.

Another lady chased around the far end of the long hallway, no doubt determined to prevent any tete-a-tete. Good for her.

"Ladies, would you both care to accompany me in a stroll around the gardens?" Acceptable, and he could make an excuse and leave them with each other. Perhaps they'd come to blows. A man could only hope.

Alex considered himself an easy-going man but these two had driven him to distraction. So much that he'd left London and taken up the invitation for a quiet gathering, only for them to discover where he'd gone and follow post-haste. The Downhollands were too genial to turn them away.

Even more reason to pursue the fascinating Constance Rattigan. He'd never met a woman before who drew him as she did. The fact that she was about to be married, or contracted anyway, made her safer than the two women who confidently came forward and took an arm each. Also infinitely better company. She conversed like a sensible woman, and while he tried to be a gentleman, he took note of her luscious figure and her lovely features almost without thinking.

Strange feeling. Must be the Yorkshire air, he decided, as he made the necessary detour to the south entrance, heading for the gardens.